D1536413

Justice for Milena

Justice for Milena

Badge of Honor

Texas Heroes
Book 10

By Susan Stoker

Cover Design by Chris Mackey, AURA Design Group
Cover Model: John DeWall
Cover Photograph: Wander Aguiar Photography
Edited by Kelli Collins

Manufactured in the United States

Table of Contents

Prologue   1
Chapter One   11
Chapter Two   22
Chapter Three   53
Chapter Four   77
Chapter Five   83
Chapter Six   106
Chapter Seven   118
Chapter Eight   132
Chapter Nine   153
Chapter Ten   178
Chapter Eleven   195
Chapter Twelve   211
Chapter Thirteen   219
Chapter Fourteen   238
Chapter Fifteen   249
Chapter Sixteen   269
Chapter Seventeen   288
Chapter Eighteen   306
Chapter Nineteen   320
Epilogue   347
Discover other titles   363
Connect with Susan Online   366
About the Author   367

Author Note

In the beginning of 2017, Lexi Blake asked if I might be interested in writing a crossover story in her Masters and Mercenaries series. I thought about it for about two seconds before agreeing wholeheartedly. Thereafter started a brainstorm of epic proportions to figure out how to integrate her character, Sadie, into one of my stories.

One thing led to another, and instead of having Sadie appear in ONE book, she ended up in two. This one, and *Rescuing Sadie*. This story is a setup for the issues Sadie has in her own book, while at the same time being TJ and Milena's story.

I want to thank Lexi for letting me play in her world, and for "giving me" Sadie. She's an awesome character, and I loved making her friends with Milena.

Prologue

Three Years Ago

TJ "ROCK" ROCKWELL sat on the tiny balcony and stared out into the dark night. He absently swirled the whiskey in his glass and wondered what in the hell he was doing with his life. He'd woken up an hour ago and couldn't get back to sleep. That was nothing new.

But instead of dreaming about the faces of the men, women, and children he'd killed while in the service of his country, he couldn't get Milena out of his head. It was thoughts of her that woke him and drove him out of bed.

She'd gotten home from her shift at the rehab facility where they'd met, and when she'd asked how his day had been, he'd jumped down her throat.

"How do you think my day's been?" he'd snarled. "I'm stuck here in this fucking apartment instead of being at Fort Benning with my team. The goddamn psychiatrist won't release me back to active duty and I'm tired of sitting around doing nothing!"

Silence had greeted his outburst. Milena had looked at him for a long moment, sorrow and confusion in her beautiful blue eyes. Finally, she'd asked, "Why are you so angry?"

He'd had a nightmare about that look on her face not too long after he'd gone to bed. There were plenty of reasons why he was angry, and not one of them was Milena's fault.

When TJ had woken up in the hospital in Germany after almost dying in an explosion, he'd found out that his entire squad had been murdered. Because he'd trusted the wrong person. Because he'd taken his attention off his teammates.

He'd wanted to go back to Afghanistan and kill as many terrorists as he could. But the doctors in the VA hospital had sent him to the States instead. To Austin, Texas, and a world-renowned rehabilitation hospital.

His first day there, TJ had met Milena. She was younger than him by a few years, blonde, and always so perky. It had annoyed him at first, but the longer he was there and the more he got to know her, the more she'd appealed to him.

One of the things he liked about her was her willingness to do whatever was needed. A patient needed pain meds? She immediately stopped what she was doing and got them, even if it wasn't her patient. When one of her fellow nurses needed to take a day off, Milena volunteered to take her shift. And it wasn't that she was a pushover; she wasn't. It was obvious she simply enjoyed doing things for others. Most people he met had some sort of hidden agenda. Not Milena. She was nice. Genuinely nice. She didn't look for what people could do for her; but what *she* could do for them.

TJ hadn't met many people in his lifetime like her. He'd found himself looking forward to talking to her when she came on shift. She smiled all the time and generally made him forget some of the awful shit he'd done while serving on his Special Forces team.

He missed his friends and teammates more than he'd ever thought possible. As a sniper, he worked alone more times than not—in high-stress situations—but his team had always been there for him. In return, he was responsible for keeping them safe while they carried out their missions. He was their "eye in the sky." TJ wasn't proud of his kill rate—one of the highest in the entire Army, he'd been told. He didn't mind killing men so much…it was the women and children who got to him.

In his mind, they were as much victims in the horrible fight against terrorism as anyone else. Forced to carry bombs to try to blow up American and British checkpoints. Or taught as young as two years old that all foreign soldiers were the enemy.

Shutting off that line of thinking before he got sucked down into the black pit in his mind, TJ tried to turn his thoughts back to Milena.

He'd been in the rehab hospital for four months, recovering from the wounds he'd received on that fateful day. Four months during which he'd gotten to know Milena. They'd both flirted and teased—and more—and when she'd found out he had no place to go when he was released, she'd offered to let him stay with her until he was back on his feet.

That was two months ago, and he was still at her apartment.

From that first night, he'd shared a bed with the generous and giving Milena. At first it had been idyllic. The lovemaking was off-the-charts good. TJ hadn't ever felt about a woman the way he did Milena.

She was adventurous and up for anything he wanted to try. They'd had sex on every surface of her apartment. The wall, the couch, the kitchen table, the shower, the coffee table, the sink in the guest bathroom, even the balcony one night when they were both drunk and their inhibitions were down.

But somewhere along the line, things had changed. *He* had changed. TJ was frustrated with his life. He didn't like relying on Milena for everything. He didn't have a job, he was officially being medically retired from the Army. He couldn't seem to go forward, and he definitely couldn't go back.

He felt like a prisoner in Milena's apartment, and he

hated that. She didn't deserve a boyfriend who was constantly on edge and hated where she lived because it wasn't in the best part of the city. She didn't deserve his anger either, but that hadn't stopped him from giving it to her anyway.

He stared out at the warm Austin night and made the decision he'd known was coming. He couldn't stay. All he was doing was hurting Milena, and she was the last person he wanted to drag down the hellish road he was on.

She deserved better. So much better than him. But he knew she'd never kick him out. It just wasn't in her. He needed to leave. Tonight.

TJ had nowhere to go, but he couldn't stand the person he'd become.

His decision made, TJ stood and put the glass of whiskey he'd been nursing on the small glass-topped table on the balcony. He entered the apartment and went straight to the master bedroom.

Standing in the doorway, TJ drank in the sight of the woman who meant more to him than anything he'd ever had in his entire life. Memories of her sitting astride him, her head thrown back as she came, blinked through his head as if he were watching a movie. The small grunts she made when he was pounding into her from behind. The way she smiled shyly up at him from between his thighs when she was giving him a blowjob.

But it wasn't just the sex he would miss. No, he'd miss Milena's caring ways. Everything she did was with him in mind. Her fridge and pantry were filled with the things he liked to eat and drink. The DVR was full of shows he frequently watched. Even the new towels hanging in her bathroom were his favorite color.

He sighed sadly. She was way too good for the likes of him. If he was ever going to be able to be in a healthy relationship, he needed to get his head on straight and figure out what the fuck he wanted to do with his life. He couldn't sit around Milena's apartment and suck the niceness out of her...because he knew that was what would happen if he stayed.

He glanced at the numerous pairs of scrubs hanging haphazardly in her closet. She loved being a nurse, loved helping people. TJ needed to let her do that and stop standing in her way.

Tiptoeing to the side of the bed, TJ sat next to Milena. She stirred and turned toward him. Her eyes opened into slits and when she saw it was him, gave him a small smile.

"Can't sleep again?" she asked.

"I'm good," he told her softly.

"I can sit up with you if you want," Milena offered.

TJ's stomach twisted. He'd been a dick to her earlier, and yet she still wanted to help him. When he'd first moved in, she'd stayed up with him when he couldn't sleep, and more often than not they'd ended up making love. It hadn't helped him sleep, but he'd felt content simply holding her as she fell asleep in his arms afterwards.

A selfish part of him wanted to say that he'd love for her to stay up with him. They hadn't made love in a week, and TJ knew it was all his fault. But he'd already made up his mind, and it would make it harder to leave if he had another taste of her. If he felt her tight pussy clench his dick as she came all over him, he'd never be able to go.

He leaned over and kissed her forehead gently, then pulled back and looked into her beautiful blue eyes. He couldn't see the color in the dim light of the room, but he knew he'd never forget what they looked like. "I'm good. You have to work in the morning. Go back to sleep, Doc."

She brought one hand up to his face and palmed his cheek. "I can call off if you want to spend the day together. I know things haven't been easy for you lately. Let me help."

TJ almost changed his mind about leaving at hearing her words. Almost.

"I'm sorry I've been a dick," he told her.

"You haven't been that bad."

He snorted. "I have, and I'm sorry. Sleep."

"Love you, TJ," she said sleepily, then dropped her

hand and closed her eyes.

TJ froze. She hadn't said the words before. But then again, neither had he.

Hearing them right before he planned to leave her was torture.

He sat next to her for the longest time, watching her sleep. Her slow, even breaths making her chest rise and fall in a gentle rhythm.

Feeling as if the weight of the world was on his shoulders, TJ forced himself to stand. He gathered the clothes strewn about the room and stuffed them into his Army-issued duffel bag. He went into the bathroom and quickly retrieved his toiletries. When he went back into the bedroom, Milena hadn't stirred.

He wanted to go to her. Slip beneath the sheets and gather her in his arms. Wanted to wake her with his mouth between her legs, show her how much he cared about her, show her what he couldn't say with words.

But instead, TJ walked silently to the door of the room and shut it behind him without looking back.

There wasn't much else he needed to gather, but he took his time, making sure he removed as much of his presence in her life as he could.

TJ knew Milena would be upset, but she'd get over him. He also knew what he was doing was cowardly, but if he saw even one tear fall from her beautiful eyes, he'd cave and stay. He was messed up, and he'd ruin her life eventually. It was better this way.

He considered writing a note, but he had no idea what to say.

That he loved her, but had to leave anyway? That he was leaving *because* he loved her? That she should find another man and live happily ever after?

The thought of anyone else touching what was his made TJ angry all over again. And that right there was why he needed to go. The anger was eating him alive. He was afraid one day the rage festering inside would break free, and Milena would be caught in the crossfire. He'd rather die than hurt her in any way.

TJ took the key to her apartment off his key ring and placed it on the kitchen counter. It looked almost obscene sitting there. He stared at it for a long moment, knowing if he walked out the door, there was no coming back. If he left, he was giving up Milena forever. She'd never forgive him for leaving without a word, and he couldn't blame her. He wouldn't deserve to be forgiven if he snuck out in the middle of the night, leaving no trace he'd ever been there.

Closing his eyes, TJ turned and slipped out of the apartment without a sound. He made sure the knob was locked and shut the door behind him.

The second it snicked closed, he wanted to throw up.

Don't do this, asshole. She'll understand, and will

stand by you until you get your life figured out. She's meant to be yours. Go back.

TJ ignored his inner voice and turned toward the parking lot. He didn't have a car, but it didn't matter. He didn't have a destination in mind, and for the first time since he'd woken up in the hospital in Germany in pain and confusion, he felt lighter.

He was a dick for feeling that way, especially after all Milena had done for him. But now he didn't have to worry about disappointing her. About seeing the love in her eyes slowly die.

He looked back once. Her apartment was completely dark. He mourned what could've been if he were a better man.

Then TJ "Rock" Rockwell turned his back on the best thing that had ever happened to him, the woman he knew deep in his gut could never be replaced, and headed for downtown Austin…and whatever the future held for him.

Chapter One

Present Day

A LOUD SCREAM pierced the air from outside the room, then abruptly fell silent.

Milena looked up in surprise at the sound. The entire time she'd worked at the Bexar County School and Orphanage for Girls, she'd never, not once, heard any of the girls raise their voices.

It was just one of the many uncomfortable and odd things about the place.

"Is it almost out?"

The desperate question brought Milena's attention back to what she was doing. Namely, helping a four-teen-year-old girl give birth.

"You're doing great, Christine," she soothed. "Take deep breaths, that's it. When you feel the need to push, don't fight it." Milena looked up from the task at hand and met her friend Sadie's eyes.

The noises coming from the other side of the door were increasing in intensity. She had no idea what time it was, having left her watch at home on the table beside her bed. She'd been jolted out of a deep sleep by her phone ringing. It had been Master Jeremiah. Christine had gone into labor and she was needed at the school.

Her normal hours were one to five, three days a week, but Milena knew she could be called at any time to attend one of her five pregnant charges at the school. The girls ranged in ages from fourteen to eighteen, and their pregnancies ranged from fifteen to thirty-six weeks.

She hadn't hesitated when she'd heard Christine was in labor. She'd woken Sadie, who had reappeared in town a month ago. She'd claimed to be going through a rough patch, and Milena simply couldn't turn her away. Besides, it was nice to have someone near her own age to talk to. She'd asked Master Jeremiah if Sadie could assist her with the girls on a voluntary basis, and he'd reluctantly allowed it. Currently, Sadie was sitting at Christine's side, holding her hand and encouraging her quietly.

If Milena was honest with herself, she'd asked to have Sadie help her out at the school because being there by herself gave her the creeps. It wasn't anything she could put her finger on, but something wasn't right at the Bexar County School and Orphanage for Girls.

Christine grunted, and Milena shook her head and forced her attention back on what she was doing. "I can see the head!" she told the exhausted teenager. "Just a couple more pushes and you'll be done."

The crash of a door being kicked open sounded from somewhere near the closed entrance to the make-shift delivery room. Milena startled, but couldn't stop what she was doing to investigate.

Her eyes met Sadie's again in concern. She had no idea what was happening, but whatever it was, it didn't sound good.

There were some muffled voices from outside the door, and Milena was about to send Sadie out to see what was going on when the door to the small room was suddenly thrown open.

Christine and Sadie both screamed in surprise, and Milena couldn't stop the screech that left her own mouth at the intrusion.

Looking to her left, she stared incredulously at two armed men standing in the doorway. They were both wearing black from head to toe, including helmets with dark-tinted shields covering their faces.

Milena was scared out of her mind, but she tried to suppress her fear in front of Christine. The poor girl was having a hard enough time at the moment as it was. There was nothing Milena could do to protect herself or the other two women in the room, but she tried bravado to project a sense of control over the situation. "Get out! This is a sterile environment!"

When the men didn't shoot her or otherwise act in

any way aggressive toward them, Milena tried to calm her erratic heartbeat. They didn't leave, but she figured if they were there to harm them, they would've fired their weapons by now.

With a loud scream, Christine gave one last push and a wet, squirmy baby slid out of her body into Milena's waiting hands. She tried not to give the men another thought and turned her attention to the new life in her arms. She clamped the umbilical cord and cut it, her motions quick and efficient. Turning to the table she'd prepared earlier, Milena set the infant down on a fluffy towel and began sucking mucus and fluid out of his little nose and mouth. Within seconds, the boy opened his mouth and protested his not-so-gentle entry into the world.

Milena heard Sadie talking softly to the teenager, reassuring her, while she finished up with the baby. Gently wiping him clean, she picked him up and turned back to Christine. She noticed one of the men who'd stormed into the room was still standing there. He hadn't come any closer to the table, but he also hadn't left. His rifle was now pointed toward the ground instead of at them, but it didn't make Milena feel any better.

She had no idea what was going on. Was the school being taken hostage? The children and all of the other inhabitants being held for ransom? She wanted so badly to ask what was going on, but she didn't want to antagonize the man with the gun. She glanced over at Sadie and was reassured when her friend wasn't panicking. Sadie used to work for a security company, and Milena figured if she wasn't frantically trying to send her a nonverbal message about ducking for cover or something, they were probably okay for the moment.

Her fingers shaking with fear, Milena took a deep breath. She needed to let Christine bond with her baby, then deliver the afterbirth.

Trying to ignore the man's presence, Milena brought Christine's baby to her. "Hold out your arms," she told the teenager.

Christine did as requested, and Milena put the tiny baby in her arms. "Meet your son, Christine."

The teenager looked up at her with wide brown eyes. "A boy?"

Milena smiled nodded. Master Jeremiah's rule was that the pregnant women weren't allowed to find out the gender of their babies ahead of time. Milena didn't know why, but wasn't brave enough to go against his wishes. Besides, the girls didn't seem to care one way or another. It was all very weird.

"Yes, a healthy seven-pound, three-ounce baby boy."

"A boy," Christine breathed, then her eyes filled with tears.

"Are you okay?" Milena asked.

The teenager nodded. "Yeah. I'm just so happy it's a boy."

Milena shook off the uneasy feeling in her gut and moved back down the bed to complete the birthing process.

Not too much later, Milena stood and stripped off the gloves she'd been wearing. Sadie had wrapped the infant in a blanket, and mom and son were quietly bonding.

Taking a deep breath, Milena turned to the man in the doorway.

Putting a hand on her hip, she asked rather belligerently, "Well?"

In her defense, she normally wouldn't have been so abrupt or rude to a man with a gun, but she was tired, and more than a little uneasy about the appearance of the men. She had no idea what was going on, and desperately wanted to protect Sadie, Christine, and the newborn baby.

"What's someone like you doing in a place like this?"

Milena blinked. It almost sounded like a pick-up line. Except they weren't in a bar and the weapon in the man's hands made it more than clear he wasn't trying to impress her.

"I work here."

He made a noise that sounded like a snort, but with

the shield over his face, Milena couldn't be sure. It annoyed her that she couldn't see him. Generally, people tended to broadcast some of what they were thinking through their facial expressions, but she was flying blind here.

Milena had no idea if the man had planned on responding to her snarky answer to his question, because they were interrupted by another man appearing in the doorway.

"Milena Reinhardt?"

She nodded. "That's me. What's going on?"

"You and your friend need to come with me."

Shaking, Milena crossed her arms over her chest and pretended to be braver than she was actually feeling. "I don't know who you are or what you want. We're not going anywhere with you."

The man turned away, looking at her over his shoulder, and pointed to the letters on the back of the vest he was wearing. "FBI. As of right this moment, the Bexar County School and Orphanage for Girls is officially shut down. And as employees, there are some tough questions you're both going to have to answer about exactly what's been going on here for the last decade."

Milena blanched, and she reached out to prop herself up on the bed next to her so she didn't fall flat on her face. She turned to look at Sadie—who didn't look nearly as shocked as Milena felt.

"Will I get to keep my baby?" Christine asked softly from the bed next to her. "Master Jeremiah took my last boy away and I never saw him again."

This time, Milena gaped at the teenager.

Christine and the other girls in the pregnancy unit, as it was called, were typically shy and didn't act like any teenagers Milena had ever known. They never spoke out of turn and were always polite, especially to Master Jeremiah and the Misters. They *never* questioned authority, especially a man's. So for Christine to speak up like she had, to an unknown male authority figure at that, was shocking.

The man who had observed while Milena helped Christine give birth spoke before the FBI agent could. His voice was low and rumbly...and something about it sounded familiar. "You'll get to keep your baby."

Too many thoughts were tumbling around Milena's brain. She had no idea what was going on, but she had a feeling it was bad. She and Sadie had discussed their suspicions about the school, but that's all they were—suspicions. They had no concrete proof of anything. Milena also knew her friend had talked to her uncle and some of his friends and relatives who owned a security company up in Dallas, but Sadie hadn't been sure they could find out anything about the school.

Master Jeremiah was an upstanding member of San

Antonio society. He'd received a commendation from the mayor for the work he was doing for the girls at Bexar. There was a steady stream of important men from the city who came to observe. Police officers, politicians, businessmen.

If all those authority figures had been there, and hadn't found anything out of order, what could she and Sadie do?

Looked like they didn't have to do anything. Whatever was happening was big. Especially if the FBI was involved.

"I need to get changed, and make sure Christine and her baby—"

The FBI agent interrupted her. "There are paramedics outside. They'll take care of them."

"Oh, but—"

The agent took a step toward her as he said, "Come along, Ms. Reinhardt. Stop stalling."

"Alvarez," the mystery man growled, as Milena almost tripped over her own feet trying to back away from the menacing agent reaching toward her.

The agent stopped in his tracks and dropped his hand. "There's nothing more you can do here," the man called Alvarez said, obviously trying to temper his impatience. "Please come with me now."

"I don't understand what's going on. Where are the other girls? They're pregnant. Stress isn't good for them." Milena thought she heard a snort from Christine, but ignored it, her gaze going from the FBI agent's face to the other man still standing by the door.

"They're fine. They're being looked after. You're wasting time," Alvarez said, his impatience barely held in check.

Swallowing hard, Milena looked over at Sadie. The other woman was still standing by Christine's side and had one hand on the teenager's shoulder. "It's okay," Sadie said. "They just want to ask us questions."

Milena narrowed her eyes at her friend. She sounded completely at ease and not at all freaked out.

When she'd shown up a month ago out of the blue, Milena had immediately invited her to stay with her at her parents' house. Bob and Missy Reinhardt had welcomed the addition to the household without question. Then again, that was how they were. They didn't judge, and had never made Milena feel bad about moving back in with them two and a half years ago. Besides, they'd loved Sadie when the girls were in high school, and seemed pleased to see her again.

Milena had a million questions, but instead of asking them, she merely nodded. She'd find out soon enough what was going on. Until then, she just had to play it smart and keep quiet. She'd figure out what to do as soon as she learned exactly what had happened at the school that night.

Straightening her shoulders, she walked out of the delivery room, refusing to look at either of the intimidating men as she passed.

Chapter Two

THOMAS JAMES "TJ" Rockwell stood at the window to the interrogation room and clenched his teeth. Hard.

Milena was sitting in a wooden chair, slumped over the cold metal table in front of her. She'd been there for an hour and was losing the battle to stay awake. Her blonde hair was in disarray and hung limply around her face. Her head would bob as she began to fall asleep, then she'd jerk awake and catch herself. This had happened several times over the five minutes TJ had been watching her.

She was still wearing the stained light blue scrubs she'd had on when she'd delivered the teenager's baby. Every so often, she'd rub her hands up and down her arms and shiver in the obviously cold interrogation room.

Without turning to look at the man next to him, TJ said, "She's not a part of this, Cruz."

"I know," his friend responded immediately.

At that, TJ finally looked at the other man. He'd known Cruz a while. His friend was taller than TJ's own six feet by a few inches, but TJ knew if push came to shove, he could win in a hand-to-hand-combat situation against him. Not that they were going to come to blows there in the FBI field office, but TJ was on edge.

It had been three years, one month, and twelve days since he'd been as close to Milena Reinhardt as he was right now, and the only thing he wanted to do was bust into the small, cold room, gather her into his arms, and tell her that he was an idiot for leaving her—and he'd never let her go again.

But he couldn't do that.

Because she was about to be interrogated by the FBI about her role in the revolting child-abuse ring at the school.

At one time, it was thought the school was some sort of cult. TJ almost would have preferred that over the sick exploitation of children they'd discovered. The only thing keeping him semi calm was the fact that his friend Cruz would be the one interrogating her.

"If she knew what was happening at that fucking place, she wouldn't have stood for it. I know that for a fact," he told Cruz.

"I *know*," Cruz repeated. "But you know as well as I do that she has to be questioned. We have to play this by the book because of how high up the corruption has apparently gone. We need to figure out how she got involved with them in the first place. A lot of heads are going to roll, and the FBI wants to make sure they've got as much information as possible on every asshole who visited that depraved place to make sure they pay."

TJ took a deep breath and turned back to the window to stare at the only woman he'd ever loved. The woman he'd screwed over, and who he had no doubt would never forgive him. Hell, he couldn't forgive *himself* for what he'd done. "Any word on Jeremiah or his son?"

Cruz pressed his lips together and shook his head. "No. They're in the wind. The SWAT team checked the school from top to bottom and couldn't find them. They got a ton of evidence to put them in jail for the rest of their fucking lives, but those two assholes somehow slipped away."

"Is Milena or her friend in danger? What about the girls who were at the school?" TJ asked urgently.

Cruz shrugged. "Honestly, it's hard to say. I'd like to believe Jeremiah and his son have enough on their plates getting out of town and staying ahead of law enforcement, but the bottom line is that I just don't know."

"Fuck," TJ said. "I want to be assigned to Milena."

Cruz held up his hand. "The bureau isn't taking that step yet. Until there's proof the Joneses are still around or are targeting anyone, we can't authorize any extra budget to go toward bodyguards."

"You don't need to pay me a dime. All I need is someone from the bureau to have a word with my supervisor so I can get the time off."

Cruz stared at him for a long moment before nodding. "I'll see what I can do."

"Appreciate it. I'm taking the next week off. Vacation. But after that, I need the official approval to stick close to her side."

"I'll do what I can."

"Thanks."

Cruz turned to go.

"Go easy on her, Cruz. She's had a hard night," TJ said softly.

Cruz nodded again, and clapped TJ on the shoulder before turning to leave the small observation room.

"Cruz?"

The other man stopped at the door and turned back.

TJ shrugged out of the brown leather jacket he'd been wearing and held it out to the other man. "Turn up the air in there. You don't need to use any fucking interrogation techniques on her, like making the temperature too cold or hot. She's freezing. Cut her some slack."

Cruz hesitated for a second, then grabbed the jacket

TJ held out to him. Without a word, he slipped out of the room to question Milena.

TJ resumed his position in front of the mirror and fisted his hands in his pockets. He hated this. Loathed it. Wanted nothing more than to be in there with Milena himself. But this had quickly become the government's operation. He'd been invited to participate in the raid only because he knew Cruz. TJ suspected that Chase Jackson, the Army Captain stationed up at Fort Hood, had something to do with his involvement in the raid as well.

Jackson had called and asked him to keep an eye on the comings and goings at the school. After learning Milena—*his* Milena—had been linked to the school, he'd spent every spare moment he had watching the property. It was only after talking to his friend, Cruz, that he'd discovered the school was already part of a low-priority FBI investigation.

Using the skills he'd learned in the Army as a Delta Force soldier, TJ had found a spot on a ridge about a mile away where he could watch over the school. He'd told Cruz about the location, and the two of them had spent the last month observing and taking notes—often together—on the comings and goings of every car. Repeat visits from some of San Antonio's highest officials was enough to make them suspicious. They'd never seen the children playing on the expensive playground off to the side of the school, and in fact, rarely saw any glimpses of the kids at all.

Audio captured by a wired city councilman sent in by the FBI—in exchange for a lesser sentence on his recent embezzlement charge—instantly changed the case from low-priority to an extremely high-priority one.

He'd watched as Milena had driven onto the grounds promptly at twelve forty-five, three days a week, Sadie in the passenger seat of her red Subaru Forester. She'd always gone into one building, which sat some ways away from the large main building. When five o'clock came, she and Sadie exited the building, got back in her car, and drove away.

TJ had been tempted to follow her. See where she was living. Who she was living with. But had talked himself out of it every time. He knew himself, and knew seeing firsthand that she'd moved on, probably gotten married, maybe had a family, would kill him.

He knew Cruz had questions about his intense interest in Milena, but the other man had let him have his privacy.

After tonight, however, TJ had a feeling the space Cruz had given him was going to be a thing of the past. But talking about Milena, and the best and worst times in his life, wasn't something he'd ever be comfortable doing.

TJ watched, a silent shadow, as Cruz entered the

small, brightly lit interrogation room and handed Milena his jacket. She looked surprised, and TJ couldn't blame her. She'd been sitting in the small, windowless room for an hour while the agents were busy talking to some of the children and teachers who'd been at the school. She was low on their priority list.

There weren't a lot of "teachers" at the school, but that was because they weren't actually instructing the students in reading, writing, or math problems. Everyone knew what was happening behind closed doors and they'd all go down for it.

As she shrugged on his jacket, he saw her eyes widen right before she turned her head to bury her nose in the collar.

MILENA WAS EXHAUSTED. Not only tired, but scared out of her mind at the same time. She had no idea how long she'd been sitting in the sterile room, but it seemed like an eternity.

Not only that, but she was freezing. Living in Texas, she'd gotten used to buildings being overly air conditioned to combat the heat outside, but this was ridiculous. It had to be fifty degrees inside the tiny room. Her hands shook and her nose was ice cold. All she wanted to do was curl up in her bed at home and hide under the covers. But she was stuck in the ice-box room until someone came and questioned her.

Maybe they'd forgotten about her. Maybe everyone had gone home and she'd be found in the morning when a bad guy was dragged into the room to be questioned about some awful thing he'd done, and they'd be surprised to find her frozen, dead body lying on the floor.

Shaking her head, Milena tried to concentrate. She was being overly dramatic. She wasn't going to freeze to death. She was chilled, yes, but she honestly wasn't all that surprised. And all things considered, she'd rather be cold than hot. She wasn't an idiot. The temperature had probably been turned down on purpose to make her uncomfortable. She'd watched enough forensic and cop shows to know how it worked.

Jumping in her chair when the door to the room was suddenly opened, Milena turned toward it. A tall man with short black hair entered. He was wearing a pair of jeans and a long-sleeve, black button-down shirt. He held out a leather jacket as he came closer.

"I apologize for the temperature of the room, Miss Reinhardt."

She stared at the jacket for a beat, then reached for it before he changed his mind. As the man got settled in the seat across from her, Milena shrugged on the jacket.

She froze when a familiar scent wafted up from the leather.

Turning her head to see if she was simply losing her mind or if she'd smelled what she thought she had, Milena brought the collar of the leather jacket to her nose and inhaled. An earthy, musky scent filled her nostrils.

Goosebumps broke out on her arms and she squeezed her eyes shut, lost in the memory of the only man she'd ever loved. A man who had crushed her heart.

His parting gift was the only thing that had kept her from falling into a pit of despair after he'd left.

"My name is Agent Cruz Livingston, and I work for the FBI. I need you to tell me everything you can about your employment at the Bexar County School and Orphanage for Girls."

His words brought her out of her reminiscing.

"Where's Sadie?"

"She's fine. She was questioned and sent home thirty minutes ago."

Milena nodded and relaxed. She might be in trouble for working at the school, but since she'd brought Sadie there, she didn't want her to be in hot water as well.

"I don't know where to start," she said quietly.

"How long have you been working there?" Cruz asked.

"About three and a half months. I was working at the women's clinic downtown and was approached by

Mister Jonathan…he's Master Jeremiah's son. Anyway, I'd noticed him before, kinda hanging out around the clinic, and when I approached to find out what his deal was, he told me that he worked at the school and they were looking for an experienced nurse to help with the pregnant teenagers. I sent him away, but researched the school when I got home. Everything seemed on the up and up. Did you know Master Jeremiah was given the key to the city a couple years ago for the philanthropic work he's done over the years?"

The FBI agent in front of her didn't nod, but didn't shake his head either. "So did Jonathan come back after that?" he asked.

Milena nodded. "Every day. He begged me to come work for his dad. Said they were desperate, and that his father had looked into my credentials and decided I was just the person they needed." She shrugged self-consciously. "I'm not stupid. I found out as much as I could about their philosophy, entry requirements— which I now know were completely bogus—and history before I agreed to talk to Master Jeremiah."

"And how did that conversation go? Did you go out to the school for an interview?"

Milena shook her head. "No. He came to the clinic one afternoon. He was well-spoken and genuinely seemed to care about the girls at his school. I still wasn't sure…I mean, he wanted me there three days a week for only four hours at a time. Twelve hours a week wasn't all that much, and it would mean sacrificing my full-time hours at the clinic, taking me down to part-time there. I'd be losing my insurance and everything."

"Let me guess, he made you an offer you couldn't refuse," Cruz said dryly.

Milena blushed but nodded. "Yeah. Said I could go on the school's insurance, and the pay was more than what I was making at the clinic, full-time. I thought it was too good to be true, and said so. He reassured me that my expertise was worth it, and that I'd also be on call. If one of the girls needed me, he said I'd be expected to come out to the school no matter what time it was. I finally agreed."

"Why?"

"Why what?"

"Why did you agree? No offense, but you live with your parents. You can't actually be hurting for money."

Milena's hands clenched into fists in her lap. She hated when people judged her. *Hated* it. They had no idea what she'd been through and how much she owed her parents for helping her without making her feel like a burden. "I pay my way," she said firmly. "I pay for groceries; I give my parents rent money even though they don't ask for it. I haven't taken a cent from them."

"Then why live at home?" Cruz asked, leaning back in his chair.

Milena glared at the agent. "Why not?" she countered, not wanting to tell this man her reasons if she didn't have to. She wasn't ashamed of why she'd moved in with them, but she wasn't about to tell this stranger her secrets.

Cruz was silent for a long minute. Milena refused to squirm under his assessment and resisted the temptation to ease the awkward silence by speaking.

Finally, he smiled, as if he was impressed with her ability to keep quiet. "Right, so...tell me about your job there at the school."

And she did. She explained how she was responsible for the pregnant teenagers' well-being. That she taught them what to eat and not eat while they were pregnant. She answered their questions about the upcoming birth and what would happen.

Cruz leaned forward when she was done speaking and put his forearms on the table in front of him. His eyes narrowed and he asked, "Did you ever come into contact with the other girls at the school? The younger ones?"

Milena shook her head.

"Not ever?" Cruz insisted.

"No. I wasn't allowed to go anywhere but the C ward."

"Why was it called the C ward?"

Milena shrugged. "The only thing I can guess is because the names of all the girls there started with the letter C."

"And you didn't think that was odd?" Cruz asked, his brown eyes piercing in their intensity.

"Well, yeah, but that's what they told me their names were. Christine, Cora, Callie, Cathy, and Claire."

"Did the girls ever talk about their lives before they got pregnant?"

Milena shook her head again. "No. They seemed…scared to, if I'm being honest."

"By all means, please be honest," Cruz drawled.

She flushed, but forced herself to continue. The sooner she told this guy everything he wanted to know, the sooner she could go home to her family. "The girls were really well behaved. They were almost too obedient. They weren't like the teenagers I treated in the downtown clinic. They seemed almost too innocent to be pregnant. The other weird thing was that Master Jeremiah didn't want me to tell them what gender their babies were, although he insisted I tell *him*."

"And you didn't find *that* odd?"

Milena was getting sick of his suspicious tone. "Actually, I found it really odd. But by that point, I had already signed a nondisclosure agreement and had received my first month's pay. I'd told the clinic director I'd be working part-time, and I was reliant on the school for my living expenses and insurance. Ultimately, I figured it didn't matter if the girls didn't know the gender of their babies. How I treated them wouldn't change."

"Hmmm," Cruz murmured, leaning back in his seat and staring at her again. He chewed his lip for a moment before seemingly coming to a decision. He took a breath and began to speak. "The Bexar County School and Orphanage for Girls was a front for a massive child-abuse and sex-trafficking organization. Jeremiah Jones was orchestrating the abuse of every girl living under the school's roof. Not only that, but when they 'aged out,' the girls were sold online to the highest bidder."

Milena felt the blood drain from her face—and all she could do was stare at the agent with her mouth open in disbelief.

He continued. "He had separate sections of the school for the girls, depending on their ages. The babies were kept in one room. They generally weren't abused. But on a girl's second birthday, she was moved to the 'littles' room. From the ages of two to five, those girls were slowly introduced to the 'rules' of the school and how life would be for them from that point on. If the students were lucky, they weren't raped...but *all* of those girls were exposed to the attentions of the 'visiting teachers.' Then, when they were five, the littles became 'smalls.' That's where the more physical abuse started. For two years, those girls had to attend 'classes' with the visiting teachers."

"Oh my God," Milena said, covering her mouth with her hand. She felt like she was going to puke. But Agent Livingston wasn't done.

"Some of the men who visited the school preferred the younger girls, but Jeremiah catered to everyone's tastes. When the girls turned eight, they were called 'bigs.' As a big, they were expected to have learned all the rules. They weren't allowed to speak unless ordered to. They did whatever the perverts who paid Jeremiah big bucks wanted them to. These girls literally didn't know any other kind of life. All they knew was doing what they were told by Jeremiah and his 'friends.'

"When they were teenagers—known as 'misses'—the abuse slowed down, but it didn't stop altogether. You were hired to make sure the babies they carried were healthy. If the baby was a girl, it was placed in the school system to suffer the same fate as her mom. If it was a boy…" Cruz shrugged. "It conveniently disappeared. Adopted by a couple desperate to have a child. And they paid handsomely for the privilege of having Jeremiah Jones broker the deal."

Milena was afraid to ask, but she did anyway. "You said when they got too old…they were sold?"

There was no emotion on Cruz's face, but somehow Milena knew he wasn't as stoic as he appeared. "Yeah. When they turned eighteen or so, too old to appeal to

Jeremiah's…*customers* anymore, he set up an online auction on the dark web. Sold them to people all over the globe as sex slaves."

The tears Milena had been holding back slipped over her lids and down her cheeks. "Have they been found?"

Cruz scoffed. His voice wasn't harsh, but he definitely wasn't holding back in order to spare her. "Miss Reinhardt, these girls had no names. No *real* names, that is. When they were babies, they were only assigned a number. Baby One. Baby Two, etc. Then when they were littles, their names started with L's. Smalls started with S. Bigs started with B. Misses with M. When they got pregnant, their name was changed yet again to start with a C. If they were young enough, they went back to being a miss. When they were put up on the web to be sold, they were merely numbers once again. Full circle. We're trying to find Jeremiah's records on the sales but for all intents and purposes, those girls are gone. Probably dead…or wishing they were."

Milena dropped her face into her hands and sobbed. She thought about Christine, and how she'd been so surprised and hopeful that she'd get to keep her baby when the school had been raided. Milena hated the thought that the baby boy could've been taken away to be adopted by someone without the girl's consent, but that was better than the alternative. If the baby had been a girl, it would've gone into the "system" and had a lifetime of abuse in front of her.

Then something occurred to her—and her head whipped up. "I was helping him abuse those poor girls?"

Something shifted in Cruz's eyes, and he said in a surprisingly gentle tone, "No. If anything, you were giving them a taste of what it was like to be treated like a human being, instead of a sex slave."

"Oh God," Milena moaned. She stood suddenly, knocking her chair backwards in the process. It fell to the floor with a loud clang but she didn't seem to hear it in her agitation. "Oh God," she repeated. "I didn't know. I swear I didn't know! I can't believe he was doing that to kids. I never even saw the children! He said there was a doctor employed full-time to take care of…" Her voice trailed off and she moaned once again.

"The doctor was abusing them too, wasn't he?" She waved off Cruz's answer when he opened his mouth. "Never mind, you don't have to tell me. I know he was. The first time I examined the girls, they were terrified. I don't know what that so-called doctor did to them, but it had to have been bad. Jesus…all those men who showed up at five when I was leaving were there to abuse the girls, weren't they?"

Cruz nodded.

"The politicians, the cops, the businessmen…*all* of them?" Milena asked.

Cruz nodded again. "Every single one. And at the moment, they're all being investigated and rounded up. One by one. They're going to pay for what they've done."

"How do you know who they are?"

"Jeremiah kept meticulous records on everyone who came to the school. Had cameras in all the rooms. A couple...clients...got nervous, and to make sure they kept quiet about what was happening, he blackmailed them. He held the careers of over a hundred men in this city in the palm of his hand."

Milena bit her lip and stared at the FBI Agent. She'd thought he looked friendly enough when he'd first entered the room. He was good-looking and tall. She had a weakness for tall men. But at the moment, he looked ruthless. She had no doubt he'd do just as he said—make sure all the perverts who partook of Jeremiah's immoral and hideous scheme would go to jail.

But wait...she was also a part of it, even if indirectly. Was she going to be arrested too? Was that why she'd been held for so long? "Am I going to jail?"

"Should you be?"

Milena stood on the other side of the room and stared at Cruz, honestly not sure how to respond. She opened her mouth to speak when a loud *thump* came from the mirror behind the agent.

Intellectually, Milena knew the mirror wasn't really

a mirror, but a window where someone, or several people, watched from the other side, but she'd blocked that out. After the bang on the window, she couldn't ignore the fact that there was, indeed, someone observing her interview.

Someone who wasn't happy about the turn in the conversation.

Another heavy *thump* sounded, and Milena jumped. Whoever was on the other side definitely wanted attention.

Surprisingly, Cruz smirked. Milena stared at him, totally confused.

"You're not going to jail," he told her, standing. He walked over to her chair, still lying on its side on the floor, and righted it. He held the back and gestured to the seat. "Come. Sit back down. I'll explain what's going to happen next and answer any other questions that you have."

Warily, Milena inched toward the chair and sat at the very edge. Without commenting, Cruz walked back around the table and sat down. "It's obvious you had no idea what was going on at the school. Not only that, you don't exactly meet the criteria to be an insider."

"The criteria?"

"You're female, for one thing, so you obviously aren't a customer of Jeremiah's and his stable of girls," Cruz told her.

Milena swallowed hard at hearing the poor abused children being described as belonging to a "stable." It was appropriate though, as they'd been treated like animals…with no feelings or rights for as long as they'd resided at the school.

"And, I'm not trying to be rude, but you're simply too old for Jeremiah's tastes. You're what…twenty-six?"

"Seven," she told him.

"Right, you and Sadie are of no interest to Jeremiah. The school has been under investigation for quite a while, and what you've said you did there matches up with the records we confiscated from Jeremiah's office."

"I saw some of the men who came at night," Milena said shakily. "Do I need to be worried about that?"

Cruz immediately shook his head. "I doubt it. They have enough to worry about. You weren't blackmailing them, and they're going to be more than aware that the evidence against them isn't based on anything you saw. The videos, pictures, and bank records are going to do them in without any eyewitness testimony from you."

"And the children? What's going to happen to them?"

For the first time since the interview had started, Milena saw true anger on the agent's face. "They'll be placed into foster care. They all need extensive psychological help. Even the babies, who weren't touched sexually, were still abused. A lack of love and comfort can be just as harmful as any other kind of neglect."

"And my girls?"

Cruz knew who she was talking about without needing her to clarify. "They're being placed into foster care as well."

"Can I see them?"

Cruz shook his head. "It's not a good idea. Any reminders of where they were and what happened can't be good for them right now. Maybe in time, but for now, no."

Milena sighed. She'd expected that answer. She didn't like it, but she understood why. "You said Sadie's been released?"

"Yeah. She was interviewed earlier. I'm sorry it took so long to get to you. We're almost done here and you'll be free to go. But Miss Reinhardt, I'll ask that you don't leave town. You and Sadie need to be accessible in case any other questions come up."

Milena nodded. "No problem on my part. I live here. Sadie's uncle's might want her home...back in Dallas."

"She said it wouldn't be an issue for her to stay. I understand she's been living with you at your parents' house."

"Yeah, she's been helping me with...uh...yeah, she came down to see me and decided to stay for a while." Milena swallowed, not wanting to get into what Sadie had been helping her with. It was nobody's business but her own. It wasn't something she was embarrassed about, not in the least, but it also wasn't something she advertised.

"One more thing…since Jeremiah and Jonathan haven't been located, you need to be extremely careful."

"You think they're going to come after me? I thought you just said you didn't think I was in danger."

"I *do* think that. I'm not saying those two will care about you or your friend, but since they're in the wind, you still need to be careful."

"Yeah, all right. That makes sense. I do have to work though. I can't just sit at home," Milena told him.

"I didn't think you would. The bureau can't offer you a full-time bodyguard at this point, but if it looks like you're in danger, you'll be assigned protection."

"I will?" Her head tilted to the right in confusion. "Who?"

"All of the law enforcement agencies in the area worked together on this bust," he said, not really answering her question. "SAPD, the state highway patrol, FBI, Texas Rangers…it was truly an interagency effort to bring this sick operation down. I'm not one hundred percent sure who would be assigned to you, if it comes to that. But rest assured, we won't just leave you vulnerable for those assholes to get ahold of."

"Oh, well…thank you," Milena said, somewhat surprised.

"As I said, at this point, I think they've hightailed it out of town. Just be alert for anything odd happening and let me know if you ever feel as if you're in danger, and I'll make sure you get that protection. Now, if you'll just sit tight, I'll arrange for you to get a ride home," Cruz told her, standing.

"Oh…my car. Can I…will I get it back?"

"Of course. The FBI doesn't go around stealing cars, Milena."

It was the first time he'd used her name, and somehow it changed the whole atmosphere of the room. Made him seem more…approachable. Friendly.

"I do suspect it'll take a couple days for it to be towed back to FBI headquarters. It'll need to be searched, you understand."

"Of course." Milena inwardly winced at what the investigators would find in the backseat. Lord only knew what was back there. She hadn't had the time or inclination to clean it out recently. Not having her car would be a pain, but she was sure her mom would let her use hers in the meantime.

"If you'll wait here, I'll be back in a bit."

"By a bit…you don't mean a few hours, do you?" Milena asked. "I have no idea what time it is, but I need to get home."

"I don't mean a few hours," he reassured her. Then

Cruz stood. He looked down at her with an expression Milena couldn't identify. Just when she was feeling uneasy, he said softly, "You have a big heart, Milena Reinhardt. My girlfriend is a lot like you. Lucky for me, she's as forgiving as she is tenderhearted."

And with those cryptic words, Agent Cruz Livingston nodded at her and left the room.

Milena stared at the door he'd disappeared through, then turned to face the huge mirror on the opposite wall from where she was sitting. She looked tired. Her hair was a mess, her scrubs were stained with Christine's blood. Even from across the room she could see the dark circles under her eyes, advertising to the world her exhaustion.

Dropping her head, Milena took a deep breath, and once more inhaled the smell emanating from the jacket she was wearing.

This time when the tears came, she didn't bother trying to hold them back. The subtle musky and earthy scent of the jacket she was wearing wafted up to her nose and made her feel even more off center. The smell reminded her of the man she'd once loved with all her heart, and she remembered how safe and secure she'd felt when he'd held her in his arms. She wished he was here right now. If she ever needed him, now was the time.

As soon as Cruz Livingston stepped foot into the observation room, TJ reached out and shoved against his chest as hard as he could. The other man took a step back, but grinned at his friend.

"You asshole. You made her cry," TJ accused.

Cruz merely shrugged. "It's not like we were having tea, TJ. She was being questioned about a fucking sex-abuse scandal."

"Yeah, but you shouldn't have made her think for one fucking second she'd be arrested. You knew before you went in there she didn't know shit about what was happening."

Crus smirked. "You know you're not supposed to do anything to bring attention to the fact you're observing the interview."

"Whatever," TJ mumbled. He turned back to the window and stared at Milena. Her arms were around her waist now and her head was lowered. She looked so vulnerable and scared, he wanted nothing more than to go to her. Now wasn't the time and it certainly wasn't the place.

He might've been doing nothing but watching over her for the last month, keeping her safe from afar, never letting her know he was there, but that shit was done.

He knew she wouldn't be happy to see him, not after the way he'd left, but he didn't care anymore. TJ still loved her, hell, had never *stopped*. And although he knew he had an uphill battle getting back into her good graces, and that she might never feel for him again the way she used to, he was going to give it his best shot.

"Be straight with me, is she in danger from those two assholes?" TJ asked abruptly.

Cruz picked up the change in conversation without missing a beat. "At this point, it's hard to tell, but I'm thinking no. The Joneses would be idiots to be within a thousand miles of San Antonio."

"Seriously, if a protection detail is necessary, I want it."

"Of course. If it comes to that, which I seriously doubt, I'll reach out to your boss."

"Appreciate it," TJ told his friend.

Cruz waved off his thanks. "I think it's obvious that no one would protect her as well as you would. It's late. Agent Bennington said he'd give Milena a ride home. I need to let him know she's ready." Cruz paused for a second, then said, "TJ…"

TJ turned and looked at Cruz. He didn't like the intense way his friend was staring at him. "Yeah?"

"You know if you need anything, all you have to do is ask. You've got a friend in every law enforcement agency in this city. Rangers, Sheriff's office, FBI, SAPD…hell, even the Warden service. With one word, we're all there."

"I know, and I appreciate it. Me and Milena…we

have a history," TJ reluctantly told him.

"No shit."

TJ's lips quirked. "Unfortunately, I fucked up, and she's not going to be happy to see me."

"She'll forgive you," Cruz said with certainty.

"I'm not sure. I was a colossal dick. It's not like I didn't put the toilet seat down or something."

"If Mickie forgave me for not telling her I was undercover when we met, Milena will forgive you."

TJ wanted to believe his friend, but he honestly wasn't sure. If the tables were turned and she'd walked out on *him* in the middle of the night without even a note, he wasn't sure he'd be able to find it within him to forgive her, never mind start up where they'd left off.

But that's what he wanted. He wanted Milena back. In his life. In his bed. By his side. He hadn't appreciated her then, but he wouldn't let even one day go by without making sure she understood how much she meant to him…if she let him.

Cruz put a hand on his shoulder and squeezed. "I'll make sure she gets home safe. Let her get some sleep, then go see her."

TJ looked at his friend and nodded absently. The door to the observation room shut behind Cruz and TJ turned his attention back to Milena.

A pane of thick two-way glass separated them, but it had been a long three years since he'd even been *this* close to her. He'd take what he could get. He watched as an agent opened the door and told Milena he was there to take her home. She stood and reluctantly—at least it seemed that way to him—removed his jacket and draped it over the back of the chair she'd been sitting in.

It took everything in him not to storm out of the observation room and confront her right then and there, but he refrained.

As soon as they'd had time to exit the hallway, TJ opened the door and went into the interrogation room. He picked up his jacket and brought it to his face. He inhaled, and the scent he'd missed more than anything made its way into his lungs...and heart.

Milena had always smelled like lemons. Her lotion and shampoo were infused with the stuff, at least that's what she always told him when he'd complimented her on her scent. Shrugging the jacket on and reveling in the way her lemony smell had seeped into the leather even during the short time she'd been wearing it, TJ resolved that tomorrow—no, later this morning; it was already three-thirty—he'd reacquaint himself with the love of his life.

He might've been a dick and given her up for all the wrong reasons in the past, but that shit was done. He wasn't going to walk away again, not without one hell of a good reason. And the *only* reason he'd walk away was if she was married. He didn't care if she was dating someone or engaged. Until she was wearing a ring on her finger, she was fair game.

And he planned on doing whatever it took to not only make her forgive him for being an ass, but to love him once again. She had to—any other outcome was unacceptable.

"COME ON, JONATHAN. The coast is clear, we can't stay here." Jeremiah Jones's voice was low and calm as he looked at his son. They were hidden in one of the secret passageways under the school, built for just such a situation as the one that had occurred tonight.

Jonathan knew from the moment his father had opened the school they might someday need a way to escape the cops.

Jeremiah had made the engineer sign a nondisclosure agreement, but after the work was completed, had him killed anyway. He'd justified it by saying there was no way he wanted anyone other than his own flesh and blood knowing about the tunnel.

"Are we going to leave the weapons here?" Jonathan asked, gesturing back the way they'd come, where an arsenal was stored. Guns, semi-automatic rifles, ammunition, rocket-propelled grenade launchers...they had it all.

"For now, yes. But if we need them, we'll come back

for them."

"Where are we going? Mexico?"

"Eventually, but not yet. I have some unfinished business to attend to first," Jeremiah said with a hard glint in his eyes.

Jonathan remembered being a child and feeling scared when his dad got like this. He'd simply learned not to question him, and to do whatever he said as soon as he said it. The punishments he'd suffered as a kid had been enough to make him extremely careful around his father even today.

The father turned to look at his son then. "I made a mistake, Jonathan."

"A mistake, Father?"

"Yeah. I hired that bitch of a nurse—*and* allowed her friend to accompany her when she came to look after the pregnant bitches. I *know* one of them called the cops on us. Probably the nurse. She ruined what I built here! It's all *her* fault I lost my girls. It's not going to be easy to get new ones, but we will. First, I have to fix my mistake before we start over in Mexico." He narrowed his eyes at his son. "You once told me you liked the redheaded bitch." It was a question without sounding like one.

"I don't like *her*," Jonathan told his father. "She's too old and tall. But…I think she'd make beautiful baby girls. Girls with red hair and green eyes. I want *them*."

Jeremiah grinned. "I'm proud of the man you've become, Jonathan. If you want her, my son, you'll have her. I'll make sure the nurse can't tattle on anyone else, then we'll take the redhead with us to Mexico. She can be the first contributor to our new stable of girls."

A slow, evil smile spread across Jonathan's face. He pushed his too-long, greasy blond hair behind one ear. "Yeah, I like that idea."

"I thought you might. Come on, son. We need to regroup and visit some of our supporters. We'll watch and wait for the right time to strike. I'll find the best way to make her pay for ruining what I've built. I don't know how yet, but mark my words. She'll wish she'd never heard of the Bexar County School and Orphanage for Girls. Or Jeremiah Jones."

The two men slipped out of the tunnel into the trees on the back side of the vast property. Jonathan had thought his father was crazy for building the tunnels under the school, but now he was glad. Instead of being locked up behind bars, they were on their way to a better life.

He followed behind Jeremiah silently, thoughts of red-haired little girls swirling through his mind as he walked.

Chapter Three

M ILENA TIPTOED INTO her parents' house and shut the door quietly behind her. She threw the lock and heaved out a huge sigh. She was numb from everything she'd learned after talking with the FBI agent. And stressed. It was extremely selfish of her, especially with everything the poor girls at the school had been through and were *still* going through, but she couldn't help but think about the money she wouldn't be making now.

She'd been so close to finally being able to move out of her parents' house and making it on her own. Hopefully the clinic would let her go back to full-time. But for now, she only had a part-time job. Not only that, but she didn't have any health insurance at the moment.

That thought was the one that made her heart rate pick up and the panic attack that had been hovering nearly get the best of her. Milena took a deep breath. Then another.

No, she was fine. It wasn't ideal, but her parents

would let her stay as long as she needed. She knew that. Just as she knew they'd help her out with any bills that might arise, as they'd done in the past.

That didn't mean she had to like it.

She was twenty-seven. Well past the age when she should be living on her own.

Milena walked into the living room and glanced at the clock on the wall. Four-thirty in the morning. She groaned softly. If she was lucky, she had an hour and a half before she needed to be up.

Detouring by the laundry room, she stripped off her stained scrubs and started the washer before heading to her room in nothing but her underwear. She closed the door to her childhood room and sighed. She made a quick trip to the bathroom, then grabbed the T-shirt she slept in every night. It was way too big to wear in public, but it was perfect to sleep in. The black letters on the front were faded and it had long since lost the smell of its previous owner, but Milena couldn't bring herself to stop wearing it.

It was stupid.

All she was doing was torturing herself.

But she couldn't make herself throw the thing out.

The Army T-shirt was all she had left of the man she'd once loved with all her heart. She'd been wearing it when he'd left. He'd taken every other scrap of clothing, leaving no trace he'd ever lived in her apartment. Except for the shirt.

Knowing she was feeling maudlin because of all the excitement from the day, Milena forced herself to crawl under her covers and close her eyes. She didn't think she'd be able to sleep, not with all the awful things she'd learned about her former employer running through her mind, but within minutes, she was out.

Milena was unceremoniously awoken some time later when a small, warm body threw itself on top of her.

Her arms instinctively closed around her two-year-old son even while she was turning to her side. She opened her eyes and looked down at James Thomas…JT for short. He was grinning up at her. He put his little hands on her cheeks and said, "It morning, Mommy."

Milena yawned. "I know, little man. Did you sleep good?"

"'Ungry."

"You're always hungry."

He clapped his little hands together and squirmed, trying to get out from under her arm.

She let him up and watched as he scooted his butt to the edge of the bed then turned on his belly. He dropped his legs down and slipped over the side of the mattress. He was a little daredevil for sure. He loved to climb up and down whatever he could. Knowing she had to get up and take care of her little boy, Milena took a deep breath. She hadn't gotten nearly enough sleep, but mornings were for her and JT. She loved their routine.

Her parents usually slept in, giving her one-on-one time with her son, and Sadie had quickly learned that mornings were sacred to Milena. With more enthusiasm than she felt, Milena threw back the covers and stumbled out of bed. She needed to get JT changed and then fix him something to eat.

Her eyes felt as if they were weighted down with lead and she knew if she looked in the mirror, she'd see huge bags under her eyes. She had to go down to the clinic this morning and grovel for her full-time job back, and hoped she'd be able to hide her exhaustion.

Milena made a quick bathroom pit stop then headed for JT's room. He knew the drill, he was extremely smart, and she knew he'd be waiting for her. He was.

He'd climbed up onto the changing table all by himself and was lying on his back. She'd tried everything in her power to dissuade him from climbing up on the furniture, but when nothing worked, she'd done what she could to make the area around it safer, putting a squishy mat below the changing table and even having her dad shorten the legs. Milena made a mental note to try to speed up his potty training.

As was their routine, JT was holding a small pillow.

As she got to work changing his diaper, he held it out to her. "Kiss Daddy."

Milena dutifully leaned forward and kissed the fabric picture sewn onto the front of the pillow by her mom. "Now you," she told her son.

Milena smiled as JT brought the pillow to his own face and kissed/slobbered all over it.

For some reason, the ritual made Milena's heart hurt that morning.

Her mom hadn't understood why she'd wanted her to make the small pillow for JT. She'd tried to explain, but wasn't sure she'd succeeded when her mom had shaken her head and sighed.

Milena wanted JT to know his daddy. Even if he'd never meet him. Even if he'd never know him. She wanted her son to know his father was a hero. A man who'd given his all for his country. But mostly, she wanted JT to know that he was created out of love. That even if his father wasn't physically in their lives, it didn't mean JT wasn't wanted.

Milena had been shocked to find out a week after TJ had left that she was pregnant. They'd been pretty careful with condoms, but there had been a few times when they'd both been too excited, too eager to bother. She thought she knew the exact moment they'd created JT...

They'd been out to eat, and something had happened. TJ suffered from PTSD, even though he'd refused to tell her what had occurred during his last mission. The one that had put him in the VA hospital where they'd met. Milena didn't know what had set him off at the restaurant that night, but he'd been on edge. She'd suggested heading home early instead of going to the movies as they'd planned.

They'd arrived back at her apartment and he was still obviously not himself. Desperately wanting to help, Milena had grabbed him behind the neck and kissed him as passionately as she could. That was all it took. He immediately took over as the aggressor and she'd found herself stripped of the sundress she'd been wearing and naked on the living room floor before she knew what had happened.

TJ had gone down on her, pulling two orgasms from her before sitting up and stripping off his own clothes. Neither of them had spoken, the moment too intense for that. He'd brought her to her knees and encouraged her to lean over the couch cushions. Then he'd taken her from behind. Hard. Rough. Deep.

And it had felt amazing.

She'd never been as turned on as she was that night. TJ had pounded into her as if she was the only thing holding him together. And she'd loved it.

But even as he'd taken her how he wanted, he hadn't been selfish. One of his hands had snaked around her body and roughly fingered her clit, forcing her to come with him. Then, after he'd exploded deep inside her, and she thought they were done, he'd stood, picked her up as if she weighed no more than a child, and carried her into her bedroom.

There, he'd made slow, sweet love to her, wringing another orgasm out of her before planting his cock as deep as he could go and looking into her eyes as he'd emptied himself inside her once more.

They hadn't talked about it afterwards. Hadn't discussed the fact that he hadn't used a condom. The next time they'd had sex, and every time after that, he'd made sure to glove up.

Milena knew without a doubt they'd created their son during that intense night when she'd let him use her to fight his demons.

She'd loved TJ Rockwell with every fiber of her being. And, even though he'd left her without looking back, she wanted his son to love him too. So, she'd had her mom make the special pillow. One JT could hold, hug, and not worry about breaking.

She told her son stories about how brave his daddy was. How handsome. He would have questions later. He'd want to know why his daddy wasn't there. Why he'd left. Milena wasn't sure what she'd tell him. She didn't want to lie and tell him that his daddy was dead, but she also didn't want him to ever feel anything other than love and pride for his father.

Milena had put pictures of TJ all around their son's room. Everywhere she looked, she was confronted with his handsome face. It was torture, but she'd done it for JT. The little boy looked exactly like his dad. Light brown hair that, at the moment, was too long and sat in large ringlets all over his head. He'd inherited her blue eyes, but his lips, nose, cheekbones, and even his ears were all TJ's.

Tears welled up in Milena's eyes as she finished changing the diaper. She normally didn't get so sentimental, but after hearing about how awful the babies' lives were who'd lived at the school, and because she was so tired, she couldn't stop the tears that fell down her cheeks.

"Mama sad?" JT asked, bringing the small pillow up to her face. "Daddy help."

Milena choked back a bitter laugh. If only.

She allowed her son to press the pillow against her face a couple times, then pulled back. She lifted him and grunted with fake exertion. "Man, you're getting big, little man!" She placed him on his chubby feet and wasn't surprised when he took off for the door. Her son hated wearing clothes. He much preferred to walk around in nothing but his diaper, and if he could get away with it, he'd tear that off too.

She put his dirty overnight diaper in the trash can

and picked up one of his shirts and a pair of shorts, then followed her son down to the kitchen.

An hour later, when her mom wandered down the stairs, Milena had managed to get JT into his shirt and fed. They'd had snuggle time and he was now watching a cartoon.

"Hey, Mom," Milena said.

"Hey, baby," Missy Reinhardt said, stopping to kiss her daughter on the head as she went past the couch on her way to the kitchen. She poured a cup of coffee, then came back into the living room and sat next to her daughter. "You okay?"

Milena wasn't surprised her mom knew something was up.

"Yeah. Just tired."

"What time did you get in last night?"

Milena cringed. "Four-thirty."

Her mom's eyebrows shot up. "Seriously?"

She nodded. Her mom didn't demand to know why, but Milena didn't expect her to. Her mom had always been pretty laid-back. Oh, she wasn't a pushover, but she had learned over the years to let her daughter share on her terms.

Milena took a sip of the lukewarm coffee in her cup and sighed. "You know that new job that was too good to be true?"

"Mm hmmm."

"It *was* too good to be true." Then she went on to tell her mom everything she'd learned about the Bexar County School and Orphanage for Girls, making sure JT was fully engrossed in the show and speaking quietly so he didn't overhear.

"Oh, baby girl, I'm so sorry."

"I…" Milena swallowed hard before continuing. "I'm going to need to stay here longer than I thought."

"You're welcome here as long as you want. This will always be a home for you. You know that," Missy said gently.

Tears sprang to Milena's eyes. "I know, but I can't help but feel as if I'm interfering with you and Daddy's life. I should be living on my own. It's not fair that you have to help me raise my son. You already did your time with poopy diapers and a messy house." She waved her hand at the room, indicating the toys that were scattered willy-nilly on the floor in front of them.

"Look at me," her mom demanded.

Milena took a deep breath and did as ordered.

"Having you and JT here is a gift. Being able to get to know my grandson as well as I do is not a hardship. I love having him, and you, here."

"And Sadie too?" Milena joked.

"Sadie too," her mom said immediately. "I've always liked her, you know that. And honestly, I'm thrilled she's here to give you a friend to talk to. I'm more than aware of what a hermit you are, Milena. You go to work and come straight home. You never go out, and you spend all your time talking to JT. He's great, but you need friends too. Since she's been here, you've changed. Relaxed more. It's a good thing."

"There's something else," Milena said, not wanting to keep this from her mom.

"What, hon?"

"The agent last night said Jeremiah and his son are missing. They weren't arrested after the raid."

Missy stiffened. "Are you in danger?"

Leave it to her mom to cut to the chase. "The agent doesn't think so. He said they would probably be trying to get as far from San Antonio as they could get. But, he also said that if necessary, I could have some sort of protection detail."

"Good," her mom said. "The last thing you need is to worry about being snatched off the street by those assholes."

"Mom!" Milena exclaimed. "You never swear!"

"Yeah, well, I didn't really have much to swear about before now."

Milena couldn't help it. She giggled. Her mom was kinda funny.

"This isn't funny."

Milena sobered. "I know it's not. But I didn't know anything about what was happening right under my nose. There's no reason for Jeremiah to be mad at me. I was totally clueless."

"You'll take the protection if you need it, though," her mom ordered.

"Of course I will. I'm not an idiot."

"Good."

Milena gave her mom a weak smile. "I have to go to the clinic this morning. See if I can grovel enough to get my full-time hours back. Get back on their insurance."

"You're exhausted, honey. Are you sure you can't take today off?"

Milena tiredly shook her head. "I'm sure. I don't think an FBI raid on my new place of employment is an acceptable reason to not be at work."

Missy Reinhardt reached out and took the cup of coffee from Milena's hands. "Well, go on then. Take a long shower, you'll feel better afterwards. I'll take JT out this afternoon so when you get back, you can take a nice long nap."

Milena smiled. "Thanks, Mom."

"I love you, baby. You're one of the strongest people I know, and I'm not just saying that because I wiped your butt when you were little."

Milena laughed and stood. "Thanks, I think."

"All I'm saying is…this too shall pass. It sucks right now. It's hard. But we'll always have your back. Okay?"

All she could do was nod. If she tried to say anything, she'd burst into tears. Trudging up the stairs to her room, Milena could only be thankful things had turned out how they had. Last night could've been very different if Master Jeremiah had expanded her duties. If she'd known more about what was going on at the school, she might be a lot more scared right now and in a lot more trouble. So many "ifs" in her life.

Taking a deep breath, Milena tried to remember that she truly believed everything happened for a reason.

The love of her life had broken her heart, but had also given her JT.

Having a truly awful pregnancy had brought her closer to her parents.

The things she'd gone through in JT's first year of life had led her to her new career.

She didn't know the reason behind her being hired by Master Jeremiah, but she truly hoped it wasn't something bad.

Maybe it was a lack of sleep, or maybe it was just residual feelings of unease from being interrogated last night, but she had a feeling something big was just around the corner. Something good-big or something bad-big, she wasn't sure yet.

Shaking her head and deciding to just go with the flow, Milena stepped into the shower and tried to wake herself up. She had to get through a long morning shift at the clinic, then an uncomfortable talk with her boss.

She needed to be on her toes, no matter how much she simply wanted to crawl back into bed and sleep.

TJ HAD SPOKEN with his supervisor and managed to get a week's vacation on short notice. Lord knew he had the time saved up. It had been a while since he'd requested to take any time off, and since his supervisor knew he'd been working a lot of overtime surveilling the "School of Horrors," as the press had dubbed the Bexar County School and Orphanage for Girls, he'd granted the request without a quibble.

He had no doubt if Milena ended up needing full-time protection, Cruz would get in touch with his supervisor and set it up so *he* could be the one assigned to her. The FBI wouldn't need to pay him overtime, he'd continue to take his regular pay to do it. It might be a lot of red tape and maybe a pain in the ass for Cruz, but TJ didn't care. He was, hands down, the best person to protect Milena because he genuinely cared what happened to her.

Deep down, TJ knew it would take more than a week to get back into Milena's good graces, but once he'd made the decision to try, he couldn't put it off. Didn't *want* to put it off. He'd made a mistake in not contacting her before now. He'd used excuse after excuse to justify keeping his distance from her or even looking her up to see where she was living.

But the bottom line was, he'd been an idiot. He hadn't been with a woman since Milena. Hadn't *wanted* to be with anyone else. He'd had plenty of offers, but no one made his heart race like she had.

He knew it probably wasn't the same for her. Milena was beautiful. Not only that, she was a good person. To the core. Any man would be lucky to have her, even if it was for a short time. TJ hated the thought of her being with anyone else, but he had to be honest with himself. She was beautiful and he'd left her. She'd probably dated plenty of men since he'd disappeared.

But ultimately, it didn't matter. As he'd decided earlier, the only way he'd back off was if she was married. He didn't even care if she was engaged. It made him an ass, he knew that. What kind of asshole would try to interfere with an engaged couple?

Him. *He* would.

He'd just have to remind Milena of their good times. Prove to her he was a changed man. That the shell of a soldier she'd met back in that VA hospital was different now. He'd found his calling with the highway patrol.

There was some danger, which called to the daredevil that lived deep inside him, but he no longer had to kill on a daily basis. Even if those he'd killed deserved it.

Refusing to think about that last day—the mission

that had sent him back to the States and landed him in the VA hospital in the first place—TJ took a deep breath and focused on the clinic in front of him. He'd been watching for an hour now, waiting for Milena to come out. He didn't have a plan, which was unlike him. He *always* had a plan. But she'd done that to him. Made him live in the here and now rather than in the future. She made him stop and enjoy what was happening in the moment. It was one of the many things he loved and missed about her.

He needed her in his life. Needed her optimism. Needed her goodness to counter the bad shit he'd done. Hell, he just simply needed *her*.

Just when he didn't think he'd be able to keep himself from barging into the clinic, she came out.

She looked tired—really tired. As he watched, she scrubbed a hand over her face and her shoulders slumped.

TJ was on the move before he'd even thought about what he was doing.

He wanted to ease her burdens. Take care of her. Make sure she was eating and getting enough sleep. It was silly, she'd always been able to take care of herself. Hell, she took care of *him* more than he'd ever taken care of her, but he wanted to change that. Needed to. It was a bone-deep conviction that he wanted to be the man she turned to when she was upset, angry, sad, as well as happy.

He was striding toward her and standing in front of her before he'd figured out what he was going to say. He'd opened his mouth, but didn't get the chance to say anything before she looked up and saw him.

For a second, she simply stared up at him.

Then turned on her heel and walked away without a word.

Startled, as that wasn't the response he'd expected— not that he knew *what* her response was going to be, though he wouldn't have been surprised if she'd smacked him—TJ strode after her.

When he caught up to her, he said the words that had been festering in his soul since the day he'd walked out. "I'm sorry, Doc. I'm so fucking sorry. I shouldn't've left. I should've talked to you, explained what was wrong with me. I've missed you every fucking day since I walked out. Regretted it even more."

She stopped abruptly, and TJ almost tripped over her, but caught himself at the last second. Milena turned, hands on her hips, glaring up at him. She was so petite, especially next to him. At six feet, he wasn't super tall, but compared to her five foot five, he was a giant. He loved how she fit against him, as if she were made just for him.

"You're an asshole," she told him.

"I know," he agreed.

His immediate acquiescence threw her, he could tell. He pressed on. "I went back to your apartment a month after I left, ready to throw myself on your mercy. To apologize. But you were gone. Poof. Without a trace. Your landlord wouldn't tell me anything, and your neighbors were just as close-lipped."

She looked up at him in confusion. "You came back?"

"Yeah, Doc. I never should've left in the first place, but I came back. And you were gone. I asked around, but no one knew where you were, or they wouldn't say. I should've dug deeper, but I didn't have time."

He could tell she wanted to ask, and was impressed when she merely shook her head. "It doesn't matter."

He went on, wanting to explain everything before she told him to fuck off. "After I left, I got shit-faced drunk. I didn't have anywhere to go and felt like dog shit for leaving without a word. I woke up in an alley with two assholes going through my pockets, trying to rob me blind. I was too drunk to fend them off, but luckily there was a law enforcement convention going on that weekend. Two highway patrol officers who were in town for the conference chased the pickpockets off and took pity on me. I have no idea why, but they hauled my ass out of that alley and back to their hotel. They threw me in the shower, saw the Army tattoo on my back, and when I woke up—on the floor, by the way—got me some coffee, then forced me to talk. Refused to let me leave until I explained why I'd been so drunk that I let myself pass out in a fucking alley."

TJ took a breath, then continued. He hadn't told this story to another person since the day it had happened, and he knew he only had another minute or so to get to the point before Milena shook herself out of her surprised stupor and took off on him.

"I told them everything. About my last mission. About my injuries. About you. About leaving. They told me I was a dumbass then promised to help me…if I wanted it. I almost told them to fuck off, but then I remembered how you always used to tell me that everything happened for a reason. That I'd been hurt because it allowed us to meet. I wanted to believe you. So I agreed. I signed up to attend the next deputy academy. The men who'd picked my worthless carcass off the street were from El Paso. They introduced me to a couple friends of theirs who were stationed in Austin, and suddenly I found myself living in a piece-of-shit motel and working my ass off every day to get in shape for the academy.

"I had to pass a shitload of tests, and I think one of my new friends pulled some strings, but I was accepted. Before I was set to start training, I went back for you. But you were gone. I wanted to look for you, but I was about to start a six-month intensive program. I vowed to find you after I graduated, but by then you were long gone."

He stared at Milena, willing her to believe him. To give him another chance. "There hasn't been one day that's gone by that I haven't thought about you. Wondered where you were. Who you were with. What you were doing." His eyes went to her left hand—which he'd been too agitated to notice during her interrogation—but she had crossed her arms in front of her and he couldn't see if she was wearing a wedding ring or not.

She sighed. "You left without saying goodbye. Without a note. Nothing. I thought you were hurt, sick...*dead*. And you *let* me suffer that way."

TJ knew this would be hard, but he'd had no idea *how* hard. "I'm sorry."

"Sorry just doesn't cut it," Milena said in a harsh tone.

"Where'd you go?" he asked.

"Too little, too late," she told him. "Go away. Please. Leave me alone. You've done enough. I can't endure what you put me through again."

"No," TJ told her in no uncertain terms. "I'm not going away. I'm going to make amends for everything I've done."

"Don't you get it? I don't *want* you to make amends," she said, her chest heaving with emotion. "There's nothing to make amends for. We're done. It's over!" She flung her arm out as she spoke. "I hate you, TJ! I hate what you did to me! Hate what I suffered through because of you. I don't like to even *think* about that time in my life. I've moved on."

He reached out and snagged her hand in midair and held it in front of him. His thumb brushed back and forth over the base of her ring finger. Her blessedly *empty* ring finger. "Are you married?"

"What? No."

One side of his mouth twitched up in a satisfied smile. "Then I'm not leaving," he insisted. "Everything happens for a reason, that's what you always said. Well, I got a call from an acquaintance up at Fort Hood. He informed me about a possible dangerous situation in my district. *He'd* gotten a call from Ian Taggart up in Dallas, who was worried about his niece. Turns out she was good friends with a Milena Reinhardt. Can you imagine how it felt to hear your name after all that time? We've come full circle—and I have another chance to prove to you how much you mean to me."

"Don't," Milena begged, trying to pull her hand from his. "Just leave me alone."

"I watched over that school for several weeks, Doc. Saw you coming and going, and it killed me to do nothing but sit there. That place was bad news, and every time you set foot in there, you were in danger. I fucking *hated* it, but I did what I was told and stood back, giving the Feds as much information as I could, if only to make them move faster and get you out of there."

"You were there last night, weren't you?" Milena asked, her voice quivering. "When I was being questioned."

"Yeah, Doc. I was there. Cruz is a friend of mine. I told him to go easy on you, and he did, until he let you fucking think you were going to jail." TJ took a deep breath and tried to get a hold of himself. "Give me a week. Talk to me. Ask me anything. I'll tell you everything you want to know. Everything I refused to tell you three years ago. I'm an open book to you. Give me a chance."

Milena swallowed and shook her head. "I can't."

"You can. I'm not going anywhere this time, Doc. I have a full-time job, I'm a highway patrol officer with the Texas Department of Public Safety. No one knows where Jeremiah and his son are. I'm going to make sure you're safe until they're caught and put behind bars."

Her eyes widened in shock. "Please tell me you aren't the protection the FBI guy talked about last night…er…this morning."

TJ nodded. "I am. I volunteered. There's a chance they're long gone, but there's no way in hell I'm going to let them hurt one hair on your head."

"Great, just great," she mumbled.

"I'm here to stay, Doc. I'll take things as slowly as you need me to. Just give me a chance. *Please*."

He was getting to her, he could tell. Shifting his hold on her hand, he stepped a little closer and rubbed his thumb against her palm this time, remembering how much she used to love it when he did that when they'd held hands. Her lemony scent wafted up to him, and he almost felt dizzy smelling it once again. It brought back so many amazing memories, it made his heart hurt.

Just when he thought she was going to agree, Milena ripped her hand from his grasp and took a step away from him.

"No. You hurt me so bad, TJ. You have no idea what I've been through since you left."

"Then tell me," he begged. "Let me make it up to you."

"You can't." She actually sounded sad. "Leave me alone."

She began to step away, not turning her back on him, as if he was a wild animal she had to keep her eye on.

"I'm not giving up, Doc. I'll see you tomorrow."

Milena pressed her lips together and shook her head, but she didn't say anything.

TJ let her back away from him, and when she turned and practically fled down the sidewalk, he didn't follow. He watched as she climbed into a dark green mini-van parked in a public lot across the street. An older man sat in the driver's seat, watching him. TJ knew it was her dad because he'd looked up everything he could about Milena a couple weeks ago.

He wasn't holding back now. He'd use every scrap of information he'd ferreted out about her to win her affection. She might've said she hated him, but the look in her eyes and the way she'd leaned toward him rather than away belied those words. No matter how long it took, he'd be patient and prove to her once and for all that he wasn't the man he used to be. He was better.

She *had* to forgive him. She just had to. The alternative was unthinkable.

Chapter Four

—————◆—————

"THAT WAS HIM, wasn't it?"

Milena sighed. Her dad wasn't going to give it up. She adored him, but he was super protective of those he loved. And he was stubborn. Probably where she'd gotten it from.

"Yeah, dad. That was him."

"What does he want? Does he know about JT? Is he trying to intimidate you into letting him have custody? Well, that's not going to happen. Not as long as I have anything to say about it! I'll refinance the fucking house eight times over before I let anyone take our little boy away. No fucking way."

Milena didn't want to smile, but she couldn't help it. She reached over and patted her dad on the shoulder. "Calm down, Dad. He doesn't want custody of JT."

"Why not? Does he not think he's the father? Idiot."

"It's not that."

"Then what? Talk to me, Milena."

She sighed again, then blurted out the truth. "He

doesn't know about him."

There was a long pause, and Milena was scared to look at her dad. She fiddled with her fingers in her lap.

"What?"

"He doesn't know about him. I…he left before I knew I was pregnant. I never saw him again until today."

"Baby…" Her dad's tone had turned sad…and even a little accusatory. "I can't say I like the man, not after what he did. The way he left you. But your mom and I thought all along that he *knew*. That he *chose* to not be a part of his son's life. As much as I hate to say it, baby, he deserves to know. Then we can decide what to do depending on how he reacts."

"I know," Milena said quietly. And she did. She'd been so surprised to see him, and it had brought back so many hurt feelings she'd thought she'd dealt with. The *last* thing she'd been thinking about was telling the man she still loved that he had a son.

"What did he want if it wasn't about JT?"

"He apologized for leaving. Told me some of what happened. He wants to talk to me more."

After another long pause, when she didn't elaborate, her dad asked, "And?"

"I told him no."

"That's your right," her dad said.

Milena relaxed. She loved the support her parents

always gave her. No matter what decisions she'd made, they'd been behind her one hundred percent. "I don't think he's going to take no for an answer," she admitted softly.

"I don't think he is either," her dad said.

Milena's head whipped up and she stared at her dad. "You don't? Why?"

"Honey, I saw the way he was looking at you. With longing, remorse, and regret."

"You could see all that from all the way across the street?" she asked dubiously, not sure what to believe anymore. TJ *had* sounded sincere, but she'd trusted him once, and he'd hurt her more than she'd ever thought possible. She couldn't do it again.

"What I saw was a man determined to right a wrong. I thought he was being intense because he wanted his son, but if he doesn't know about JT, then that's not what was happening."

"He said he'll be the one assigned to protect me until Jeremiah and Jonathan are arrested."

"I have no doubt he'll do what it takes to keep you safe."

"He hurt me, Daddy," Milena said quietly.

"I know. And that makes me want to beat the fucker into the ground."

Milena held back the chuckle that wanted to escape. Her dad wasn't exactly Arnold Schwarzenegger. He was a couple inches shorter than TJ and definitely wasn't in any kind of shape to be taking on anyone. His gut was prominent on his frame and he'd only get hurt if he got into any real altercation. But the fact that he *wanted* to hurt TJ actually made Milena feel good. Protected.

"I'm not sure you could beat him up," Milena said dryly.

"I know. But I'd give it my best shot if it came to that. I can't deny I'd feel better knowing he'd be looking out for you until those assholes are put behind bars where they belong. But, honey, you need to tell him about his son. Even if nothing else comes from you talking to him, he deserves to know. Not only that…but JT deserves to know his father. I'm not saying that young man will even want to be in his son's life, but it's his decision to make. Not yours."

Her dad was right, Milena knew he was, but it scared the shit out of her.

"Besides, I think you need to talk to him for your own sake."

"Why?"

"Why? Milena, JT's room is filled with pictures of his father. He carries that little pillow around with him everywhere. You tell your son bedtime stories about how brave and good his father is. You wouldn't do any of that if you didn't still have feelings for the man."

Milena swallowed. Hard. Her dad was right. Of

course he was.

"What are you scared of, honey?" Bob Reinhardt asked softly. "If he tries to take him from you, we'll take him to court. He hasn't paid a cent in child support in two years. He wasn't there when you were sick. He hasn't changed one diaper, sat up one night with JT when he cried, nothing. He's not going to get custody."

"I'm not afraid of that," Milena said honestly.

"Then what?"

She blinked back the tears in her eyes. "I still love him. Even after he left without a word. What if I let him back in and he doesn't want anything to do with me? If I tell him about JT, I might have to see him for the rest of my life. I'm not sure I could handle it if he married someone else and had kids with her. It'd tear me apart, Daddy."

Her father didn't say a word as he pulled into the driveway of the huge suburban house he'd bought for his wife so many years ago. He cut the engine and reached a hand out to his daughter. Palming her cheek, he said, "If you forgive him and let him back into your life, there's no way he'll be able to resist falling back in love with you."

Milena wanted to believe him. Wanted to believe it with every fiber of her being, but she honestly wasn't so sure. TJ had left her so easily before, what would prevent him from doing it once more? If she let him back into her life, and their son's, and he left again, it wouldn't just be *her* heart broken this time. She knew that like she knew she needed oxygen to breathe.

She didn't respond to her dad's words, but he didn't seem to expect her to. He merely ran his hand over the top of her head as he used to do all the time when she was little and climbed out of the van.

After taking a deep breath, Milena did the same. Eager to get inside, see her baby boy, then not think about anything for a while. Her mom had promised to take JT out of the house so she could take a nap, and that's just what she was going to do. Not think about Jeremiah Jones, his son, the awful things that had been done to the girls at the school, her job at the clinic that she still didn't know if she'd get back, and certainly not Thomas James Rockwell.

Chapter Five

———————— ◆ ————————

"**Y**OU SURE THIS is a good idea?" Daxton Chambers asked his friend.

"Yes." TJ's answer was short and to the point. He'd called the Texas Ranger for some moral support. He'd admitted that he'd been watching the school for weeks and gotten all of Milena's contact information from the law enforcement database. He'd been there when Dax had met Mackenzie for the first time, and for some reason he'd felt the urge to call his friend to talk about the situation with Milena.

"You haven't ever mentioned this chick before," Dax said.

"Because I thought she was a part of my past. I didn't think I'd ever see her again."

"But now you have."

"Now I have," TJ agreed. "In a nutshell, I met her when I was in the VA hospital after I got hurt in the Middle East. We lived together for a couple months before I made the worst decision of my life."

"Let me guess," Dax said dryly. "You thought she was too good for you. That you'd fuck up her life. So you left."

TJ huffed out a breath. "Yeah, that's about it."

"Good luck then, man. You're gonna need it."

"Aren't you supposed to be all supportive and shit?" TJ asked grumpily. "That's why I called."

"I *am* being supportive. Would you rather I lie and tell you that I think this'll be a cakewalk?"

"No. But you know, maybe a little bit of positivity wouldn't go amiss here."

"I could tell the second you said her name that you're serious about this woman, TJ. I absolutely will not blow smoke up your ass about her or the situation. If I thought you didn't give one shit about her, I would've told you to have a one-night stand and get her out of your system, but this one's different."

"Yeah," TJ agreed. "She is."

"Right, so I'm gonna be straight with you. And by the way, I want to meet her. And I'm sure Mack will too," Dax said.

"I think it's a bit early to be setting up meet and greets," TJ returned.

"I didn't mean today, asshole. After she forgives you. After you're back in her good graces."

TJ couldn't help but smile. Dax couldn't see it, of course, but it felt really good that his friend was absolutely certain he could get Milena to forgive him. "Deal."

"Call me later," Dax ordered. "I want to hear more about this fucking child-abuse bullshit."

Being reminded about Jeremiah Jones and his equally perverted son—and the fact that Milena and her friend had been in the middle of that shit—made his teeth clench. "I will. Cruz thinks the perverts who ran the place are long gone, but I've got a bad feeling about them. They slipped away in the raid, and so far, no one can find them. I don't think Milena needs full-time protection, but I'm doing what I can to keep my eye out for her in the meantime."

"Fuck. Anything you need, all you have to do is ask," Dax said.

"Appreciate it. She's at the clinic now, but I'm going to head over there when she gets off. I'll let you know if I think I need to step up my surveillance."

"You better. You'd do it for me or any of the others. I'll talk to you later."

"Later." TJ hung up and took a deep breath then looked at the clock. He had a couple hours to kill before Milena would get off work at the clinic. He knew she'd been working mornings downtown ever since she took the job at the school. He was betting on the fact that she'd head home after her shift, and that was where he was planning on attempting to talk to her.

She wasn't going to be happy when he simply showed up at her parents' house, but he'd been serious when he told her he wasn't giving up. He was going to do whatever it took to make sure she knew how sorry he was.

TJ CLIMBED OUT of his black Mustang and strode toward the front door with determination. The neighborhood was older and very well-kept. The house was a two-story, probably around four thousand square feet. Big, especially for a couple who only had one child, but Missy and Bob's reasons for having such a large house were the least of his worries at the moment.

He was nervous. Determined, but nervous. The last time he'd seen Milena it hadn't gone well, and showing up on her doorstep probably wasn't the smartest thing to do, but he couldn't stay away. He needed to reassure her that he was serious about making amends and having her back in his life.

He pushed the doorbell and stepped back, making sure he could be seen clearly through the peephole. The last thing he wanted to do was worry her parents.

The time it took for someone to answer the door seemed like an eternity, but finally it opened. An older woman, probably in her early fifties, stood there. TJ would recognize Milena's mother anywhere. She and her daughter looked a lot alike.

She was probably a couple inches taller than Milena, but had the same blonde hair and blue eyes. TJ swallowed and had the brief thought that this was what Milena would look like in twenty-five years. And he wanted to be by her side to see it.

"Good afternoon, ma'am. My name is Thomas James, and I'm here to see your daughter."

She stared at him for a long moment, a worried look on her face. Then she glanced behind her. When she turned to him again, she was biting her lip.

TJ didn't like the vibe she was giving off. He immediately went on alert. Was there an intruder in the house who had forced her to open the door? Was Milena all right? He couldn't stop his mind from going there, not with his background and training.

"Now isn't a good time, young man."

TJ blinked. He had suspected that he wouldn't be a welcome sight on their doorstep, but he hadn't expected an outright snub. "I apologize for showing up unannounced, but I really do need to see Milena."

"I don't think now is—"

Whatever she was going to say was interrupted by the high-pitched, happy squeal of a toddler. A little boy ran past Missy Reinhardt and out the door.

Acting on instinct, TJ crouched down and snatched the fast-moving child.

He let out an *umph* as the toddler hit him, but his arms closed around the small body protectively, keeping him safe from tumbling down the stairs at the front of the house.

"JT, come back here! You know you're—" Milena's voice halted mid-sentence as she appeared next to her mom.

Her eyes had been filled with laughter, but TJ saw panic replace the carefree, happy look on her face when she saw him.

TJ put his hands on the boy's upper arms and held him steady in front of him. "Looks like you've got a runner on…"

His voice trailed off as he got a good look at the child. He was naked except for a diaper. He had light brown hair, almost blond, and bright blue eyes.

His gaze went from the boy to Milena in shock.

The three adults stared at each other without a word for a long moment before the boy broke the silence.

"Daddy!"

TJ swallowed hard as he looked into eyes so like Milena's, it was uncanny. The toddler had her blue eyes…but he could see parts of himself in the boy's face as well, especially the shape of his nose.

TJ didn't need the child's exclamation to prove what he knew in his heart was true.

This was his son.

His. *Son*.

"Daddy!" the boy squealed again.

"Hi," TJ managed. Then the little boy did something that made TJ's battle-hardened heart crack down the middle. He threw his little arms around his neck and squeezed.

TJ couldn't have said anything at that moment if his life depended on it. All he could do was wrap one arm around the little boy and hug him back. Of course, being two, the toddler didn't tolerate being confined for long. He giggled, pulled back, and ran back inside the house, past his mom and grandmother, who were standing as still as statues.

TJ slowly stood, trying to process what had just happened.

"I think you should come in," Missy Reinhardt finally said.

TJ nodded, still too choked up to say a word.

He followed the women into the house, past a formal dining room, through an obviously remodeled kitchen and into a spacious living room. There were toys strewn all over the floor, and a half-eaten muffin on the low coffee table, along with a sippy cup.

The toddler was standing in front of the television, dancing along to an animated movie playing on the screen. His little butt bobbed up and down and his arms occasionally raised to make a sort of flapping motion. It was the cutest thing TJ had ever seen.

Milena's friend, Sadie, was sitting on the couch, and her eyes comically widened when she saw him enter the room. "I can take him upstairs to—"

"No," TJ interrupted, suddenly afraid that if he lost sight of the boy, he'd never see him again.

"It's okay. Mom, Sadie, give us some space?" Milena asked quietly.

The other two women nodded immediately. "I'll be in the kitchen," Missy said.

"I'll just...I'll be upstairs," Sadie told everyone.

TJ didn't watch the others go, he only had eyes for his son. He knew Milena's mom would probably be able to hear whatever they talked about, but he couldn't care less at this point.

He had a son. A *son*.

TJ slowly sat on the edge of an armchair and watched his son dance.

"I wasn't purposely keeping him from you."

TJ took a deep breath and shut his eyes, trying to control his emotions. He wasn't sure what he felt. Joy. Excitement. Bitterness that he'd missed so much of his son's life. Anger. "How old is he?" TJ asked in a low voice.

"Twenty-five months."

Two years. He'd missed two years. "And his name is JT?"

"It's short for James Thomas," Milena confirmed.

TJ's eyes popped open and he turned to Milena in surprise. "You named him after me?"

He watched as Milena licked her lips nervously, but she held his eyes. "Yeah."

Before he could say anything, JT waddled over to where TJ was sitting and started to climb onto his lap. In surprise, TJ opened his legs, giving the toddler room to maneuver, and wrapped an arm around the little boy when he settled against him. When JT was comfortable, he rested his head on his dad's shoulder and stuck a thumb in his mouth, content to watch the movie from his lap.

"Why isn't he scared of me?" TJ asked Milena quietly.

Milena looked away from him then, as if embarrassed. "You're not a stranger to him."

"Why?"

"I made sure he knew you. Knew that his daddy was a hero."

"How?" TJ knew his questions sounded abrupt, maybe harsh, but he couldn't help it. He'd come here to try to convince Milena to give him a second chance, only to find out he was a father. All the speeches he'd prepared in his mind had disappeared like puffs of smoke the second he'd looked into his son's eyes.

"Pictures. Stories." She shrugged. "I didn't know

where you were, TJ. You disappeared without a word. I figured someday he'd want to know his father, and as much as you hurt me, I was proud of you. Still am."

TJ had so many questions—questions only Milena had the answers to—but with the slight weight of his son in his arms, he didn't want to move, and he definitely didn't think the boy should be privy to the inevitable conversation.

So for the next twenty minutes, he kept his eyes on his son while the boy watched television. TJ reveled in the emotions that crossed his son's tiny face. Happiness, delight, humor, seriousness.

His mind was spinning. He'd made a human. A tiny person. It was mind-boggling.

Even though he'd been blindsided, this was the best day of his life.

He couldn't think beyond this moment. Had no idea what would happen in the future, but he knew without a doubt that he'd remember today for the rest of his life. It wasn't the way most men found out they were fathers, obviously, but he cherished the experience for what it was.

When the credits began to play on the television screen, JT squirmed in his lap. Reluctantly, TJ lifted the boy and placed him on his feet on the floor in front of the chair. His son looked up at him for a moment and smiled. "Daddy," he said matter-of-factly, then turned and raced toward the kitchen screaming for his "nana."

TJ's eyes followed his son until he couldn't see him any longer, then he finally turned to Milena. He wanted to hate her. Wanted to rail at her for keeping his son from him. Wanted to know if she'd ever planned on telling him…but the words wouldn't come. He was simply too overwhelmed.

"I was going to tell you," she said softly, as if she could read his mind.

"You should've told me long before now."

Her eyes met his, and instead of seeing remorse, he saw anger. It surprised him.

"Really? When, TJ? When should I have told you? I had no idea where you *were*. *You* walked out on *me*."

"Did you even try to find me?" he asked, the anger and disappointment he felt at being blindsided by the knowledge she'd had his son leaking through in his words.

"Yeah, I did." Her words were just as angry. "I called the hospitals, police stations, even the fucking morgue to see if maybe you'd been hurt or killed, and that's why you hadn't gotten ahold of me. To my disappointment and despair, I finally figured out that you hadn't been in an accident. You weren't dead. You'd simply gotten tired of me and *left*."

The emotion in her words got to him, and somehow made his own anger dissipate a little. "I didn't get tired of you."

She snorted in disbelief. "Could'a fooled me."

"I didn't," he insisted. "I was a mess. I was so angry back then. You didn't deserve that. I wanted to be the man you needed, instead of a man you had to deal with."

"I would've done anything for you," she said sadly.

"Don't you get it? I didn't want to drag you down with my issues."

She didn't respond that time, just stared at him.

"But I was wrong."

She blinked in surprise.

"Yeah, I can admit it. I told you before, I realized it within a week of leaving. It took me a few more weeks to man up and go back to you, but by then, you were gone."

She nodded. "I couldn't stay. Not in that apartment, where I saw you everywhere I looked. My sheets still smelled like you."

"I wish you would've tried harder to find me," he said sadly.

It was apparently the wrong thing to say. Milena stood and glared down at him. "Yeah? When should I have done that? When I was throwing up from the morning sickness I had all freaking *day*? Oh, I know, maybe when I started bleeding so badly, I thought I'd lost my baby. Or how about when I had to quit my job at the VA and move back here because I was put on bed rest? I had to be waited on hand and foot because I was scared if I moved even an inch in the wrong direction, I'd kill our son. How about when I started labor four weeks early and my parents had to rush me to the hospital? Or when JT wasn't breathing when they finally got him out? Maybe I should've been trying to find you then, huh?"

"Doc," TJ said softly, trying to stop her tirade, with no luck.

"Or maybe you think I should have resumed the search for my baby's daddy—after he left without a fucking word—when I was up trying to soothe JT in the middle of the night? He was colicky, TJ. Do you know what that means? It means he cried nonstop. *Literally.* For hours, and nothing I did could calm him down. There were times I had to step away from him so I wouldn't hurt my baby. Should I have tried to find you *then*?"

TJ didn't think, he just stood and stepped into Milena's personal space. But he didn't stop there. He wrapped his arms around her and pulled her close until her head was resting against him, much like his son's had earlier.

He felt her hands clench the sleeves of his T-shirt in her fists, but she didn't push him away.

"Why should I have tried to find you, TJ?" she

asked sadly, a little calmer now. "You threw me away like I was *nothing*. I didn't think you wanted anything to do with me. Why would I have gone out of my way to find you when my world felt like it was ending, to put myself through the agony of hearing that you didn't want anything to do with me *or* your baby?"

"I want you. I want you *both*."

She stiffened, and he hurried to clarify. "I'm not going to take him away from you, Doc. I would never do that. You're his mother. The one person in this world I have no doubt would die for him if necessary. No…I take that back. One of *two* people in this world who would die for him."

Milena picked her head up at that. She looked at him with tears sparkling in her eyes, but didn't say anything. She just stared at him as if she were trying to read his mind.

"I'm so sorry I left. So fucking sorry I wasn't by your side, holding your hair back as you got sick because of our child. Sorry I wasn't there to take you to the hospital when you started bleeding. Sorry for not being there to spoil and pamper you when you were bedbound. You'll never know how damn sorry I am that I wasn't around to share the stress and worry when our son wouldn't stop crying. But I'm going to make it up to you, Doc. Mark my words."

"How? You can't turn back the clock, TJ. You can't

go back in time."

"I know, but starting from this moment, I can damn well be sure not to miss another second of his life. You need anything, and I mean *anything*, you call me. If you're too tired to get up and change his diaper, call me and I'll come over and do it. You need someone to watch him? I'll do it. If he has a doctor's appointment, I want to be there. If he skins his goddamn knee, I want to be there to kiss and make it better.

"And not only that, I'm going to take care of you too. You look tired, Doc. You need to sleep more. I'll make sure you get the naps you need. I'll treat you to a spa day. Get your hair done. Get your nails done. Hell, you want to take a girls' trip out of town with Sadie, I'll pay for that too. Whatever you need, whenever you need it, I'll make sure you get it."

"You can't make up for all that you've missed with money."

Her words pierced his heart, but not for the reason she might think. "I am perfectly aware that I can't get the last two years back. And, Doc, I don't blame you. You're right, it wasn't your responsibility to find me. I should've tried harder to track *you* down. If I had, you wouldn't have been alone. And that's all on me. But I'm here now."

"Because Jeremiah and Jonathan are still on the loose."

"Yes and no. Nothing would keep me from protecting you against those assholes, but even if they weren't in the picture, I'd be here."

"I want you in JT's life," Milena said softly. "I wouldn't have told him about you for the last two years if I didn't, but you and me...we aren't meant to be."

TJ tightened his arms around her. "You're wrong. You were the reason I pulled my head out of my ass and applied to be a patrolman. I did it for *you*. To be a man you could be proud of."

"TJ," she protested weakly.

"I love you, Doc," TJ admitted, letting everything he was feeling show in his eyes. "I loved you practically from the first time you gave me shit in the VA hospital. I loved you even more after our first kiss in the supply closet in that damn place. I agreed to move into your apartment when I didn't have any other place to go because I loved you. When you made the first move and stood in your doorway with nothing on but one of my T-shirts and invited me to sleep in your bed, I thought my heart would burst with how much I fucking loved you."

He brought his hands up to her face and framed it, tilting her chin up in the process so she had to look into his eyes.

"When we went out to eat that one night, someone dropped something in the kitchen. It freaked me out—

and you didn't even blink. We went home and you knew exactly what I needed. You took off your red sundress and let me take you how I wanted. I loved you when I was fucking you as you leaned over that couch. I knew I wasn't wearing a condom, but I didn't care. I needed to mark you. Needed to leave a part of myself inside your body. And I loved that you let me. I needed you desperately, and you gave me *you*. All of you. That was the night JT was created, wasn't it?"

She nodded, her head still in his grasp.

"And I know this is hard to believe, but I loved you even when I left that night. So much, I thought you were better off without me. But I was wrong. We're better when we're together. I felt it then, and I feel it now. I never stopped loving you, Doc. *Never.* I fucked up, I know it. You know it. Your parents know it. Hell, JT probably even knows it somehow. But there's no way I'm walking away a second time."

"I don't think I can do it again."

"You can do anything you set your mind on, Doc."

She didn't respond, just stared up at him with sad eyes.

TJ took a deep breath and forced himself to drop his hands and step away from the love of his life. He'd hurt her, badly. It wasn't going to be as easy as apologizing to have her take him back, that was obvious. He knew his Milena was stubborn, but he was more so. He'd sat on rooftops in the scorching Middle Eastern heat for hours before taking a shot. He could take as much time as needed to get her to trust him again. To love him.

"I'm going to call my Human Resources department and get you and JT put on my insurance."

"What?" she asked.

"I also need to update my will and make sure you're listed as my next of kin on the departmental paperwork."

"TJ—" she started, but he talked over her.

"I don't know anything about it, but what do people normally pay in child support?"

She didn't say a word, just stared at him in disbelief.

He waved a hand. "It doesn't matter. I'll write you a check for ten thousand to start with. That should cover some of what I should've been paying all along."

"I don't want your money."

"Tough. You're getting it."

"You can't buy me back," she said snarkily.

"I'm not trying to," he replied immediately. Her words hurt, but he refused to be nasty back to her. She had every right to be pissed at him. He'd abandoned her when she'd needed him most.

"Then what are you doing? JT and I have been just fine without you."

"I know." And he did. It was more than obvious she didn't need his help, and that stung. A lot. He pushed through it. "You told Cruz at the station that you took that whack-job's offer because you needed the money. You quit working at the clinic full-time to start at the school. All I'm doing is giving you some breathing room to figure out what you want to do next. If you want to use it to get your own place, great. If you want to buy a newer model car, that's fine. If you want to work full-time again at the clinic, no problem. But if you want to continue with less hours so you can spend more time with our son, then I'm going to make sure you have the means to do that."

He knew he wasn't playing fair, but *all* was fair in love and war. And this was a war to gain back her love and trust. He'd play dirty if he had to.

Not giving her a chance to respond, he said, "I need to go. The bank closes at five and I want to get to the station and start the paperwork to add you and JT to my insurance." He took out his phone and asked, "What's your number? I want to send you a text so you have mine in case you need anything."

She stared at him for a long moment, and TJ wasn't sure she was going to tell him her number, but finally she relented.

He punched it in and sent a quick text. "I mean it, Milena. You let me know if you need anything. I won't let you down again. Even if I'm working, I'll find a way to get you what you need. Understand?"

She nodded woodenly.

Deciding she'd had enough and needed to regroup, he asked, "Do you think it'd be okay if I said bye to JT before I go?"

Milena stared at him with big eyes and swallowed before saying, "Yeah. He'd probably like that."

"Thank you." TJ leaned in close and gave her a chaste goodbye kiss on the cheek. "See you tomorrow, Doc." Then he strode toward the kitchen where he'd last seen his son heading.

JT was sitting at a high chair at a small table in the corner of the spacious room, and TJ went to his side. He kneeled down next to him and smiled when his son held out a Cheerio.

"Daddy, eat."

He leaned forward and caught the snack in his mouth, gumming the little fingers as he did. JT giggled loudly and clapped his hands in delight when his dad let him go.

"She was in a bad place when we moved her in."

TJ stiffened, but he'd known this was coming. He stood and turned to face Milena's mom. "I didn't know."

"I realize that, but it doesn't make it any less true."

"I'm adding her to my insurance and giving her the money she and my son should've had all along, that they *would've* had if I'd known she was pregnant."

"Money won't buy their love."

Missy Reinhardt sounded so much like her daughter, TJ couldn't help but smile. "That's what she said. And I know that," he informed her. "I won't let her down again."

He refrained from shifting in place like a naughty child under her stare, barely.

"See that you don't," she finally said.

Feeling as though he'd somehow earned the older woman's approval, even though it didn't look or sound like it, TJ merely nodded. "I'll be back tomorrow after she gets off work."

"Why don't you come over while she's working? You could get to know your son better."

TJ's heart lurched. Oh, he wanted that. Badly. But he said, "No. That would make Milena nervous. I'm not here to take our son away from her. I can't deny I want to spend time with him, but I'll do it with Milena or not at all. She needs to know she can trust me before she'll want me being alone with him."

"Then I guess we'll be seeing you tomorrow," Mrs. Reinhardt said with a slight smile, and TJ couldn't help but feel as if he'd passed some sort of test.

He nodded, then turned back to JT. He leaned over and kissed the top of the boy's head and turned to leave. At the last minute, he asked Milena's mom, "Would you take a picture of us? I'd love to be able to show it to my friends. They'll never believe my ugly mug helped make something so perfect and beautiful."

It was obviously the right thing to say, because her smile grew and she reached for his phone. TJ crouched down next to his son's high chair and looked at him for a long moment. God, he still couldn't wrap his mind around the fact that he was a father.

He turned to face Missy and saw that she was already holding his phone up. He dutifully smiled for the photo. He was still smiling when he felt a slimy hand touch his cheek. Turning to JT, he laughed outright when he saw that his son had stuffed as many Cheerios into his mouth as he could and was drooling all over himself...and had shared that drool with his old man.

"Don't choke, little man," he drawled, wiping his tiny hand with a paper towel sitting nearby.

When he'd wiped off as much drool as he could, he stood. Milena's mom was still grinning like a loon, but she didn't say a word as she handed him back his phone. He didn't bother looking at the picture, simply put his phone back in his pocket.

"I'll see you tomorrow."

"Bye, TJ."

He strode out of the kitchen and back to the front door. TJ knew he'd be having a serious conversation with Milena's dad at some point, and the man wouldn't be as easy on him as her mom had been, but he didn't mind. He liked that Milena and JT had people who loved and looked out for them.

His thoughts were chaotic, but he hadn't ever been happier. He had a son! And he'd made the first step toward getting Milena back.

He didn't have any illusions; this was going to be the hardest thing he'd ever done. More difficult than hitting his target from a mile and a half away. Tougher than getting over what had happened to him and the things he'd done in the Army. But it'd be worth it. *They* were worth it.

Chapter Six

———————◆•———————

SADIE SAT CROSS-LEGGED on Milena's bed later that night. JT was asleep and the room was lit only by a lamp on the bedside table.

"He flat-out said he loves you?" Sadie asked, her eyebrows drawn down in disbelief.

"Yeah. Just threw it out there like I was supposed to fall at his feet or something," Milena said caustically. She knew she was being unfair, but she felt off kilter. She'd about had a heart attack when JT had run past her mom straight into TJ's arms. She'd thought about trying to deny JT was his, but when her son had opened his mouth and called him Daddy, and after the look of awe on TJ's face, she knew she couldn't do it.

The years had been good to him. When they'd been together three years ago, he was still healing from the wounds he'd gotten overseas. But since then, he'd healed completely and had filled out. His arms were thick and muscular, and she had a feeling if she ever saw him without a shirt, she'd see that he was even more chiseled than he'd been in the past. His brown hair was shorter than when they'd been together before, and he seemed to have a perpetual five o'clock shadow now, which was sexy as all get out.

But it wasn't just his looks that were slightly different. He seemed even more intense than he'd been back then…if that was possible. His brown eyes were penetrating. Whereas before, he frequently looked away from her when he was talking, as if he felt guilty about something, now he had no problem holding eye contact. All that attention on her made Milena feel as if whatever she was saying was the most important thing he'd ever heard. It was a little discomfiting, but also made her feel all squishy inside.

"And did you?" Sadie asked.

"Did I what?" Milena repeated, not sure what they were talking about as she'd gotten lost in memories of TJ.

"Fall at his feet?"

"Of course not!" Milena said quickly—maybe a bit *too* quickly.

"But you want to." It wasn't a question.

"No, I don't." The look of skepticism was easy to read on Sadie's face. "Look, he's just here because he feels guilty or something. And he might be assigned to look after me until Jeremiah and Jonathan are found."

Sadie shook her head. "I'm sure he does feel some

guilt, and he should. He was a dick. But, Milena, he doesn't have to protect you. The Feds can assign someone else to you. There are thousands of law enforcement officers in this city. Any one of them can protect you."

Milena blocked out the common sense her friend was using. "He's arrogant to the nth degree. He strode into the house and practically told me I was his…like a caveman or something. He thinks that throwing money at me and putting me on his insurance will fix everything."

Sadie shifted until she was lying on her side and her head was propped up by a hand. She was about as different from Milena as she could get. Her dark auburn hair fell messily around her shoulders and her green eyes were piercing in their intensity. She was almost five inches taller than Milena, and slender in a way Milena would never be.

"Let me tell you something about dominant men…once they decide they want something, they're gonna get it one way or another."

Milena shook her head. "That's not how things work."

"It is," Sadie insisted. "Let me guess, he told you he left for your own good, right?"

"Yeah, pretty much."

"Men like TJ have crazy high standards for themselves. It's ridiculous, really. They think they have to be perfect. I'm guessing he was really good at what he did in the Army…" Sadie's voice trailed off, as if she was asking a question without coming out and actually voicing it.

Milena nodded. "Yeah, I got that impression. He was a sniper."

"Oh Christ," Sadie murmured, and turned to flop onto her back. "Yeah, so he was probably *very* good at his job. He got hurt and was sent home…to him, I'm sure that felt like a massive failure. He was frustrated he wasn't over there still fighting, and then he was chaptered out of the service altogether. When he had healed enough, he lived with you, right?"

"He didn't have anywhere else to go," Milena told her friend defensively.

"Don't you get it?" Sadie asked. "There he was, still healing, no home, no job, he probably felt like he'd let his friends and country down. He was lost. I'm frankly surprised he stayed as long as he did."

Milena couldn't help but flinch. That hurt.

"Oh sweetie," Sadie said, and leaned over and put her hand on Milena's knee. "I didn't mean that in a bad way. What I meant was that he *had* to have loved you to have stayed for as long as he did. He left because he didn't feel like he was man enough for you. He was trying to be noble. Men like him don't like to feel vulnerable. At all."

"I didn't judge him, Sadie. Not for one second. I would've been there by his side as he worked through whatever he had to, but he didn't give me the chance."

Sadie turned back over and stared at the ceiling once more. "You have to be sneaky with men like him," she informed her friend. "They need your support, but you have to do it in such a way that they don't really realize what you're doing. He's got a group of close friends, right?"

"I have no idea."

"He does," Sadie said with conviction. "His tribe. And I'll bet those friends have women of their own. You need to get to know them. Get close to them. They'll be your source of support when it comes to your man because TJ isn't going to come home and tell you when he's had a bad day. You'll be able to sense it, but he won't tell you why. And that's okay, but you can talk to the other women to help yourself deal with how he is. You can set up guys' nights out. Let him blow off some steam. Cook him dinner. Initiate sex. Let him take you how he wants and needs. *That's* how you help a man like TJ."

"How do you know all this? You're single!"

Sadie smiled up at the ceiling. "I'm a good observer. My aunt married a man just like TJ. Well, maybe not *just* like him, but close enough. You know I was the administrative assistant for McKay-Taggart. Everyone who works there is just like your man. Alpha, obsessive, insanely jealous, and when they fall for someone, they fall *hard*. And it might look like the men are in charge, but ultimately, it's the women who hold most of the power. I've seen my uncle leave in the middle of an important meeting because my aunt called and needed something. He's big, and sometimes scary, but my aunt and his kids mean the world to him."

Milena sighed. She wanted to believe her friend, but it was so hard. "He let me down, Sadie. Big time. I don't know that I'll ever be able to trust him again."

"You will," Sadie said with conviction.

Milena shook her head sadly. "I can't just take him back like nothing happened. Like he didn't rip my heart out of my chest and stomp on it."

"And you shouldn't." Sadie moved and sat up once again, crossing her legs and leaning forward. "He knows he screwed up. But he missed two years of his son's life as a result, Milena. If he's anything like my uncle and his friends, that's something he'll beat himself up about for the rest of his life. He missed JT's first smile, his first steps, his first word, and so many other firsts that he'll never get back. Ever. There's no need to throw it in his face because he's well aware of the magnitude of what he missed. He needs to work hard for your forgiveness and trust, and he should. He needs to prove to you that what he did two years ago will never happen again. That you can rely on him. But, girl, if you can find it in your heart to let him in again, not a day will go by where he won't show you with and without words that you're the most important person in his life. You'll never feel as loved, cherished, or protected as you will with a man like him by your side."

Milena knew what Sadie said was true. But she couldn't just forget all the pain, worry, and hardship she'd been through over the last three years. "I'm scared," she admitted in a soft tone.

"I know. That's why you should take things slow. Get to know the man TJ is today. Let him show you that you can trust him again. One day, you'll realize that the fear you're feeling right now is gone. That's when you can move forward again."

"How'd you get so smart?" Milena asked. Sadie was younger than her by a couple years, but in many ways, she seemed older. Milena might be a mother, but Sadie had a wisdom beyond her years.

"I've had good role models," she replied. "I've watched my uncles Sean and Ian and their friends. They're stubborn, badass, infuriating men. But they're all completely devoted to their women. They've set the bar so high for me, I don't think I'll ever find a man who lives up to their legacy."

"I think you will," Milena told her friend. "You're

smart. Loyal. Brave. You'll so find the man meant to be yours."

"I hope so," Sadie responded. "I'm kinda glad that FBI guy said that I had to stay in town in case they had more questions. I like hanging out with you. I've missed you."

Milena heard the wistfulness in her friend's voice and she immediately offered, "I've missed you too. I don't get out a lot, and having you here has made me realize how much I've missed talking to other women my age. You're welcome to stay longer, even if you're cleared to leave."

Sadie's eager gaze met hers.

"I mean, there's plenty of room in this house. My parents don't mind you being here at all. You could easily get a job down here if you wanted."

"I had a job up in Dallas."

"I know, but you're my only close friend here. I'd hate to see you go."

Sadie chewed on her lip for a moment before saying, "Maybe I could find something part-time."

Milena smiled, then leaned over and hugged her friend. "Thank you. I'm so happy you're staying."

"For a while," Sadie warned. "Eventually I'll go back. Uncle Ian is probably scaring off the new admin. He has a tendency to bluster when he doesn't get his way. So…think you'll see TJ tomorrow?"

It was an abrupt change of subject, but Milena didn't mind. "He said he'd come by after I got off work."

"Then you'll see him tomorrow," Sadie said definitively. "What are you going to do?"

"What do you mean?"

"What do you mean, what do *I* mean?" Sadie asked. "You can't just sit around the house staring at each other."

Milena looked at her friend in shock. She hadn't thought about *doing* anything. "I have no idea," she blurted.

"Stop panicking," Sadie ordered, obviously reading her friend well. "How about taking JT to the park? You guys can stay busy watching him and it won't be as awkward as sitting on the couch trying to figure out what to talk about."

"Yeah, okay, that sounds good."

"Then the next day, you can take him to McDonald's and let TJ experience a meal out with his son."

"The next day?" Milena asked, but Sadie went on as if she hadn't heard her.

"Then maybe you can go to the zoo downtown. That might be a bit ambitious for an afternoon, but probably better for JT, since he tends to get bored easily. And if it's nice, you could take him to that park that has the water spout thing and let JT play in the water.

Oooh, I know, another good date could be the farmers' market downtown. That would tire JT out and you could get some good fruits and veggies while you walk around and talk."

Milena held up a hand to stop her friend. "What in the world are you talking about, Sadie? He hasn't said anything about coming over *after* tomorrow. Let's take things one day at a time, huh?"

Sadie smirked. "You're so cute."

"What?"

"Of *course* he's going to be over here every day. He wants to get to know his son, but maybe more importantly, he knows how badly he screwed up, and he's going to do everything in his power to get back in *your* good graces. If he has to use JT as an excuse to see you every day, he will. Mark my words, Milena. Operation Get Milena Back will commence tomorrow."

Milena rolled her eyes at her friend.

"And just so you know, I'm happy to watch JT for you any night you want to go out, just the two of you."

"It's too early for that."

"Is it?"

Milena wanted to emphatically say yes, but couldn't deny she was interested. The man who had been at her house today, and had apologized so sweetly and earnestly, wasn't the same man she'd known all those years ago. That man had been closed off and angry, with just enough of his sweet side coming out to make her fall in love with him. She didn't see much of that old anger in him now...thankfully. Could he really be so changed? Could he really still love her as much as he claimed he did?

She wanted to believe it, but a small part of her was still afraid that maybe he was just laying it on thick so he could have access to his son.

"Maybe," she hedged, rolling her eyes again when Sadie beamed.

"Right. On that note, I'm going to call my aunt and let her know all is well down here and that I'll be staying for a while. I have a good feeling about TJ, Milena. He reminds me a lot of my uncle, and that's a good thing. Give him a chance. You won't regret it."

Milena didn't respond verbally, but simply nodded at her friend. She watched as Sadie climbed off the bed and headed to her own room, closing the door softly behind her.

Flopping backwards, Milena huffed out a deep breath and wondered how her life had gotten so complicated so quickly. A week ago, she was a single mother working two jobs to try to earn enough money to move out of her parents' house into a small, cramped apartment.

Now she was still a single mother, but that was about all that was the same. She'd been embroiled in the middle of a sex-abuse scandal, interrogated by the FBI, and had been reunited with her baby's daddy, whom she'd thought she hated but deep down still loved, but whom she definitely didn't trust with her heart yet. She had only a part-time job with no insurance, but had a feeling she'd have an influx of money in her bank account soon, a gift from TJ.

It was all so unbelievable.

Shaking her head and deciding she needed to take one day at a time, Milena checked the baby monitor. Satisfied that it was on and working, she climbed under the sheets and snuggled beneath her comforter.

She was asleep within minutes, her dreams full of the man she'd missed every day since he'd left in the middle of the night.

Chapter Seven

———————— ♦ ————————

T J KEPT HIS eyes on his son, but was very aware of the woman at his side. They were at a playground, where Milena had suggested they go when he'd shown up at her parents' door after lunch. JT seemed to be a happy child. Every time he fell, which was often, he'd pick himself up, giggle, and run off again. He was content to toddle after the older kids at the park, not even caring when he couldn't keep up.

TJ had stayed up late the night before, reading articles about colic and what caused it—and horrifying stories about parents who cracked under the pressure of the unrelenting crying, and harmed their child to make them stop screaming.

Every word he read made him feel guiltier about not trying harder to find Milena and make amends. It might not've changed the fact that JT was colicky, but he could've been there to share the load for Milena.

"I'm working on the insurance thing, but unfortunately, because we're not married, I can't get you added to my plan," TJ blurted into the awkward silence that had settled between them like a weighted blanket. "JT is fine, because he's my son."

"I expected that," Milena said without any trace of irritation or disappointment.

"I talked to the HR director this morning though, and she gave me some names of private insurers. Tomorrow when you're at work, I'll call and get information. You can decide which company and plan works best for you and I'll get that set up."

She looked at him in confusion. "You don't need to do that."

He shrugged. "Maybe, maybe not. But I am."

Milena huffed out an irritated breath and looked back toward the playground to where JT was playing. "I can take care of myself."

"I know you can. But I need to do this for you."

She refused to look at him. "You don't need to do anything of the sort."

"I wasn't there for you when I should've been. I wasn't there to hold your hand and take care of you when you were forced to stay in bed when you were pregnant. I wasn't there when you went into early labor, and I wasn't there to help take some of the stress off of you once JT was born. I know I can't fix my absence with money, but knowing that you'll be covered in case some jackass runs into you on the road, or if you fall and break a bone, is a peace of mind that I need. And I think it will take some stress off you too. Please, let me do this."

Milena sighed. "We've been over this. You can't change the past, TJ."

"I know. *Believe* me, I know. But I can change the future, or at least help shape it."

She turned to look at him again. "You're not going to let this go, are you?"

"No."

"Fine. But I want to pick the plan. You don't have any say."

TJ felt the tension roll off his shoulders at her acquiescence. "No problem." Right. He was only going to show her plans he thought were adequate, no matter the cost. "It's going to take some time to get JT added to my insurance."

"It's okay."

"It's not. I mean, he's a kid. He needs to be protected, just in case." TJ cleared his throat, not wanting to bring up the next point, but knowing he had to. "I do need to prove I'm JT's father though. The HR director said that a paternity test would probably be the quickest way to do that. I hate to think about JT having to be pricked by a needle, but—"

"Why?"

TJ blinked at Milena's question. "Why what?"

"Why do you need a paternity test? Won't the birth certificate work as proof?"

He stared at her for a second before the meaning of her words sank in. His chest immediately got tight and he pressed his lips together tightly to try to hold back the emotion threatening to overwhelm him.

Looking down at the dirt under his feet, TJ tried to swallow so he could answer Milena's question.

He felt her hand touch his shoulder. "TJ? What's wrong?"

"You put my name on his birth certificate?" he asked in a tone that probably sounded weird.

"Of course I did. You're his father. Why wouldn't I?"

Not able to sit any longer, TJ stood and paced in front of the bench. "Because you hate me? Because I left you to have my child alone without a word? Because I don't deserve it?"

He looked down at Milena in confusion, waiting for her answer.

She slowly stood and faced him. Their difference in height felt perfect to him. Her blonde hair just brushed her shoulders and her blue eyes seemed even bluer in the sunlight. For their outing, she'd worn a green tank top with a pair of cropped jeans and flip flops on her feet.

She looked casual and comfortable, and all he wanted to do was haul her into his arms and kiss her until she gave in and forgave him. She was curvier than he remembered, probably because she'd had his child. All TJ could think about was how beautiful she was—and how big of an idiot *he* was for thinking for one second that he could give her up.

"TJ, you're his father. Yeah, I was upset when you left, but I was more sad. I decided before JT was even born that he'd know nothing but good things about his father. Putting your name on his birth certificate was never a question for me."

"Thank you," TJ choked out. He wanted to say more, but wasn't sure words could adequately explain his feelings.

She opened her mouth to respond when a scream sounded from the playground, followed by wailing.

TJ was on the move before he'd even thought about it. JT was lying on the ground crying as if he was being tortured.

"What happened?" he asked a little girl, probably around eight years old.

She looked scared, but answered him anyway. "He fell. He was trying to go up the ladder of the slide."

TJ looked up where she was pointing and nodded when he saw the four or so steps. It was high, but not high enough to have done any permanent damage to JT. The ground was covered in mulch, giving the area under the playground equipment a soft, spongy place for kids to land if they fell.

He quickly felt for any blood, lumps, or bumps on his son's small body. Finding none, he scooped JT up into his arms and stood, cradling him against his chest. One hand rested under his butt and the other pressed his head into his shoulder. The screams coming from his lungs were loud. Loud enough to make TJ wince with their volume.

"Is he okay?" Milena asked from next to him calmly.

"I think so. He's got a set of lungs on him, doesn't he?" TJ asked.

"Come on, let's go sit. He'll be fine in a couple of minutes. He's just scared. It's not the first time he's fallen."

"You're being really calm about this," TJ noted as he followed her back to the bench they'd been sitting on.

"He's an active boy, TJ. He's had his share of scrapes and bruises."

TJ eased down onto the bench and rocked his son and murmured words of encouragement and sympathy in his ear until his sobs turned to the occasional sniffle. He patted his back and asked, "You better now, buddy?"

JT sniffed and wiped his nose with the back of his hand, then nodded.

"What hurts?"

The little boy shrugged.

"Did you fall on your butt?" Milena suggested.

JT nodded.

Her hand came out and joined TJ's in rubbing their son's back. She leaned forward and kissed his forehead. "You want to go home, or stay and play some more?"

JT looked over at the playground, then back at his mom. "Play."

"All right. Let go of Daddy and get going. Twenty more minutes then we need to go home."

TJ leaned over and placed his son on his feet. He ran a hand over his light brown curls and watched as he ran back to his new friends as if nothing had happened.

Neither he nor Milena said anything for a minute or two as they kept an eye on the little boy to make sure he was okay.

Finally, TJ said softly. "Okay, that about gave me a heart attack."

Milena chuckled, and the sound was so carefree and happy, and reminded him so much of how she was three years ago, it almost hurt. "You better get used to it. I swear he's part monkey. One of his favorite things to do is climb."

He turned to face Milena. "Is that what he sounded like when he had colic?"

"Pretty much. His lungs were smaller, but his cry was just as piercing then as it is now."

TJ shook his head in awe. "I'm sorry I wasn't there to help. You're simply amazing," he told her.

"What?"

"I listened to him for only a couple minutes and I thought I was going to go crazy. I wanted to fix whatever was wrong. Make him stop crying because he sounded like he was in so much pain. I can't imagine having to hold him for hours as he cried."

"If you apologize again, I'm gonna get mad," Milena told him.

TJ blinked.

"Seriously, it's done. You're sorry you left. I was upset and pissed, but I did what I had to do for my son. *Our* son. You don't have to apologize every time something happens that makes you think about what you missed. Okay?"

TJ swallowed hard, but nodded. "I'll try."

"Good."

They watched JT play for another twenty minutes before Milena called out to tell him it was time to go. TJ took the big shoulder bag Milena had insisted they needed to bring with them. It weighed a ton and he'd only caught glimpses of what was inside. Diapers, snacks, two bottles of water, tubes of some sort of cream, an extra set of clothes for JT, and who knew what else. She insisted that if she didn't bring it with them, something would happen and she'd need it. He didn't argue, but secretly thought it was crazy.

As they walked toward his black Mustang—her car

should be returned sometime tomorrow, she was told—TJ looked around out of habit. His eyes stopped on a man sitting on a wooden bench on the far side of the playground. He hadn't noticed him earlier.

He was wearing a baseball cap pulled down low over his forehead, so TJ couldn't see his face clearly. He had a scruffy beard and was tall and lanky.

TJ stopped at his car and stood aside as Milena strapped JT into his car seat.

"Do you think we could stop at the store on the way home?"

TJ turned away from the man and faced Milena. "Of course."

"Great. I'm out of Cheerios and it's JT's favorite snack."

"No problem. I told you, anything you need, whenever you need it, I'll make sure you get it."

She rolled her eyes. "Well, I need a million dollars, but I'm not going to hold my breath that you'll deliver anytime soon."

"Give me fifty years and I'll make sure you have your money, Doc." TJ's voice deepened and he leaned into Milena as he spoke, creating a little cocoon of intimacy between them.

She stared up at him for a second, then cleared her throat and took a step back.

Realizing he was pushing, TJ smiled, then allowed

her the space. As he walked around to the driver's side, he remembered the man. His gaze wandered back to the bench he'd been sitting on, only to find it empty. He looked around the area and saw no sign of the mysterious-looking man.

Vowing to be more observant in the future, TJ opened the car door and climbed inside. Just because the man was wearing a baseball hat didn't mean he was dangerous. He tried to convince himself of that, but his conscience wasn't having it.

Making a mental note to contact Cruz as soon as he could to see if there was any update on the whereabouts of the Joneses, TJ started his car and headed for the grocery store with the two people who meant the world to him.

"YOU'RE SURE IT was her?" Jeremiah asked.

"Positive," Jonathan told his dad. "I didn't see the other woman though."

Jeremiah waved off his son's words. "And there was a baby? Was it a girl or boy?"

"A boy. A real brat. He fell off a tiny little ladder and screamed his head off."

"A boy," Jeremiah mused. They were currently staying in a fleabag motel on the outskirts of San Antonio. It was a piece of shit, but they took cash and didn't ask too many questions. They'd tried to call some of the men who had been coming to the school for years for assistance, but they were all either behind bars already, or had hung up when they'd found out who was calling.

It pissed Jeremiah off, but he didn't need them.

But he decided he *did* need that little boy.

It would be the perfect revenge. He was just going to kill the bitch and be done with it, but this was even better. He needed to groom someone else to help with his new school when he set it up, and taking the son from the bitch who had brought down his empire would devastate her.

He'd take them both, show her exactly what her son's future would be, then dispose of her. He didn't want a woman around. He had no use for women, none whatsoever.

He would take the boy, and he'd allow his son to take the bitch's friend. They'd use her to get a couple babies and then get rid of her too.

Jeremiah smiled at his son. "Keep your eye on her. I want to know her schedule. Who she sees. Where she lives, and what time she comes and goes. We'll figure out the best time to catch her unawares."

"And get the redhead too, right?" Jonathan asked.

"Yeah. Her too."

"Do you have a plan?"

Jeremiah's hand was moving before he'd even

thought about it. He smacked his son across the face before the other man had a chance to move. "Seriously? After all this time, you're questioning me?"

"I'm sorry, Father," Jonathan said immediately, bowing his head.

"Just because we aren't at school doesn't mean the rules have changed," he told Jonathan, his words low and deadly.

"Yes, sir."

"Don't forget again. You might be an adult, but I can and will punish you like I did when you were young. Remember that."

"Yes, sir."

"To answer your insolent question, of course I have a plan. Don't I always?"

"Yes, Father."

"What are you still doing standing here? The next time I see you, you'd better have more information about that bitch and my new son, hear me?"

Jeremiah barely paid any attention to the son he'd fathered when he was just seventeen as Jonathan left the motel room. His own father had brought a young teenage prostitute home and hidden her in their basement. He'd tied her down and made Jeremiah fuck her until she'd gotten pregnant. Then she was kept down there until his father thought the baby could survive outside her womb. He'd cut his grandson, Jonathan, out

of her belly without mercy, leaving the woman screaming in pain until she'd fallen silent. Jeremiah still
remembered how bad she'd smelled when his dad had
forced him to clean up the mess. She'd died from blood
loss, but he hadn't cared.

He'd had a son.

Someone vulnerable to him. Finally.

He'd always been weaker than his dad—and he
loved knowing he could do everything to his son that
his father had done to him.

Jeremiah grinned when he remembered the look on
his father's face right before he'd blown his head off
with the shotgun the old man had loved to threaten *him*
with.

Maybe taking Jonathan with him when he went to
Mexico with the bitch's baby wasn't the best idea.
Jonathan might turn on him like he'd turned on his
own father.

The more he thought about his past, the more para-
noid Jeremiah got. Making the decision right then and
there to start completely over without Jonathan.

Getting a new son was the best idea he'd had in a
long time. And taking the flesh and blood from the
bitch who'd ratted him out was the perfect revenge
indeed.

Rubbing his hands together, Jeremiah imagined all
the things he'd do to the boy to show him who was

boss. Who was in charge. His dick got hard just thinking about it.

Settling into the dirty chair in the corner of the motel room, Jeremiah unzipped his pants and palmed himself. Oh yeah, he was definitely looking forward to starting over in Mexico with his new family.

Chapter Eight

THE WEEK WENT by quickly for Milena. She worked each morning at the clinic downtown and spent every afternoon with TJ and their son. He'd done extremely well so far with JT, as if he'd been a parent his whole life. He was nurturing, but didn't spoil the little boy. When she'd commented on it, he'd simply said he paid attention to everything *she* did and tried to emulate it.

Which of course made her stupid heart turn over in her chest.

He'd been attentive to her, but not suffocating. Each time they came back from whatever outing they'd been on, he made sure she and JT were inside her parents' house safe and sound before he left. He never tried to finagle an invitation to come inside, even when she kind of wanted him to. He didn't crowd into her personal space and hadn't tried to kiss her.

All in all, the week had been confusing. She could tell TJ was different than he'd been three years ago. It was as if the bad stuff about him had just disappeared altogether. He didn't seem angry, he wasn't impatient, he didn't even mind when JT threw a fit in the middle of the store. He simply stood over him in the aisle and let him scream until he'd exhausted himself, seemingly unaware of the disapproving looks from other shoppers as they passed.

Now, at the end of the week, Sadie had been visiting Milena at the clinic, and they were chatting about nothing in particular as they left when a man caught Milena's attention. He was standing down the street, leaning against a wall. Staring at them.

"Sadie, straight in front of us, see that guy in the hat?" Milena asked her friend softly as they walked toward her car.

Hearing the tension in Milena's voice, Sadie immediately went on alert. She looked where Milena indicated and stiffened. "Isn't that Mister Jonathan?"

Milena swallowed hard. "Yeah, that's what I thought too."

Sadie's hand went inside the bag she always carried on her shoulder. Milena knew she had a cute little pink gun. A gun that might be small, but was still deadly.

When the man realized he'd been seen, instead of turning around and leaving, he tipped his hat to them in what might've been a gallant gesture, except for the evil grin on his face.

"Holy shit," Milena breathed, and reached for her phone. She unlocked it and went to her contacts, clicking on TJ's name before she'd even thought about what she was doing.

"Hey, Milena. What's up?" TJ asked as he answered.

"Sadie and I are outside the clinic and I'm pretty sure Jonathan is watching us."

"Go back inside," TJ ordered immediately in a voice that had changed from jovial and happy to urgent and pissed off in a heartbeat. "Now."

"He's not doing anything, just standing there staring at us."

"Please, Doc. Go back inside. I'll be there as soon as I can."

"He's leaving now."

"Milena," TJ warned. "You had better be on your way back to the clinic."

Jonathan turned and sauntered down the street as if he didn't have a care in the world. He veered down an alley and disappeared from view. But before he did, he blew a kiss in their direction.

Milena shuddered in revulsion. "He's gone now."

"Milena, for God's sake! Go. Back. To. The. Clinic." Each word out of TJ's mouth was clipped.

"Sadie, TJ wants us to go back to the clinic and wait for him," Milena told her friend. What she really wanted to do was get in her car and go home, but it had been a long time since she'd heard that tone of voice from TJ, and she wasn't sure it would be smart to go against him.

Her friend looked at her for a heartbeat, then asked, "Is he on his way here?"

Milena nodded.

Sadie glanced in the direction Jonathan had disappeared, then at her friend once more. "Then we need to do what he says."

"Are you there yet?" TJ asked impatiently in her ear.

"No, but we're going," Milena said.

"Good."

She heard a door slam and knew TJ was now in his car. She blew out a relieved breath. Just knowing he was on his way went a long way toward making her feel better. "He didn't do anything, TJ. Just smiled and blew us a kiss as he left."

"*Fuck!*" TJ swore. "Doc, every law enforcement officer in a hundred-mile radius is looking for that asshole. He and his dad are on the FBI's Most Wanted list. No one has seen them since the school was raided. The fact that he's still hanging around in San Antonio and standing outside *your* clinic doesn't exactly give me warm fuzzies. Not to mention blowing you a fucking kiss. I hate to say this, because I know it's not going to make you happy, but this changes things."

"Changes things how?"

"In that the half-ass job I've been doing of keeping my eye on you just changed to a more full-time job. There's no way I've found you again, only to have a perverted asshole snatch you away."

They arrived back at the clinic and entered, Milena too focused on her conversation with TJ to care about her surroundings. "No one is going to snatch me away!" she exclaimed. "And it wasn't like I was hiding from you. I've been here the whole time. In plain sight. We worked in the same city, for God's sake. All you had to do was look up my name on that fancy highway patrol database and you could've found me, TJ. But no, it wasn't until I was in trouble that you even bothered. You just have to be the fucking hero, don't you?"

There was silence on the other end of the line, except for the faint sound of a siren in the background, as Milena waited for him to respond.

"What else?" he strangely asked.

"What else, what?" Milena huffed.

"What else are you pissed at me for? Go on, get it all out."

"Pretty much everything, TJ!" she told him. If he wanted a list, she'd give him one. "As I said, you had the resources to find me whenever you wanted, but you didn't. It wasn't until you thought I was in danger that you even bothered. I'm upset that you won't talk to me about what happened to you when you got hurt in the

Army. I'm mad that you seem to be perfect now, but I'm just waiting for the other shoe to drop and for you to hurt me again. I'm pissed at how good you are with JT without even trying, when I was scared every day for his first year that I was going to screw him up so badly he'd end up being a serial killer. And I'm mad that I've felt happier and safer in the last week than I have since the moment you walked out on me!"

Milena was breathing hard at the end of her tirade. Little puffs of air were coming out and she realized she'd been pacing in the lobby of the clinic as she'd gone off on TJ.

"You go, girl."

The words were spoken softly from behind her, and Milena spun around and saw three teenagers sitting in the waiting room, staring at her. Sadie was standing with her arms crossed, smirking as she leaned against a wall. Milena didn't know which of them had said the words, but was mortified that she'd spoken like that in front of other people.

Milena closed her eyes in embarrassment.

TJ's voice sounded in her ear, calm and seemingly unruffled. "I did look you up. I shouldn't have waited as long as I did though. I figured you were better off without me. No, that's a lie. I was scared to death that I'd look you up and find out you were married. I'm a coward, Doc. I was terrified to look for you and so damn depressed without you. Yeah, knowing you might be in danger was the impetus for me to get off my ass, but it's not because I think you can't take care of yourself. You're an adult, Milena. I know better than anyone that you are no damsel in distress.

"As for JT, it might seem as if I'm a natural with him, but that's only because I've been watching you. I hope there will be a time when you trust me enough to be alone with him, but I have to tell you, I'm petrified and excited about that prospect at the same time. What if I say something wrong? What if I give him something to eat that he's allergic to? What if he gets hurt on my watch and you never trust me again? What if he decides I'm a no-good bum and hates me? I'm well aware he's as amazing as he is as a result of your influence on him.

"And I'll tell you everything you want to know about my time in the Army. Every fucking thing. I don't want to; not because you don't deserve to know, but because it makes me feel like a failure. But I will. I want you to know why I left three years ago, and to get to know the man I am today.

"And lastly, I haven't been as happy and settled in my entire life as I have been in the last week. I wake up in the morning excited to talk to you, to see you, to watch you interact with our son, and I go to sleep at night eager for the hours to pass so I can be around you once more. I'll say it as many times as you need to hear, but I'm not going to hurt you like I did three years ago. I'm one hundred percent in with this relationship. That means answering any concerns you have, manning up and talking about my feelings, and doing everything in my power to make sure you and JT are safe and happy.

"Now…I'm almost there. I'm going to look around. I doubt I'll find anything, but I have to try. Go into the back, away from the windows. I'll be in as soon as I'm done covering the perimeter."

And with that, he hung up.

Milena took the phone away from her ear and stared at it for a beat before looking up at her audience a little sheepishly.

"Giiiiirl, he certainly seemed to have a lot to say after you told him off," one of the teenagers said.

"We need to get away from the windows," Milena said in a flat tone, feeling shell-shocked by what TJ had just told her. He hadn't shied away from anything she'd said. He'd laid it all on the line. The shield she'd been holding around her heart cracked, letting him in just a little bit.

Sadie helped herd the teenagers into one of the examination rooms, and then stood in the small copy and storage room with Milena.

"I take it he's outside?" Sadie asked.

Milena nodded and turned to her friend. "Am I crazy for thinking about giving him another chance?"

"If he'd blown you off when you called, I would say yes. But he didn't. The second he knew you might be in even the smallest amount of trouble, he dropped everything and raced to get to you. Do you know how rare that is? I have the best and worst role models. The best because my uncle and his friends have showed me exactly what I want. A man who cherishes his woman. Who does whatever it takes to keep her happy. The worst because that's a hell of a high standard a man has to live up to if he wants to be with me."

She walked up to Milena and put her hands on her shoulders, looking into her friend's eyes. "He fucked up. There's no denying that. But he's a guy, Milena. Unfortunately, they do that shit. And no one is perfect. It might've taken him longer than it should've to pull his head out of his ass, but he's back now. And from where I'm standing, he's back one hundred percent. He seems genuine in his remorse over what happened and how long it took him to find you. I'm not saying go out and buy a wedding dress and put money down on a venue, but I *am* saying to give him the benefit of the doubt."

"I don't think I'd survive him leaving again," Milena whispered.

"Then grab hold and don't *let* him leave again," Sadie fired back. "A relationship is a two-way street. Make him so damn happy, and reliant on you and JT for his happiness, he can't even imagine walking away. Relationships aren't all sunshine and roses, Milena. You know that. There are ups and downs, and it takes communication and a hell of a lot of work to keep things fresh and smooth. You've had more downs than ups, which sucks, but I'm fairly certain if you give him an inch, he'll more than make up for the shit he piled on you."

Sadie took a step back, put her hands in the pockets of her jeans and smirked. "Besides, I've been watching him for the last week when he's been at the house, and I have a feeling he's got a bit of Dom in him."

"What?" Milena asked, shocked.

"Don't get freaked," Sadie told her friend. "When you were with him three years ago, how was the sex?"

"Um…good?"

"Of course it was. I don't mean that. I mean, was he bossy in bed? Did he seem to take over when you guys went at it?"

Milena knew she was blushing, but nodded anyway.

"Right. That's why he reminds me so much of my uncles Sean and Ian. I'm not saying he's going to want to haul you off to a BDSM club and strap you to a Saint Andrew's Cross and flog you in front of a roomful of people, but he needs that control. Just as you want to please him, he wants to make sure he takes care of you in every way."

"I don't understand half of what you just said. What's a Saint Andrew's Cross?"

Sadie waved her hand. "It doesn't matter. You liked the way he was in bed, right?"

"Yeah, but what—"

"And forgive me this inelegant question, but if JT was in danger, who would you trust most to get him *out* of that danger? Me, you, your mom and dad, or TJ?"

Milena stared at her friend, the answer easier than she was comfortable saying out loud.

"TJ, right?" Sadie asked.

"I shouldn't. I mean, he didn't even know he had a son until a week ago," Milena protested.

"It's because you know, deep down, TJ would do anything for you and your son. He's a Dom, Milena. Maybe not a full-blown, into-the-lifestyle Dominant, just as you'll never be the kind of submissive who wants to play outside the bedroom. But the two of you fit. If you let him in enough to trust him fully, I have a feeling he'll change your life for the better. He's learned his lesson, he won't let you down again. If you let him, you'll have a partner who will kill to protect you and your son, will bend over backwards to satisfy you in the bedroom, and in return, he'll get a woman who can make him believe in himself again."

"How do you know?" Milena asked, blown away by how observant her friend was.

Sadie shrugged. "I told you. I've had some hella good role models."

They grinned at each other.

Before Milena could say anything else, they heard the bell on the outer door to the clinic tinkle. She turned to the open door of the copy room and before she could move, TJ was there.

He strode toward her and, without a word or warning, wrapped one hand around her waist and the other went to her nape. He pulled her into him and kissed her. Hard. Deep. Without apology and without hesitation. As if he were rejoicing in the fact that she wasn't hurt. That Jonathan hadn't gotten to her.

Way before she was ready, he pulled back but didn't take his hands from her. "You all right?"

Milena nodded and licked her lips nervously, tasting a hint of peppermint. He'd obviously had a mint or chewed a piece of gum in the not-so-distant past. The combination of mint and TJ was erotic as hell, and she shifted uneasily, feeling how she'd immediately gotten wet at his familiar taste.

"Sadie? You good?" TJ asked, not taking his eyes from Milena's.

"I'm good," was her slightly amused response.

Milena watched as TJ took a moment to compose himself. Every muscle was tight. She could feel how tense he was under her palms, which were resting on his chest. His breaths came in short, choppy pants and he honestly looked like he wanted to tear someone from limb to limb.

Wanting to soothe him, Milena rubbed her thumbs back and forth over his rock-hard pecs. "We're okay, TJ. He didn't come near us."

"But he was here. Watching you. He knows where you work."

"Of course he does. Remember, he was the one who found me here." She saw his jaw flex before he answered.

"There was no sign of him, but I didn't really expect there to be. Is this the first time you've seen him since the raid?" TJ asked.

Milena nodded.

"He should've been long gone before now," TJ said. "If he and Jeremiah were smart, they would be on the other side of the country or in Mexico by now."

"Maybe it was a coincidence." Milena ignored Sadie's snort.

TJ simply shook his head. "No, I don't think it is."

Milena felt his thumb brush back and forth at the base of her skull, making her heart flutter in her rib cage. That small caress brought back so many memories. He used to hold her just like this after making love to her. Her head resting on his shoulder, her arm flung across his chest, his hand at her nape, lazily caressing her as they both came down from their orgasms.

Sadie's words rattled around in her head. Dom. For-give. Trust.

Taking a huge leap of faith, and hoping like hell she wasn't making the worst mistake of her life, Milena slowly moved her arms around TJ and laid her head against him, shoving her nose into the space at his neck.

TJ WAS SO full of emotion he couldn't control it. Anger at Jonathan for daring to show his face. Relief that Milena was all right. Frustration that he couldn't take Milena to the ground and prove to her once and for all that he'd never hurt her again and would take care of her, in and out of the bedroom, for the rest of her life.

He'd acted without thinking. So damn happy to see her standing and perfectly healthy that he'd done what he'd been aching to do for the last week. He'd kissed her with all the longing in his soul, trying to say what he hadn't yet been able to convince her of with words.

Pulling back way before he was sated—as if he could *ever* get enough of her—TJ held her as he made sure both she and Sadie were all right. He couldn't bear to let her go. Couldn't bear to see the distrust and frustration in her eyes.

The second she caressed his chest to try to calm him down, goosebumps broke out all over his body. Her lemony scent soothing him, making him long for what he used to have. His thumb moved as if it had a mind of its own, using muscle memory, caressing the skin he knew was ultra-sensitive, brushing against the wispy hairs at her nape.

He was afraid he'd pushed too hard, gone too far, but then she gave him her weight and hugged him.

"Doc," he whispered, overwhelmed.

He barely noticed when Sadie slipped out of the room, leaving him and Milena alone.

"I'm scared," Milena whispered, and he felt her warm breath against his neck as she spoke.

"I'm a different man than I was back then," he tried to reassure her. "I'm not saying opening up will be easy, but I'm going to try. I'm not proud of some of the things I did when I was in the Army."

Her arms tightened and she looked up at him. "You're a good man, Thomas James."

His lips quirked in a smile. He loved when she scolded him using his full name. If anyone else dared, he'd hurt them, but he loved the way his name sounded on her lips. "I'm trying to be," he told her. Turning his head, he kissed her forehead, then reluctantly loosened his arms and stepped back from her.

"This changes things," he said gravely.

She took a deep breath and nodded.

"And I'm not just talking about you and me."

"I know," she said, not protesting his words.

"There's no reason Jonathan should've been within a hundred miles of you today. Not if he and his father were truly trying to disappear."

"I don't get it," Milena said. "That FBI guy said it himself. I didn't know anything about what was going on. Why would they care about me?"

"I don't know," TJ said in frustration, "but I'm not about to leave you vulnerable while we try to figure it out. This past week I was on vacation from my job, but starting next week, my full-time job is protecting you."

"TJ, no, that's not necessary," she immediately protested.

"Like hell. Look, the Feds don't have the resources to keep tabs on all the girls and teenagers who were at the school. Hell, they don't have the resources to protect even a handful of them. Not with budget cuts and all the bullshit going on in Washington these days. But that doesn't mean that they aren't concerned about what those two assholes have up their sleeve. I talked to Cruz the night of the raid, and he agreed that if there was any threat against you, he'd talk to my supervisor and get it approved for me to be temporarily assigned to protect you."

Milena looked at him as if he had two heads. "That's crazy. I'm nobody important. How is this happening?"

He took her shoulders in his hands and looked her in the eyes. "That's bullshit. You're important, Doc."

"I don't do well with confinement," she admitted.

"I know. And it's not my intention to spirit you away to some far-flung cabin and lock you inside, no matter how much I might want to. I'll allow you to continue with your regular activities, as long I'm by your side every step of the way."

"Seriously?"

TJ winced. "I know it sounds stifling, but the alternative is that cabin in BFE."

Her brows came down. "No one says BFE anymore, TJ."

He grinned. "I just did."

She shook her head. "Why are we even talking about this?"

"You started it," he teased.

She merely glared at him.

Sobering, he said, "I'm going to be around a lot more, Doc. And believe me, it's no hardship. I can't be with you twenty-four seven though, not unless you want to move in with me…" He let his sentence trail off suggestively, hoping that maybe she'd agree and save him a fuck ton of worry.

When she immediately shook her head, he sighed.

"I didn't think so. Therefore, when I'm not around, I need to know where you are. Every second. And I'm not trying to be a dick or controlling. My plan is to have one of my friends watch over you when I can't."

"What does that mean?"

"It means they'll sit outside in an unmarked car, keeping an eye on your parents' house, if that's where you are. It means they'll escort you to and from the clinic if I'm not available to do it myself. If you want to go to the park with JT, someone will be there with you. Me or one of my friends. I wouldn't advise you to go to big public spaces until those assholes are caught, but I won't stop you from doing it if you want to. My goal is not to make you a prisoner, but I don't want you doing anything that would make you an easy target if either Jeremiah or Jonathan decided to do something stupid."

He could tell Milena wanted to protest, but to her credit, she merely sighed. "I don't like it. I think you know that. But what I like less is thinking about what all the girls who lived at that school went through. If Master Jeremiah and Mister Jonathan were that cruel to them, I can't imagine what they might do to *me* if they thought I had anything to do with bringing down the school."

"I lost you once, I won't do it again," TJ said with feeling. Then, without giving her a chance to respond, grabbed her hand. "Come on, let's get you home. I need to call Cruz and give him an update and talk to your parents about what's going on."

Thankful she didn't protest, TJ led her out the door. He collected Sadie and the three of them headed out of the clinic and to Milena's car. He'd drive it back to her parents' house and Cruz would help him get his Mustang later. The Delta Force soldier inside him—which had only let him down once, on his last mission—was screaming that he had to keep Milena and his son by his side at all times to protect them. And that's exactly what he was going to do.

"SHE'S STILL WORKING at the clinic in the mornings," Jonathan told his father. "She gets there early, around seven-thirty, and leaves after lunch."

"She have the boy with her?"

Jonathan shook his head. "No. Just her. Sometimes her friend comes with her." He'd been so excited to see the red-haired bitch today. She was a bit tall for his liking, but just the thought of the beautiful little girls she would give him was enough to get him hard, and he knew he'd be able to fuck the woman without an issue. Especially when the end goal was so clear in his mind.

"You need to find out where the brat is when she's at work. I need him. It would be better to take them together, but if need be, we can snatch them separately," Jeremiah said without a trace of sympathy in his tone.

"There's something else, Father," Jonathan said. He

didn't want to tell Jeremiah this part, but did anyway.

"What?"

"They saw me."

Jonathan never saw the fist coming.

Jeremiah hit him in the face before he had a chance to prepare. He went flying backward and fell over the one chair in the small motel room. He looked up and saw his father, full of rage, standing over him.

Jeremiah kicked him repeatedly as he berated him. "You. Dumb. Shit! You were supposed to watch them without being seen. Now they know we're still in San Antonio and will probably be more on guard!"

Jonathan curled into a ball but didn't say anything. He knew his father would continue to beat him until he was satisfied he'd learned his lesson.

But deep inside, Jonathan was glad his redhead had seen him. Was glad she was scared. It would make it all the better when he captured her. She'd know he was in charge. Not his father—*him*. He alone had the power to impregnate her. It was a heady feeling, and one he couldn't shake. The redhead was *his*. His to do with what *he* wanted.

He'd never had a girl to himself before. He'd always had to share with the others who visited the school. The redhead would live or die because of him and him alone.

So Jonathan let his father beat on him all he wanted. Being spotted was worth it. Worth seeing the worry in her eyes.

When Jeremiah finally got tired, he scowled and said, "Get up. We need to switch motels. Because of your incompetence, this one is probably compromised. You have one more shot, boy. You screw up again and your precious redhead will become mine. I'll give her that baby you so desperately want, and you won't *ever* get to touch her. Understand?"

His father's words made a red haze fill his vision, but Jonathan nodded obediently.

No, she was his. All his. His father hadn't trusted him to train a little all by himself. He'd always had his father's cast-offs. The child the redhead would bear would be all *his*. She'd grow up knowing *he* was her master.

Hiding his anger from his father, Jonathan got up off the floor, ignoring the aches and pains from where Jeremiah had kicked him, and he quickly collected his things, stuffing them into the small backpack he'd brought with him from the school.

He tuned out his father's plans for the bitch and her son, and instead made his own.

He'd help Jeremiah, but in the end, he'd do his own thing, go his own way. He'd take the redhead and start his own school. And the first student would be his very own daughter.

Chapter Nine

———◆———

TWO WEEKS LATER, TJ had gotten into a routine with Milena. He came by early in the morning and escorted her to the clinic. One of his friends—Cruz, Dax, Quint, or Hayden—would meet him there and take over watching her for the morning. He would either go home and take a quick nap, do errands, or continue to try to find where Jeremiah and Jonathan were hiding out…with no luck.

Then he'd arrive after lunch to escort Milena back to her parents' house, and he'd spend the rest of the afternoon and sometimes the evening with her and his son.

After TJ left each evening, he would drive away as if he was going home, but then circle around and park down the street from the house. He'd spend the rest of the night keeping watch over the two most important people in his life. He'd done a piss-poor job of making sure Milena had what she needed to be happy and healthy once; he wouldn't fail again. Especially not with

Jeremiah and Jonathan still on the loose.

TJ yawned and looked at his watch. Two forty-seven in the morning. He was tired, but unlike during other stakeouts he'd done, he didn't have the slightest urge to take a quick catnap. Not when the people he was watching over were so precious.

Since he'd begun staking out the house, he'd yet to see anything out of the ordinary. He looked up from his watch—and froze. He blinked to and squinted his eyes, looking at where he'd clearly seen the silhouette of a man slinking around the side of the large house before whoever it was had disappeared.

Without thought, TJ eased out of the car and headed in the direction he'd seen the figure. There absolutely shouldn't be anyone lurking outside the house, and if it was Jeremiah or Jonathan, he wanted to catch them in the act and turn their ass over to the cops.

Taking out his pistol, TJ ran as silently as he could toward where he'd last seen the figure. Using the stealth he'd perfected during his time on the Delta Force teams, he eased around the side of the house. He didn't see anyone and continued along the bushes. When he got to the corner, he put his back to the stucco and cautiously looked around to the backyard.

Standing under a large tree was a man dressed all in black. He was holding something in his hands, but TJ couldn't tell what it was. He was looking up at one of the windows in the house.

It was…odd. He wasn't trying to break in at the moment, and because it was the middle of the night, all the lights were off…so it wasn't as if he could be watching any of the occupants inside.

Adrenaline coursed through TJ's body. He wanted this guy. Bad.

He'd taken one silent step toward him when he was spotted.

TJ didn't even have time to say a word before the mystery man turned and sprinted toward the back fence.

Without hesitation, TJ raced after him.

The likely identity of the man in black was confirmed when he easily vaulted over the four-foot-high chain-link fence without any difficulty whatsoever. It had to be Jonathan, as TJ didn't think Jeremiah would've been able to get over the enclosure so easily.

TJ had one hand on the top of the fence and was two seconds away from leaping it and continuing the chase, but stopped. Frustration coursed through him. He couldn't risk leaving Milena and the others vulnerable. What if Jonathan was the bait and Jeremiah was waiting for TJ to leave the house unprotected? He couldn't risk it.

Watching the man in black until he disappeared into the night, TJ turned back toward the house. He went back to where he'd seen Jonathan standing under the tree. Every muscle in his body tensed when he saw what had been left lying on the ground.

Zip ties.

Anger welled inside TJ. It was more confirmation that the man hadn't just been a pervert hoping to get a glimpse of someone without their clothes on. The Joneses were still out there—and for some reason, they had Milena in their sights. It didn't make sense. Milena hadn't been the one to call in the tip on the school.

TJ paused and took a deep breath. Milena hadn't...but *Sadie* had.

She'd been the one to call her uncles and let them know something wasn't right at the school, which had started the entire investigation in the first place. What if Jeremiah had figured that out? And he'd wrongly assumed it was Milena?

"Damn," he said in a whisper as he took out his phone and quickly took a picture for the evidence techs. He didn't want to touch the plastic restraints in case DNA or fingerprints could be retrieved from them. He then eased his way back around to the front of the house.

Jonathan lurking around Milena's house upped his sense of urgency. He was already protecting her full-time, but tonight's sighting just had him all the more determined to keep his eye on Milena. No way were Jonathan or Jeremiah getting their hands on his woman.

Not in this lifetime.

Frustration coursed through TJ's body. He wanted to be inside with Milena. Wanted to make sure she and his son were all right. But if he couldn't be, then sitting outside the house they were in was the second-best place.

No longer tired, TJ settled back into the driver's seat of his car. His eyes constantly scanned the area around the house. A part of him hoped Jonathan would come back and try again. He wouldn't get away a second time. TJ had underestimated the man tonight. Hadn't expected him to be as agile as he was. If he dared show his face anywhere near Milena again, he'd discover exactly what TJ had learned while he'd been a Delta.

JONATHAN STOPPED RUNNING and leaned against the side of a house several blocks away. He was breathing hard and could feel his heart beating out a frantic tattoo. That had been close, too close. He couldn't get caught now.

He hadn't realized someone was watching the house until he'd already been spotted. Luckily he was agile and had a head start, allowing him the precious seconds he'd needed to hide from whoever it was who had seen him.

Father would be pissed if he knew what he'd done. "That's why I won't tell him," Jonathan said quietly.

All he'd wanted was a glimpse of his redhead. It had been stupid to go to the house, but he couldn't help himself.

Taking a deep breath, Jonathan stood up straight and, after looking around to make sure he hadn't been followed, slunk around the back of the house he'd been leaning against to double back for his car. He needed to get back to the motel and his room before his dad realized he was gone. The sleeping pill he'd slipped into his father's nightly beer had done its job and allowed Jonathan to slip out without Jeremiah noticing, but he didn't want to push his luck.

Looking back in the direction of the house where his redhead was sleeping, he said softly, "Soon. I'll be seeing you soon."

TJ STRETCHED. HE'D been sitting outside the Reinhardts' house all night and the sun was just beginning to peek over the horizon. He hadn't relaxed since he'd chased Jonathan away, and was feeling antsy about seeing Milena with his own two eyes to make sure she was safe. He reached for his phone when it vibrated in his pocket.

"Rockwell," he answered.

"This is Captain Jackson. What's the word?"

TJ had been speaking periodically with the captain

since the raid on the school. For some reason, the other man seemed to be inordinately interested in everything that had been going on. "Chased a man who was lurking around Milena's house."

"Fuck. You didn't catch him?"

"No. I couldn't leave the house unprotected."

"How's Sadie?"

TJ cocked his head and didn't answer for a long beat. It wasn't as if Jackson hadn't asked about Milena's friend before—he had—but this time, TJ heard something more than professional interest in the man's voice.

"She's good. She sometimes goes with Milena to the clinic, but she got a part-time job in a coffee shop. She works on the weekends and occasionally in the afternoons."

"Keep your eye on her," the other man ordered. "I don't like this. And her uncles are getting antsy. They want her home. They're going to lose their shit when they hear someone was sneaking around the house."

TJ refused to get pissed at the captain. He wasn't saying that he didn't think TJ could keep her safe, just that her relatives, who were definitely able to protect her, wanted her home. He couldn't blame them.

"Of course I'll keep my eye on her. I have no proof that whoever it was I chased away was Jonathan or Jeremiah," TJ warned. "It could've just been a kid." He didn't believe that, and the zip ties sitting on the dashboard of his car inside a plastic bag mocked his words.

"You don't believe that any more than I do," Chase said. "I wish like fuck I could be down there helping with surveillance, but I can't. Let me know if you have more info. If anything else happens, call me. If she…er…they are in danger, I want to know about it."

TJ didn't even ask why. He wasn't sure the Army had any more interest in the case. They'd been concerned when they'd thought the school might be a front for some sort of anti-government cult. No one wanted a group of citizens stockpiling weapons. But after the raid, when no weapons were found, and the Army brass realized that the school was "only" a child-abuse ring, their interest had waned.

But not Captain Jackson's.

He was just as concerned today as he'd been when he'd first received the files about the school. About Sadie. Maybe more so after what happened earlier.

"Of course," TJ told the captain, reassuring him that he'd keep him in the loop.

"Later," the captain said.

"Later," TJ returned. He glanced down at the watch on his wrist. Six-thirty. It was a bit early; he usually knocked on the door around seven and they left not too long after that. But he needed to see Milena this morning. Needed to make sure she and JT were good.

He strode up the walkway to the door and softly knocked. It opened almost immediately, but instead of Milena, it was her father.

TJ didn't even hesitate. "Good morning, sir."

"It's time we talked," Mr. Reinhardt said in a solemn tone. He turned and walked back inside the house.

TJ closed the door behind him, locked it, and followed Milena's dad. He was actually glad this was happening now. He'd been expecting it for a while. Her dad had been pretty cool with him, but he wanted to make sure her father knew where he stood when it came to his daughter and grandson.

Robert Reinhardt led them to a spacious office. He immediately sat behind a desk, unconsciously or consciously giving him the place of power in the room. There were floor-to-ceiling bookshelves filled with books on either side, with a large window behind the desk.

Milena's father was in his early fifties but didn't look his age. He had a gut, but other than that, seemed to wear his age well. His hair was darker than Milena's; she'd obviously inherited her blonde hair from her mom. This morning he was wearing a pair of dark brown slacks and a pale-yellow dress shirt.

TJ sat in one of the leather chairs strategically placed in front of the desk and waited for the older man to take the lead on the conversation. He didn't have long to wait.

"When Milena called us from Austin after you left, I'd never been so worried about my daughter as I was then. She was absolutely heartbroken. Her mother and I did what we could to support her, but that was hard when she wasn't even living in the same city. Then when she moved home, it was obvious she wasn't the same. Oh, she tried to hide her depression, but it was easy to see since we know her so well.

"Once she moved in, she got better at faking being happy, but I heard my daughter crying almost every night. She was terrified she'd lose her baby, the only link she had to the man she loved with all her heart. When she went into early labor, the only thing I could do was pray she lived. You haven't known fear until you see your baby in pain and know there's absolutely nothing you can do about it.

"I didn't agree with her putting your name on the birth certificate. I thought she should've claimed she had no idea who the father was. I didn't say a word when she put all those pictures of you in JT's room. I didn't even complain when she had her mother make that damn pillow for him. But it cost her."

TJ had seen the pictures Milena had put in JT's room the previous week. He'd gone in there to grab a toy or something for his son and had stopped in his tracks when he'd seen all the photos. He'd had a hard time composing himself. No wonder JT had said "Daddy" the first time he'd seen him. He'd been looking at TJ's face since the very first day he'd come home. It humbled and awed him that Milena had done that. Even if he knew she hadn't done it for him, but for their son.

TJ opened his mouth to speak, but Milena's dad continued before he could.

"When you showed up on our doorstep three weeks ago, I saw a change in my little girl immediately. She smiled more, even though she wasn't sure of your intentions. But she's terrified, young man. Scared out of her skull that one day you're going to up and disappear again. Don't get me wrong, I'm grateful you're here watching out for her, keeping her safe from those perverts, but there's more at stake for her now.

"She has a son. A little person who, if I'm not mistaken, is becoming as attached to you as my daughter is. You might be a cop, and I know I could get in trouble for saying this, but if you hurt her again, I'll kill you. She can't go through what she did three years ago. It would be better if you were dead than for her to realize that you'd left her again." Mr. Reinhardt stopped speaking and glared at TJ, as if daring him to pull out a pair of handcuffs and arrest him for threatening an officer of the law.

But TJ had no intention of doing that.

"She won't have to go through losing me again because I'm not going anywhere, Mr. Reinhardt."

"Are you here because of the possibility she's in danger?"

"Yes." As the scowl on the other man's face deepened, TJ went on quickly. "And no. I can't deny I'm back in her life because of that fucking school, but that is *not* why I'm still here. I love her. Never stopped loving her. But three years ago, I was an asshole. I knew if I didn't get my head on straight, I'd end up hurting her. I know I *did* hurt her, but not in the same way I would've if I'd stayed. The last thing I wanted was her finding out how weak I was. I was having a hard time getting past the mistakes I'd made on my last mission. People died. Lots of people died."

Bob's face lost some of its antagonism, but he didn't interrupt.

"I fucked up, I admit it. But I left because I thought it was for her own good. Hindsight is always twenty/twenty though, and obviously, she suffered more because I left. That won't happen again. I swear to you, I'm here to stay. I want to see JT grow up to be an amazing man who knows how to treat his woman as if she's the most precious thing to him. I don't want a day to go by that your daughter doesn't know down to the very marrow of her bones that she's loved, and I would do anything for her. *Anything.*"

TJ didn't flinch as the other man stared at him for a long moment. Then he said, "We didn't know she hadn't told you about the baby. We thought all along you knew and didn't care. But I think she was scared to really search for you. Scared that if you found out, you'd want her to get rid of him."

"I would *not* have done that," TJ said firmly. "I can't say that I would've been overjoyed, especially since I was in a dark place, but I wouldn't have wanted her to abort him."

The older man nodded. "Then after JT was born, we encouraged her to do her best to find you, but I think she was scared you would try to get him taken away from her."

TJ closed his eyes in despair. He knew he'd screwed up when he'd left her, but he had no idea she thought he might've stooped low enough to do something like try to take her child from her. He snorted out a bitter laugh. "No judge in his or her right mind would've granted custody to me. Especially back then."

"I'm just telling you what was going through her mind."

TJ nodded.

"Anyway, when you showed back up, I think she was relieved. She told me she hated keeping him from you."

TJ leaned forward and rested his elbows on his

knees. He didn't look away from Milena's father as he said, "I don't blame her for any decisions she made in the past. I'm as equally responsible for those decisions as she is. All I want is to move forward. I want to get to know JT better, but more than that, I want your daughter back in my life. I'm going to keep her safe. I'm going to do my damnedest to make her happy, no matter what that means. If that means she wants ten more kids, then that's what she'll get. If she wants to move to Timbuktu, I'll get her there.

"I've learned my lesson the hard way. I lost two years of my child's life because I was an idiot. It's not going to happen again. I want to wake up every morning to her beautiful face and go to bed each night with her by my side."

TJ held Mr. Reinhardt's gaze steadily and waited for a response.

When it came, it was better than he could've hoped for. The man stood up and held out his hand. "I assume that means you're going to eventually be my son-in-law, since I won't have my daughter living in sin for the rest of her life. I have to ask you to call me Bob."

TJ smiled and stood as well, reaching for the other man's hand. They shook and TJ said, "Thank you, Bob."

"Thank *you*, son."

"For what?"

"For bringing the smile back to my girl's face."

TJ knew he had a long way to go to earn back Milena's love, but he was going to do whatever it took to get there. "Since you're her father, I need to tell you something."

Bob's brows furrowed. "Yes?"

"I think you know I've been keeping watch over the house at night. Well, last night I chased someone out of the backyard."

"Fuck," Bob swore softly.

"I couldn't follow him because I didn't want to leave the house vulnerable."

"Was it him?"

TJ didn't know which of the Joneses Bob was referring to, but ultimately it didn't matter if it was Jeremiah or Jonathan. "I think so."

"Keep my baby girl safe," Bob said, the frustration and worry for his daughter easy to hear in his voice.

"I plan on it," TJ told him.

They stared at each other a heartbeat before Bob nodded. He looked down at his watch and said, "I'm sure Milena is up and in the kitchen by now.

TJ followed Bob out of the office and into the kitchen—and froze in his tracks upon seeing Milena.

She was leaning over looking for something in the refrigerator. His eyes swung to her ass, and he couldn't tear them away. Milena had always had curves, but after having his baby, she'd obviously not lost all the weight she'd gained.

She was wearing a pair of jeans that molded to her as if they were a second skin. Her blouse had ridden up, and the image of him walking up to her and putting a hand on her back, keeping her bent over, was as clear as day in his mind. He'd reach around and unfasten her jeans and expose her luscious ass to his gaze. Then he'd take her just like that. Bent over in front of the fridge, her nipples taut with the cool air wafting over them, her fingers holding on to the sides of the large appliance as he hammered inside of her, showing her without words how fucking sexy she was and how much he loved her body.

"Hey, baby," Mr. Reinhardt said to his daughter.

His words acted as a figurative bucket of cold water, dashing the fantasy that had been consuming TJ. Knowing his hard-on would be more than obvious to both Milena and her dad, he stepped behind the long bar that flanked one side of the kitchen.

"Hi, Daddy," Milena said, standing upright and presenting her cheek to her dad. She looked from him to TJ and asked, "Everything all right?"

"Of course," Bob said, reaching around her and grabbing the container of orange juice.

Milena turned to TJ. "Good morning."

God, what he'd give to hear her say that when she

was still half asleep in his bed. He'd wake her up with a kiss, and maybe after they'd greeted each other, he'd move down her body and show her exactly how good of a morning it could be. One thing about his girl, she loved morning sex.

Shaking his head and telling himself to get it out of his ass, and to stop thinking about how much more beautiful Milena would be naked on his sheets *now* than she was three years ago, TJ did his best to smile back at her and say, "Morning."

The need to have Milena living with him was growing with every day they spent together. And after last night, he was all the more determined to convince her to move in with him.

He opened his mouth to say just that, "Move in with me," but her dad spoke before he could.

"Your mom and I were thinking…"

Milena turned to her dad. When he didn't finish his thought, she prompted, "Yeah?"

"You know we love having you here, and you'll always be welcome, but with everything that's happened, maybe it's better if you moved in with TJ…for your own safety."

TJ's mouth hung open in surprise at Bob's words. At how he'd said the exact thing he'd been thinking and hoping for.

"What?" Milena asked, obviously equally shocked.

"As much as I hate to admit it, TJ is better equipped to protect you. He's got the experience, and as big as this house is, someone could break in and hide for days and we'd never find him." The older man was joking, but TJ could see he was struggling with what he was saying.

"He's right," TJ said softly. "My apartment doesn't have half the space this house does, and I'm on the fourth floor. There's also a doorman. No one can simply waltz in without being recorded on security cameras and going through a rigorous screening. I have three bedrooms, so there's plenty of room for both you and JT."

He didn't mention that one of the rooms was currently stuffed to the gills with boxes of crap he'd never bothered to unpack after the military had shipped his belongings to him once he'd graduated from the academy. Milena would sleep in his bed, and if she wasn't comfortable with him being there to share it with her, he'd stay on the couch until she was.

"But…JT is used to *this* house. It's babyproofed. And Sadie is here," Milena protested weakly.

"He'll get used to my place, Doc," TJ said. "You'll be there with him, so he'll settle in quickly. I can buy a few plug protectors to babyproof the place."

She turned to him then, her hands on her hips. "There's more to it than a few plug protectors," she said, her brows drawn down in consternation. "He climbs everything, nothing is safe from him. If you have DVDs on a shelf, he'll take them all out and pound on them. Babyproofing is about making sure any sharp corners on furniture are covered and all knickknacks are out of reach. Cabinets have to be locked so he can't get into anything toxic. Medicine has to be put away, preferably locked as well. Do you have a bathtub? Because it's not like he can take a shower. And a balcony would be a disaster with him around, there's nothing he wouldn't like more than to climb over the darn thing."

TJ inwardly started to panic, but outwardly he kept his cool. "I don't have a balcony," he tried to reassure Milena, "and I truly don't have anything I'd give a shit about if he broke. You can come over and help me make sure it's safe for him."

Milena stared at him for a beat before turning to her dad. "You really want us gone?"

"Oh, baby girl," her dad said, and took her into his arms. "You know it's not that. I just want you and my grandson safe. And unfortunately, I'm not the man who can do that."

Milena had wrapped her arms around her dad when he'd hugged her, but leaned back to look him in the face. "I don't understand this change of heart."

"I'll just go over and say hello to JT," he told the pair, then quickly headed into the other room to greet his son.

He could still hear the conversation between Milena and her dad, but he pretended to be engrossed with JT.

"Milena, that man has been keeping watch over the house from his car every night since he came back into your life. He's proven that keeping you safe is more than a job to him."

"He has? That's crazy."

"No, it's dedication. It's stubbornness. And after what happened last night, it's obviously necessary."

"What happened last night?" she asked.

"He chased away someone who was lurking around the backyard."

Milena gasped. "Seriously? Was it them?"

"He thinks so."

There was a loaded silence between father and daughter. TJ wasn't sure he liked Milena knowing about the creeper in the backyard, but knew it was in her best interest so she could stay alert.

"I think you know as well as I do that he still loves you," Bob told his daughter.

Her voice lowered, and TJ couldn't hear what her response was to her dad's statement. And he really wanted to know what she thought.

JT sat on his lap and happily bobbed up and down as he watched the cartoon on the screen in front of them. He'd been pleased to see his dad but distracted by his show, only allowing TJ one small hug before pushing him away so he could see the television once more.

It was another couple of minutes before Milena came into the room. Her dad had gone back upstairs with two cups of coffee, one for his wife and one for him. She sat on the cushion next to him.

"I'm not sure about moving in with you," she said honestly. "It's too soon. I don't…I can't…"

"No pressure, Doc," TJ said, even though inside he was screaming, *Mine, mine, mine!* "You can come over and help me make sure everything is safe for JT. You can stay until Jeremiah and Jonathan are caught and then we can reevaluate."

"Reevaluate?" she asked, her head tilted in question, her blonde hair sliding over her shoulder to brush against her breasts.

Pulling his eyes away from her tits—God, he was such an asshole—TJ nodded. "Yeah. I want you there permanently. Being around you the last few weeks has hammered home how much my feelings for you haven't changed. I miss you. I haven't forgotten one second of the time we lived together, and how much I enjoyed being near you. I love you, Doc. I want you and JT under my roof. I want to see you first thing when I get up, and I want the right to read my son a bedtime story and tuck him into bed in the evening. If he cries in the middle of the night, I want to let you sleep while I comfort him. I want to be a real father to my son, and be a man you can count on. I know I have a ways to go with that second part, but I think if you live with me, you'll see that I'm not fucking around when it comes to us."

She bit her lip and looked away. Then she asked, "Are you really watching over the house from your car?"

"Yes." He didn't beat around the bush.

"Why?"

TJ waited, but she didn't look at him. He shifted JT on his lap and reached out to touch her chin and encourage her to turn her head. Their eyes met and he said, "Because if there's even a one-percent chance Jeremiah wants to get his hands on you, he's going to have to go through me to get to you. I think I proved that last night."

Her pupils dilated at his words, and TJ could see the pulse hammering in her neck. She wanted to say yes, he knew she did, but she was scared. He couldn't blame her.

"Me moving in is one thing. But you have no idea how much work a two-year-old is."

"I know I don't," he agreed immediately. "And that's just sad. I *should* know. I've missed out on so much. I don't care if he trashes everything I own. It's just stuff. It can be replaced. But I won't ever be able to get these years of his life back. Before I know it, he'll be a teenager and will want to sulk in his room all night playing video games, and his old man will be too dorky and annoying for him to want anything to do with."

TJ returned the smile Milena gave him. "Give it a chance," he cajoled. "Give *us* a chance. I can protect you better if I'm there with you. It's one thing to chase someone away from the house. But staying here really isn't safe. Anything could've happened last night. While I was preoccupied with whoever was in the yard, someone could've slipped inside through the front door. My apartment complex is safer. There are less ways someone could get inside. Sadie can come over whenever you want. In fact, I'll probably insist on it, as I'd love to take you on dates. She can babysit while I wine and dine you. I…" He faltered, then forced himself to continue. "I have a lot I want to tell you. About that last mission. Why I was in the hospital so long."

"You don't have to," Milena immediately said, resting a hand on his, which had dropped from her face and was resting on JT's little thigh.

"I appreciate that, but yeah, I do. I'm not hiding anything from you anymore. Anything you want to know, ask. I'll tell you everything. The only way we can work is if we don't have any secrets."

"But…you don't like talking about your time in the Army. About being a sniper."

He pressed his lips together, then took a deep breath. "I don't. And I can't say that I'll want to continually rehash it over and over, but you have the right to know the kind of man I am."

"I know the kind of man you are," Milena said softly.

"You don't. But you will. And if, after you hear what I've done you want to move back to your parents' house, I'll let you." She opened her mouth to protest, but he pressed a finger over her lips. "But if you can accept it, accept *me* as I am, I'll move heaven and earth to make you and JT happy for the rest of your lives."

Milena reached up and took his index finger in her hand and squeezed, pulling it away from her mouth. "I'm nervous about this, but I want to try. You hurt me so badly when you left, but it was because I loved you so much. I can't say that I'm fully convinced you won't do it again, but I'm willing to give you the benefit of the doubt. Besides, I'd be an idiot to turn down your protection for JT."

TJ winced at that, but immediately blanked his expression. He looked down at his watch. "We need to get going if we're going to get you to the clinic on time."

She nodded. "I'll make sure Sadie is up so she can come out and watch him."

TJ watched as Milena left to get her friend. Her ass swayed as she walked away from him and he had to look away. The longing inside him to take her in his arms and prove once and for all that he would never leave her again was strong, but he resisted.

She was moving in with him. He had time, he hoped, to slowly chip away at the bricks around her heart. The shield that he'd put there. By God, he'd dismantle that wall one brick at a time if it was the last thing he'd ever do. He'd make sure Milena knew he was serious about being there for her, or die trying.

Chapter Ten

THREE DAYS LATER, Milena nervously stood in the elevator of TJ's apartment complex with him. He'd picked her up from the clinic and told her he wanted to show her what he'd done to make his place safe for JT…and to get her approval.

She wasn't sure moving in with him was the best decision, but she couldn't deny she was excited about it. TJ had the power to hurt her, badly, but after having another long talk with Sadie the other night, she'd decided to go for it. She only had one life to live, and something her friend said really stuck with her.

She'd agreed the possibility TJ would hurt Milena was there, but then she'd said, "But what if he doesn't? What if you move in and you find that he's exactly what you've missed for the last three years?"

And Sadie was right. Milena didn't want to deny JT the chance to know his father, and she really didn't want to deny TJ the right to know his son. Besides, deep down, Milena knew she still loved the man. If there was even the slightest chance they could get back what they'd had three years ago, she'd be an idiot to not at least try.

Milena jerked when she felt TJ gently entwine his fingers with hers.

"Relax, Doc. It's going to be fine."

She nodded and gripped his hand harder, loving how it felt in hers. Startled, Milena realized she'd never held hands with TJ before.

His was big and completely engulfed hers. His calluses felt rough against her own smooth skin. But this small gesture made her feel protected and cared for.

The elevator chimed when they reached the fourth floor and TJ exited, not letting go of her hand. He nodded at a man and woman who were waiting for the elevator and continued down the hall.

His apartment was at the very end of the hallway. He pushed the door open and stood to the side, gesturing for her to enter ahead of him.

"Welcome home," he said softly. She bit her lip. God, those words sounded so good.

Instead of doing what she really wanted to—flinging herself into his arms and begging him to take her to bed—she calmly walked into his space.

His musky, earthy familiar scent entered her nose and she inhaled deeply. It was something she'd missed horribly after he'd left, and the memories from the smell left her almost lightheaded.

"Are you all right?" he asked quietly from beside her.

Milena realized she'd closed her eyes and probably looked like a dork just standing there in his entryway. She nodded and looked up at him. "Yeah....it smells like you. I just...it brings back a lot of memories."

His lips curved up at her words. He curled a hand behind her neck and leaned down and kissed her forehead, leaving his lips on her skin for a long moment before pulling back. "Your scent, those lemons, was the first thing I noticed about you too. I hadn't realized how much I'd missed it until I had it back."

Then he straightened and put his keys into a basket on a small table in the foyer. "I tried to do everything you mentioned the other day...putting away small items JT could choke on and getting those little locks for the kitchen cabinets, but I had no idea if it was enough. I called Daxton's girlfriend—you know Dax, he's been with you at the clinic a few times. Anyway, Mackenzie and Dax don't have any kids yet, but she has a ton of nieces and nephews. She came over and helped me babyproof everything."

"Really?"

"Yeah. Why are you so surprised?"

Milena shrugged. "I guess I just thought you'd be upset at having your place disturbed."

TJ leaned in close. "I told you once and I'll tell you

again, as many times as you need me to, I don't give a shit about the stuff in my apartment. It's just that, stuff. I care about you and my son. I want him to be safe and happy here. And I want you to be able to relax when you step through that door. And you can't do that if you're constantly worried about what he's putting in his mouth or if he's going to be hurt."

She swallowed. Hard. God, he was going to be impossible to resist.

Milena made a decision right then and there. Standing in his front foyer, before she'd even seen his apartment. She decided to give their relationship everything she had. She couldn't do it halfway.

He'd gone above and beyond to try to prove that he'd changed. He'd arranged it so he could be by her side every day for the last month or so. He'd spent every night for the last few weeks in his car, watching over her and JT. He'd gone out of his way to be nice to her parents and Sadie, and he hadn't gone overboard, insisting she quit her job and hide out at home until the threat from the Joneses was over.

Not only that, but he'd done his best to keep a respectable distance between them, even though she'd caught a look of such longing and lust in his eyes a few times it had made her knees weak.

No, *she* was the one who'd been holding back. Guarding her heart and not letting him make even the smallest headway. She'd been the one to keep his son a secret from him. She'd been the one to keep him at arm's length when he'd shown no indication he was the angry man he'd been three years ago.

"I'm sure whatever you've done to the apartment is perfect," she said softly. "As long as you've done the basics, we can figure out what else needs to be done once we move in."

He seemed to relax at her words, as if he'd expected her to be unbending and over-the-top about the apartment safety, and Milena realized once more how much she'd kept him at arm's length.

TJ then gave her a thorough tour of his space. He pointed out every electrical outlet and security cover and told her that he'd actually given his old coffee table to one of his friends because he thought the corners were too sharp. The new table was wood with curved edges. He had moved all of his DVDs and CDs to the highest shelves of the built-in entertainment center. Room after room showed his careful attention to detail in making sure his son would be safe in his home.

He showed her an empty room, which he explained would be JT's. There was a faint outline of a picture on one of the walls. It was a rough pencil drawing, the kind of thing artists did before they started actually using paint.

"What's that?" Milena asked.

TJ shrugged a little self-consciously. "One of the guys I work with is married to an artist. I asked if she could come over and make the room a little more boy-friendly. She should be here tomorrow to finish it up."

Milena stepped closer to the wall and her eyes widened as the picture came into focus. She knew without a doubt it was going to be a masterpiece when it was finished. The art would take up the entire wall, and was going to literally be a jungle. And within the trees were dinosaurs. They peeked out from behind bushes and rocks.

Turning to TJ, she said, "This is perfect."

"Really?" he asked.

Nodding, not sure how he could think otherwise, she tried to reassure him. "My God, TJ, he's going to adore this. He loves dinosaurs. He's never going to want to leave his room."

"I didn't want it to be too much, but when I saw the sketch of what she wanted to do, I told her to make it bigger, to make it cover the entire wall."

Without thought, Milena stepped toward TJ and stood on her tiptoes. She brushed her lips over his in a light kiss. "It's perfect."

She froze as his arms came around her waist and he hauled her against him. She was still on her toes, and felt as though the two of them were in some sort of weird time bubble. A memory seared into her brain of another time they'd stood like this. She'd made him dinner and he'd come up behind her, kissing her neck suggestively. She'd turned in his embrace and stood on her tiptoes so she could reciprocate.

Dinner had burned, but neither had cared.

Milena felt her nipples peak and her panties grow damp from the erotic memory.

She stared up at TJ, trying to read his emotions in his eyes. He moved then, slow enough that she could pull back if she wanted. His head dropped toward hers.

But Milena had no desire to pull away from him. She licked her lips. After her decision mere minutes ago, she wanted this. Wanted his lips on hers. Wanted to know if the desire coursing through her veins was only one-sided.

Her eyes closed as she felt his warm breath against her cheek. He kissed her there, then his lips lightly brushed over her sensitive skin as he inched his way to her mouth. Then he was there. His mouth covered hers and they both moaned.

At first, the kiss was tentative, as if they were both unsure. But when Milena opened to him, any reticence on either of their parts was lost. TJ's tongue surged into her mouth as he took control. One hand came up to her head and held her to him as the other tightened on her back, pressing her harder into him so there wasn't an inch of space between their bodies.

Milena could feel his erection against her stomach, hot, hard, and oh so familiar. One of her hands shoved under his shirt and her fingernails raked against the small of his back as she tried to get closer to him. The other held on to his biceps as he bent her backward.

All the while, his tongue dueled with hers. He refused to let her pull away from him. When she gasped for air, he nibbled on her lower lip. He thrust his tongue in and out of her mouth, imitating the act of making love to her. When she tried to push inside his mouth, he blocked her, twining his tongue around hers, forcing her to take what he gave.

Milena went boneless in his arms, letting him do what he wanted. She loved it. Every second. She wanted to tear her clothes off and beg him to take her however he needed. She was ready, more than ready. One kiss was all it had taken for all her pent-up lust to come roaring to the surface. She wanted him. All of him.

To her disappointment, instead of ripping her clothes off, he took his mouth from hers, hauled her upright, and buried his face into the space between her neck and shoulder, and held her to him in an embrace so tight, she didn't know where he ended and she began.

They stood like that for at least a minute, both breathing heavily, their chests moving in and out in tandem. Milena swore she could feel his dick throbbing against her stomach. Her breasts hurt because her nipples were so hard and she knew if she even brushed against her clit, she'd come.

But still TJ didn't move. Finally, she whispered, "TJ?"

She felt him shake his head against her shoulder.

Now she was worried. "TJ?" she tried again. "Are you okay?"

She leaned her head away from him, as much as she could since he wouldn't let her go, and turned to stare at his face.

He finally looked up, and Milena was alarmed to see that his eyes were wet as if he was on the verge of crying. She never thought she'd ever see the day when Thomas James Rockwell cried.

"Oh my God, what? Are you hurt? What's wrong?"

He shook his head, but didn't take his gaze from hers. She saw him swallow hard before he spoke. "I never thought I'd have that again. I've dreamed about it for three years, but didn't think you'd ever give me another chance."

Milena relaxed now that she knew nothing was seriously wrong.

He took a deep breath and used his shoulder to wipe his face, then ran his palm down her arm until he reached her hand, clasping it in his own. "Ready for the rest of the tour?"

Milena nodded, shell-shocked. She'd just seen TJ as

vulnerable as she'd ever seen him before. He hadn't seemed ashamed of his tears, which blew her away. She'd made the decision to give their relationship another chance, and it seemed as if letting down her guard had in turn lowered his. For the first time since he'd come barreling back into her life, Milena thought they just might have a shot.

He showed her the second guest room, which was filled with boxes. He assured her that the room could and *would* be locked, so JT didn't get into mischief in there. She hadn't really thought about the ramifications of that second guest room being so filled with crap until he opened the door to the master bedroom.

The huge king-size bed immediately drew her eyes. The bedframe was nothing fancy, a simple solid head and footboard. But Milena couldn't take her eyes off the mattress. It was covered with a navy-blue duvet, which looked ultra-soft and luxurious. It made her want to immediately go and lay down, test to see if it was as comfortable as it looked.

And that made her think about the sleeping arrangements. Her eyes whipped up to TJ's.

As if he could read her mind, he said, "I want you here. In my bed."

"I'm not sure...I just..." Milena wasn't sure what she wanted to say. Minutes ago, she'd been ready for TJ to take her however he wanted, but now, after she'd had a chance to rein in her raging libido, she wasn't sure about taking their relationship to the next level so quickly.

"It's a big bed. We could sleep next to each other and not come close to touching."

She smiled, a memory flashing through her brain as if it had happened yesterday rather than over three years ago. "Really? You think that'll work? I seem to remember you always hogging my side of the bed."

He blushed. TJ actually *blushed*, but he didn't pull away from her and he didn't try to hide his embarrassment. "Yeah, you're right. It's probably not possible. I might be able to keep my hands to myself, but the second I fall asleep, I know I'd unconsciously sneak over to your side and pull you into my arms and hold you as close as I could."

There went her pesky heart again, pumping out of control at his words.

"I can sleep on the couch," he went on, as if he hadn't rocked her world. "I'll have to ask you to keep the bedroom door open though, so I can hear if you need me in the night. I'm pretty confident in the building's security, but I'm not putting anything past those assholes. With my luck, they'll figure out a way to levitate and come in through the window in the middle of the night to get at you."

Milena really didn't like that image.

Her thoughts must've shown on her face, because TJ brought a hand up and brushed the back of his fingers down her cheek. "You're safe here, Doc. From Jeremiah and Jonathan, even from me. I'll give you as much space as you need. We can take our relationship slow. I'm just so fucking thankful you're here. It seems appropriate that when I needed a place to go, to feel safe, you opened up your home to me, and now here I am doing the same for you. Full circle."

Milena nodded. She wasn't sure what she wanted anymore. One second she wanted to jump TJ's bones, and the next she was freaked simply by looking at a bed. It made no sense, and she was sick to death of her own thoughts.

"You've done a good job, TJ. I don't think JT could be any safer."

"Really?"

"Really."

"So you'll move in?"

Milena nodded. "Yeah."

"When?"

She couldn't help it. He looked so eager and excited, it was as if he were a kid waiting to go trick-or-treating or something. "I don't know. I'll have to look at my schedule and talk to my parents."

"Soon though, right?"

"Yeah. Are you sure you aren't going to regret this?

You've been a bachelor for a long time," Milena said.

"I'm positive. I can't wait to have you both here with me all the time."

"Well, maybe not all the time," Milena teased. "We do have to work you know."

"You know what I mean," he retorted, wrapping the hand that was holding hers around her waist.

She stood there in his embrace, one hand held captive in his behind her back, and simply soaked in the contented feeling of being with him.

"Do you think your folks will be willing to continue to watch JT during the day? I don't want to take advantage of them, and we can start looking for a good, safe daycare for him if we need to."

"They're willing. My mom actually talked to me about this the other night. She was worried they wouldn't get to see him as much if I moved out."

"Okay, Doc. We'll plan on taking him to your parents' house in the mornings before we go to work and one of us can pick him up when we get off."

She smiled up at him. "You're being awfully accommodating."

"Don't you understand? I'd do anything for the two of you. Anything. You and JT are the most important people in my life now. No one and nothing comes before your well-being."

Milena blinked. She'd been teasing, but his answer

was one-hundred-percent serious. She'd lived a good life. Had great parents, good friends, had never really wanted for anything. But TJ's proclamation made goosebumps break out on her arms.

She couldn't speak, so she simply nodded.

He leaned down and brushed his lips over hers in a brief caress. The look in his eyes said he wanted more, but he stood up and twirled her, breaking her out of her surprised stupor and making her laugh. "Come on, let's go. It's been too long since I've seen my son."

"It's only been like six hours."

"Like I said, too long," TJ retorted.

He held her hand as they left his apartment, during the elevator ride, and all the way to his car. And once he'd settled into the driver's seat and they were on their way, he took her hand in his once more.

Milena stared down at their entwined fingers and smiled. She liked this new TJ. A lot.

Jonathan sat in the car he'd stolen the day before and stared at the redhead through the large picture window of the coffee shop. Going to the house she was staying at had been impulsive. He hadn't seen her then, but the thought of snatching her away and saying to hell with his father's plan had been swirling through his head ever since that night.

He didn't want to wait anymore.

He watched as his redhead laughed with the people in the small shop, and he wanted to kill each and every one of them. She was *his*. She belonged to *him*. They shouldn't be looking at her.

Jonathan fingered the plastic zip ties in his lap without thought. Once he got them on her wrists, he'd never take them off. She'd be his to do whatever he wanted. And while the physical act of making babies with her didn't appeal, the fear in her eyes and how she'd obey his every order *did*.

He watched as she changed out the plastic bags in the two trash cans inside the coffee shop then headed toward the back.

He hadn't really planned on today being the day he made his move, but she was giving him the perfect opportunity. Jonathan had scoped out the shop earlier and knew the Dumpster was in an alley behind the shop. He could grab her right now. Take her south of the border and never have to see his father again. His new family could be started as early as that night.

His heart beating overtime with excitement, Jonathan eased the car door open and put one foot on the hot asphalt—then stopped short.

A truck pulled up a couple of car lengths down from him. A woman he recognized leaned over and kissed the man behind the wheel, and then hopped down from the truck.

She had a similar shade of hair to his woman, but he wasn't attracted to her at all. She was too muscular, too...hard. Not to mention, she was a cop. She headed straight for the coffee shop, and Jonathan knew his chance to snatch the object of his obsession had faded away.

He pulled his foot back inside the car and sat there fuming.

He *hated* that he was denied access to his redhead, but clenched his fists and tried to control his temper.

The more he watched her, the more he wanted her. It had been too long since he'd been able to sate his needs, not since the school had been closed down. It wasn't easy to find a girl who wouldn't go to the cops after he was done with her. That's why he needed the redhead to make one for him.

His eyes closed as he fantasized about a little red-haired girl calling him Master Jonathan, and doing whatever he told her to.

Just like the other night at the house, Father didn't know he was here today, but Jonathan didn't care. He'd lie and tell Jeremiah he'd been watching the other bitch and her brat. He had no use for the baby boy. None. He knew his father was going to replace him, but that was okay with him.

His chance to snatch the redhead had been lost with

the arrival of the cop, but he'd get another. Deciding to stick with his father's plans for now, Jonathan continued to watch through the window of the shop. "I can't wait to make you mine," he murmured.

Chapter Eleven

————————◆————————

MILENA HAD TRIED to get TJ to stay the night at her parents' house, but he'd refused, saying it just wasn't right. She had no idea what was "wrong" about it, but he'd refused to budge. She was a little irritated that he preferred to sit outside in his car all night rather than be inside with her and their son, especially after all his talk of it being easier to protect her if he was with her.

It was Saturday night, and she and Sadie were alone in the house with JT. Her parents had gone downtown for a date night, something they'd done periodically over the years. They'd spend the night at a fancy hotel and "reconnect." Their words, not hers.

She and Sadie were hanging out on the couch and chatting. JT had fallen asleep an hour before and they were enjoying the girl time.

"I just don't understand why he won't come inside," Milena bitched to Sadie for what seemed like the hundredth time.

Her friend merely shrugged. "It's a guy thing."

"Seriously?"

"Seriously," Sadie said with confidence. "Look, I'm not going to pretend I know exactly what he's thinking, but I'm guessing it has something to do with the way he looks at you."

"How does he look at me?" Milena asked.

"As if he wants to tear off all your clothes and have his wicked way with you."

Milena blushed. "He does not."

"Yeah, Milena, he does. And he probably doesn't want to risk losing control and doing just that when you're still living under your dad's roof."

"But I'm twenty-seven, not fifteen."

"Doesn't matter. It's still your dad's house."

"That's just stupid," Milena complained.

"Remember how I told you about my uncle and how alpha he was?"

"Yeah."

"Then trust me. I know what I'm talking about."

Milena huffed out a breath. "I just don't want him to be uncomfortable and I don't like thinking about him sitting out there in his car all night."

"When are you moving in with him?"

"Probably next week."

"He'll live until then," Sadie declared.

Milena laughed. "You're so mean."

"Nah. Besides, it's good for him. A man never died from being horny, no matter what they might claim otherwise."

Both women laughed.

"You're sure you're okay with this?" Milena asked.

"You moving in with him? Definitely. It's about time you went after what you want. And what you want is TJ."

"I just feel bad about leaving you here."

"Don't," Sadie said. "I'll probably be going back up to Dallas in a month or so. My uncle Ian is threatening to haul me back up there tomorrow if I don't give him an exact date on when I'm returning."

"He sounds scary."

"Uncle Ian? Nah. He just likes to have his way."

"What about your other uncle? Sean?"

"He likes to have his way too, but he's not as in-your-face about it as Ian is. He'll get my aunt Grace to cry and tell me how much she misses me until I feel so guilty I have no choice but to go back."

Milena smiled at her friend. "You're lucky to have them."

"I know."

Just then, Milena's phone rang. She leaned over to the coffee table and picked it up. It wasn't too late, nine o'clock on a Saturday, but getting a call at this time of night wasn't usual.

"Hello?" She listened for a minute, then said, "I'll be there as soon as I can. Call her back and tell her to meet me there."

As soon as she hung up, Sadie asked, "An emergency?"

Milena nodded. "Yeah, the clinic's answering service got a message about one of the homeless teenagers I've been seeing. Apparently, she's been in labor for a while and didn't tell anyone. The woman she's been hanging with on the streets called and said she can't wait until tomorrow when we open. Can you stay and watch JT while I go in?"

Sadie shook her head. "No. You can't go by yourself. It's dark, Milena. TJ would lose his mind. I'm coming with you."

Milena chewed her lip. "I can't call my parents, it's not fair to them. Maybe I could bring JT with me."

"Call TJ," Sadie ordered. "If you don't, I'll march my ass outside and drag him in here myself."

"I don't want to bother him," Milena protested.

"You aren't alone anymore," Sadie said reasonably. "You don't have to do everything by yourself. Call him."

Milena nodded reluctantly and tapped on TJ's number in her contacts.

He answered after only one ring. "What's wrong?"

"Nothing. Well, sorta. I need some help."

"Hang on, I'm coming in."

Milena stared down at the phone in disbelief. She looked up at Sadie. "He hung up on me."

The doorbell rang.

Sadie giggled. "He might've hung up, but he sure doesn't mess around when it comes to getting to your side when you need him." She stood and headed to the front door to let TJ in.

Milena had just stood up when TJ was there. "What do you need?"

"I just got a call from the clinic's answering service. I need to go into work and I need Sadie with me to help."

TJ immediately understood her dilemma. "You can't go downtown by yourself."

"I know, that's why I called you."

Some of the tension in his face eased at her words. He brought his hand to the back of her neck and pulled her into him, as he'd been doing more and more. He hadn't ever done it in the past, but now he did it all the time. Milena loved it. It was tender and loving, and never failed to make her feel closer to him. He rested his forehead against hers for a second, then pulled back and took a deep breath.

"This sucks," he said, surprising her. At her raised brows, he explained. "I don't want you out of my sight, but I'm not keen on having anyone else watch JT either. If it's okay with you, I'd like to call two of my friends and have them go with you and Sadie to make sure you're safe and this isn't Jeremiah's way of getting his hands on you. I'll stay here with JT."

"You're *asking* me if it's okay?"

"Yeah, Doc. I'm asking you."

Milena slowly nodded. "Okay, that'll work. But I need to get down there quickly. I really don't think this is Jeremiah. The kid in question really is pregnant. It's a bit early for her to be in labor, so I want to make sure something isn't wrong."

TJ nodded and pulled his phone out of his back pocket and clicked on a contact.

Within five minutes, he'd arranged for Hayden, the sheriff's deputy, and Quint from the SAPD to meet at her house. He'd called Cruz, but he was currently on a stakeout and couldn't help.

Milena felt humbled that TJ's friends would drop everything on a Saturday night to help her. They didn't even really know her. She said as much to TJ.

"They're my friends, and they know I'd do the same for them if they asked." He shrugged. "It's what friends do."

"I know, but it's a pain in the ass," she protested.

"I told you once that I'd do anything for you, Doc, and this is part of that. If you need something and I can't provide it for you, I'll call every friend I have and turn in any marker in order to get it for you."

She was beginning to understand a little of what

Sadie had talked to her about earlier. TJ was a man who took care of his own. No matter what that entailed. "Thank you."

"You don't have to thank me. Not for this. If I buy you a giant diamond necklace, you can thank me. If I go with you to the opera, when I hate the opera, you can thank me. But you never thank me for taking care of you and our son and making sure you're both safe. Got it?"

She nodded.

"Good. Now, before you need to leave, give me the rundown real fast on what to do if JT wakes up."

Milena spent the next fifteen minutes making sure TJ knew where the extra bottle was and what to do if he woke up hungry or with a dirty diaper. The toddler was getting better at sleeping through the night, but sometimes still woke up. Something occurred to Milena. "You *have* changed a diaper before, haven't you?"

TJ shrugged. "No, but how hard can it be? I've seen it done on television."

Milena resisted the urge to laugh. He was completely serious. Well, if their son woke up, he'd find out for himself soon enough how hard it could be.

A knock sounded on the door and Sadie went to answer it, letting in both Hayden and Quint. After explanations of what was going on, TJ walked Milena to the door. Sadie had gone on ahead with Hayden and

Quint.

"Stay safe," TJ implored. "Now that you're back in my life, I don't know what I'd do without you."

"Nothing is going to happen. I'm just going down to the clinic to assess Julie. I'll call the ambulance if it looks like she's really about to give birth. Most of the time, especially when it's their first child, it's a false alarm."

"What do you know about the woman who called the answering service?" TJ asked. "Is she trustworthy?"

Milena shrugged. "I don't know her all that well, but her name is Blythe and she's brought Julie in a couple times."

"And she's homeless too?"

"Yeah. But she doesn't seem like a typical homeless person."

"What do you mean?" TJ asked.

Milena shrugged. "Just that she doesn't seem like she's hit rock bottom, like a lot of the homeless I've met. She honestly seems like someone who had some bad luck in her life and is trying to dig her way out."

TJ studied her for a second, then nodded. "Okay. Do whatever Hayden and Quint tell you to. If they say to get down, drop to your belly immediately. If they tell you to run, you run and don't look back. Got it?"

"I'm going to be fine."

"Got it?" TJ asked again in a harder tone.

"Got it," Milena dutifully repeated.

Then for the third time since he'd come back into her life, TJ kissed her. *Really* kissed her. His head tilted and he took her mouth with as much intensity as he had the last time they'd made out, only this time their kiss was shorter, and thus way less satisfying.

"Come back to me, Doc," he whispered. "I'll keep our son safe."

Milena nodded and backed away from him. She turned so she wouldn't fall down the steps that led up to the front door and looked back. TJ was still standing in the doorway, his intense gaze on hers.

Even when Quint was backing down the driveway, TJ still stood there, watching.

SIX HOURS LATER, Milena and Sadie pulled into the driveway back at the house. They'd arrived at the clinic and Blythe and Julie had been waiting for them. Hayden and Quint had made sure the clinic was safe and empty, and then she and Sadie had gotten to work.

Julie had been given a thorough examination, and even though she was several centimeters dilated and in a considerable amount of pain, because her water hadn't broken, Milena wanted to try to stop the labor. Julie was only thirty-three weeks along and it would be better if the baby had more time in her womb.

Julie was freaked out, Blythe was worried, and Milena was on edge. It was pitch black outside and, for the first time, she was worried that this *would* make an excellent opportunity for Jeremiah and Jonathan to make their move…if they were even after her.

Three hours later, despite all of Milena's efforts, Julie's water had broken and Sadie called the paramedics. Julie hadn't wanted to go to the hospital at all, and it had taken both Blythe and Milena to convince her she needed to for the health of her unborn baby.

Wanting to make sure all was well, Milena and Sadie had convinced Hayden and Quint to take them to the emergency room.

It was now three in the morning. Julie hadn't had her baby yet, but she was being looked after by the doctors in the hospital and they reassured Milena they had things well in hand. Blythe was allowed to stay with Julie, and Milena and Sadie had just been in the way.

Quint and Hayden had accompanied them home and refused to leave until they made sure everything was still secure. Expecting to see TJ when she let everyone into the house, Milena was surprised when he was nowhere to be seen.

Quint made her and Sadie stand in the large foyer while he and Hayden cleared the entire house.

Several minutes later they returned, both with huge grins on their faces.

"What?" Milena asked.

"Nothing," Quint said.

"The house is clear," Hayden told her, still smiling from ear to ear.

Something was up, but Milena had no idea what.

"Where's TJ?" she asked the officers.

"He's in JT's room," Hayden said.

Milena nodded and put her purse on the front table. "Thanks for coming over tonight. I really appreciate it."

Quint waved off her thanks. "We'd do anything for TJ. He's gone above and beyond for us, and it's actually nice to be able to do something for *him* for once."

"He's a good man," Hayden told Milena. "Not the most open guy I've ever met, but I know it's because of his background. He's crazy about you and JT though. Don't doubt that."

"He's talked about us?" Milena asked.

Quint laughed. Threw his head back and laughed as if she'd said the funniest thing ever.

"What?" she asked, confused.

Hayden pulled out her cell and clicked on a few buttons before handing it to Milena. "Right after he met him, he sent this group text to all of us."

Milena took the phone and scrolled. Her eyes widened as she realized what she was looking at. He'd sent a crap-ton of pictures to his friends. She knew these were photos her mom had taken, she'd told her all about how

TJ had asked if she would take a picture of him and his son. And she'd snapped more than one. She'd taken a dozen or more. They were candids, and the awe and love that shone in TJ's eyes as he looked at JT was clear to see.

But it was what he'd typed to his friends that made her eyes tear up.

TJ: I'd like you to meet my son. James Thomas.

TJ: Good thing he takes after his mom because otherwise he'd be an ugly bastard.

TJ: He's smart as hell.

TJ: I've never been so humbled or so happy in all my life.

TJ: I can't wait for you all to meet him.

Each line was accompanied by a different picture. JT with his messy hand on TJ's cheek. TJ laughing at something his son had done. Only one picture had both father and son looking at the camera, but Milena thought all of the others were better.

"He'd definitely talked about you two," Quint unnecessarily concluded, still chuckling at her earlier question.

"You've got our numbers, right?" Hayden asked as she took her phone back.

"Yes."

"Use them if you need to. If you can't get ahold of

TJ or if something happens, don't hesitate to contact one of us."

Milena nodded. "I will. Thanks."

Hayden and Quint nodded at her, and Quint said, "We'll show ourselves out."

Milena thanked them once more. She wasn't stupid enough to turn down Hayden's offer to contact them if something happened. If Master Jeremiah somehow got to her, she'd fight tooth and nail and do whatever it took to get away from him and back to TJ and JT.

"I'll lock up," Sadie said softly from next to Milena. "You go on up and check on JT."

"Thanks," Milena told her friend. "You don't have to work tomorrow, do you?"

"Yup. But not until eleven. I'm good."

Milena hugged Sadie. "You're the best."

"I know," Sadie returned with a smirk. "Go on. I'll see you in the morning before I head out."

Milena tiptoed up the stairs and hesitated in front of her son's door before taking a deep breath and pushing it open. What she saw stopped her in her tracks.

The room was a disaster. If Quint and Hayden hadn't been so relaxed and sure that the house was clear, she would've panicked.

There were diapers strewn all around JT's changing table. A couple of them were open but unused. Baby powder covered the changing table like a fine mist. Toys were everywhere, and even the rocking chair she'd used all the time when JT was younger was tipped over.

Milena couldn't even process what she was seeing. Her eyes went to JT's crib. She needed to make sure her son was all right.

She could only gape in surprise at the sight that greeted her.

JT was sound asleep, both arms thrown over his head, his legs splayed open. He was naked except for a small towel wrapped around his waist.

But it was the man wrapped around the boy that stopped her heart. TJ was lying inside her son's crib. *Inside the crib.* He was on his side and his legs were drawn up in what looked like an uncomfortable position. One arm was under his head, being used as a pillow, and his other hand was resting on JT's chest. He was curled around his son, as if he were protecting him even in his sleep. There were a few stuffed animals in the crib with them, and Milena could see the edge of a book under one of TJ's thighs.

She stood there for what seemed like an hour before she moved. And it was only to slowly reach around to her back pocket and pull out her phone. The light in the room was dim, JT's nightlight giving her enough light to see, but not really enough for her to take a good-quality picture. But she wanted to try anyway.

Seeing TJ wrapped around his son after what could

only be described as one hell of night, if the room around her was any indication, was something she'd remember for the rest of her life. She snapped a few pictures, then put the phone back in her pocket. As quietly as she could, Milena righted the rocking chair and moved it closer to the crib.

It had been a long time since she'd stayed awake and simply watched her son sleep, but she couldn't make herself leave. She was exhausted, utterly drained, but seeing TJ scrunched up inside the crib made her heart melt.

She'd never understood when women posted comments on social media about their ovaries exploding under pictures of hot guys, but she got it now. Boy, did she.

Milena suddenly wanted another baby with TJ more than she wanted to breathe. She wanted to see him cradling their infant in his muscular arms. Wanted to see him get all googly-eyed over a little girl. She was sad that he'd missed out on the first two years of JT's life, but she absolutely wanted to gift him with experiencing it with another baby. Or two. Or three.

Hell, she had it bad.

Milena eased her body back in the rocker and stretched her legs out, her eyes focused on the sleeping man and boy. She fought sleep for the longest time, not wanting to miss one second of the beauty in front of her. But eventually she lost the battle, her eyes closed, and she drifted off to sleep, dreaming about blonde-haired little girls with brown eyes like TJ's and little boys who acted just like their daddy.

Chapter Twelve

———————— ◆ ————————

TJ WOKE WITH a groan he instinctively muffled. He was stiff as hell and couldn't figure out where he was for a split second. For a moment, he thought he was back with his unit overseas. Many a time he'd woken up uncomfortable and stiff from sleeping God knows where.

But the night before immediately came back to him in a flash. He'd been so cocky, thinking he'd be able to handle things if JT woke up while he was there.

How wrong he'd been.

JT had woken up screaming, and nothing he'd done had made him stop. The little boy kept asking for his mommy, and no amount of hugging, bouncing, or cuddling could calm him down. TJ had even tried to change his diaper, thinking maybe that was what was irritating his son so much, but that had been a bigger disaster.

JT wouldn't stop crying and wiggling all over the changing table. TJ dropped the basket with the diapers in it, scattering them all over the floor. And the poop. Oh my God, it was horrible. It was everywhere, in every crevice. TJ had used about three dozen of the little wipes to try to clean JT up, and had gagged every other second. It was horrifying, disgusting, and a hundred other adjectives.

Then TJ couldn't get the new diaper on his son. He gave up after the third try and just let the stupid thing fall to the ground with the others. He'd wrapped JT in a towel and continued to do everything he could think of to distract him and get him to stop crying. All without luck. He'd finally crawled into his son's crib with him and rubbed his chest until he'd fallen asleep. TJ knew it wasn't anything he'd done; the boy had simply exhaust-ed himself.

TJ felt like a complete failure. On top of everything, he'd been so exhausted and worried, he'd slept like the dead. Fat lot of good he would've done if Jeremiah had burst into the room.

He was so disgusted with himself, TJ didn't imme-diately notice he wasn't alone in the room. When he did, he wasn't sure if he should be embarrassed or relieved Milena was back.

Relief won out.

As carefully as possible, TJ sat up. He had one leg over the edge of the crib when Milena woke. She shifted in the rocking chair—the chair he remembered kicking over in frustration the night before when JT was crying—and opened her eyes.

"Hey," she said softly, sitting up.

"Hey," TJ repeated, finishing his escape from the crib.

"Rough night?" she asked, indicating the room with her eyes.

TJ stood for a moment, stretching his back, trying to get the kinks out, then he got down on his knees in front of her and inched his way toward her until she had no choice but to widen her thighs to give him room. He wrapped his arms around her waist and laid his head in her lap.

He felt her hands running over his scalp and sighed. "My God. I suck at this dad thing."

She chuckled softly. "Why don't you tell me what happened and how the room got to look like a hurricane came through."

And he did. Leaving nothing out. He admitted to feeling helpless and scared when JT wouldn't stop crying. How disgusted he was with the diaper change. How he'd kicked the chair over in frustration. "I have no idea how you did it, Doc. I've read a lot about colic, and I feel so damn guilty you had to go through that on your own."

"I wasn't alone," she said. "My parents helped."

"Yeah, but it's not the same." How he knew that, he

didn't know, but the guilt he felt that she'd gone through that period of time without him wouldn't ease. He didn't know if he'd ever get over it. "I had one night of it, and I'm sure he was crying because of something I did wrong or wasn't doing for him. All he wanted was you, and I couldn't give that to him."

"Look at me," Milena ordered.

TJ obeyed, looking up at her. He saw nothing but love in her eyes. He had no idea how he'd gotten so lucky. She shouldn't be looking at him like that. She should be disgusted at the fact he couldn't hack one night with his son. Should still be pissed that he'd left her. But by some miracle, she didn't seem to be.

"It gets easier with practice. You should've seen the first time I tried to change his diaper. It was a disaster."

"As disastrous as that?" TJ asked, not taking his eyes from her but motioning to the diapers strewn about the room and the powder covering the changing table.

"Almost."

TJ doubted that, but appreciated her trying to make him feel better.

"All I'm saying is to give yourself a break. You'll get better at it. You'll learn to read what he needs. When he's around you more, he'll allow you to comfort him too."

She was being extremely generous. TJ brought a hand up to her head and ran it over her hair. "How was last night? When did you get in?"

"Long and tiring. We ended up calling the paramedics and Julie was admitted to the hospital. We got back around three."

TJ winced. "I'm sorry I didn't hear you get home."

"You were exhausted."

"But I still should've heard you. It's inexcusable that I didn't."

"I'm fine," Milena said, letting him off the hook when she probably shouldn't. "I have Wednesday off…would that work for us moving in?"

TJ closed his eyes, saying a short prayer of thanks before opening them and nodding. "Absolutely. That's perfect. Better than perfect. JT's mural should be finished this weekend. I can see if some of the guys will help."

"And you really don't mind us moving in?"

"No. A thousand times no. I'm looking forward to it."

JT stirred in his crib, and TJ winced.

Milena laughed. "I've got him. Why don't you go shower?"

TJ shook his head. "No. I want to watch you change him. See how to do it. Then I'll clean up this mess and you can get him some breakfast. I'll watch him while you get dressed."

She stared at him with a look he couldn't interpret.

"What?"

"Thank you," she whispered.

TJ stood and held out his hand. He helped her out of the rocking chair. Then he leaned down and kissed her forehead. "You don't have to thank me for doing what I should've been doing all along."

And with that, he went to the crib and picked up his fidgeting son. JT's forehead wrinkled when he saw his dad. His eyes swung right and then left, as if looking for his favorite human.

TJ chuckled. "She's right here, buddy." He handed his son over to Milena and smiled when JT sighed in relief. "I feel the same way, son."

Milena smiled at him, then turned her attention to JT. She cuddled him for a moment, then asked TJ, "Will you get me a clean diaper? And some talcum powder?"

TJ got her what she needed and watched in rapt attention as she quickly and easily put the diaper on JT. What had taken him over fifteen minutes to screw up, she'd completed in one. "You make that look so easy," he said in awe.

"After you've changed thousands of diapers, it *is* easy."

And TJ supposed it was. Just as chambering a bullet was easy for him. Just as being able to read the wind currents and gauge the distance between him and a target through the scope of his rifle was easy.

He shook his head, ridding his mind of his past. "Go on," he said quietly. "Get him settled downstairs. I'll be down once I clean up this disaster."

He remained still as Milena came toward him with JT in her arms. The toddler was content now that his mom was home. He sucked his thumb as he rested his head on her shoulder. Milena was wearing the same clothes she'd had on the night before, her hair was in disarray and her eye makeup was smeared, but she'd never looked as beautiful to him as she did right that second, with their son in her arms and the relaxed look on her face.

"Thanks for looking after him last night."

TJ couldn't resist her. He placed a hand on her nape and gently brought her face to his. He kissed her lips then murmured, "Don't ever thank me for that, Doc. He's my *son*. It's my job to be here for him. I'm not 'helping you out,' I'm not 'babysitting.' I'm simply doing what a father should."

She brought a hand up and laid it on his cheek. He could see an abundance of emotion in her eyes, but she didn't say a word. She simply nodded and backed away.

TJ let them go, and once they were out of the room, he looked around in disbelief. Sighing, he got to work cleaning up the mess he'd made the night before.

"IT's GETTING CLOSER, boy," Jeremiah told his son. "The cops have finished their investigation of the school and left, so we can sneak back in and prepare. There's just one more thing we need to do, then we'll be ready."

Jonathan nodded. He was eager to get on with it. Every day that passed was one less day he had with his little girl. The faster he got his hands on the redhead, the faster he could get her pregnant.

That was now all he could think about. He'd searched the Internet until he'd found the perfect website. *Ginger Girls for Daddy*. He was obsessed with it. The videos made him crave his own little ginger girl. And he'd have her...as soon as Father got on with the plan.

Jeremiah continued to blabber about what he was going to do with the bitch once he had her in his clutches. He talked about how her son would become *his* son, and how he'd start a new and better school in Mexico.

Jonathan tuned his father out once again. He wasn't an idiot. He knew as soon as his father had the little boy he had his eye on and killed his mother, he'd have no more use for him. He was expendable.

But he didn't care. Jonathan would have his own family.

Chapter Thirteen

ILENA HAD AGREED to move in with TJ, but hadn't been completely sure if it would work out. Sure, she loved him, and recently he'd done everything in his power to make her feel comfortable around him, but this was a big step.

But a week after he'd gotten a bunch of his law enforcement friends to help move her things to his apartment, she was amazed at how...*easy* it was to integrate her life with his again.

Their routine had been set from the first morning. Breakfast, they'd take turns in the shower while the other watched JT, then he'd drive them to her parents' house and drop off their son. Then TJ would bring her to the clinic and wait with her until one of his friends showed up for security duty. After lunch, he'd reappear, and even if he had to wait an hour as she dealt with unexpected patients, he never acted irritated or pissed at the delay.

They'd then go and get JT and spend the rest of the

day together. Sometimes they did errands or let JT run around a park to release his pent-up energy, but more often than not, they came back to the apartment and hung out.

TJ was getting better at changing JT's diapers, and had yet to show any irritation at the quirks of a toddler. His previously pristine apartment had been taken over by plastic toys, diapers, and sippy cups. The huge, expensive, fancy television was now mostly used for videos and cartoons for their son instead of sports or action movies.

And not once had he complained.

In fact, Milena hadn't ever seen TJ look so happy and content.

But her absolute favorite moments were in the middle of the night. TJ had done his best to learn how to deal with JT and his up-and-down emotions. When the toddler was happy, he was the sweetest child ever. When he was mad, he was a demon child, as was typical for most two year olds. TJ was learning when to give in and coddle him and when to stand tough.

Milena hadn't been ready to sleep with TJ yet, even though deep down she really wanted that. She might've decided to do what she could to make their relationship work, but sleeping in the same bed, smelling his unique scent, knowing he was within inches of her, she just couldn't do yet. That was the last step for her, a line that she knew, if crossed, she couldn't come back from.

TJ hadn't seemed upset with her decision and hadn't pressured her in the least. Milena had the baby monitor on the table next to his huge king-size bed so she could hear if JT needed her in the middle of the night. The first night, when she'd woken up to TJ's whispered words, she'd been confused. Then she realized she was hearing him speaking to JT through the baby monitor.

She'd cried as she'd listened to him talking to his son. He spoke of his love for the toddler, of how he'd be by his side as he grew up. How he'd teach him to throw a football, and be protective and gentlemanly to women, and he'd be there if JT needed a sounding board about girls.

But it was his whispered, one-sided conversations about *her* that reached straight to her heart and practically ripped it out of her chest.

Your mom is the strongest person I know, and she loves you so much. You are the luckiest little boy in the whole world to have a mommy like Milena. No matter where you go or what you say to her, she will always love you. She has a huge heart and is the most forgiving person I've ever met. Even when you do stupid shit that you know is wrong, she'll still forgive you.

It was as if TJ was speaking right to her, but she knew he wasn't. Knew he thought she was still sleeping soundly in his bed.

I'll teach you to cherish her. To never back-talk. To always tell her how much you love her when you leave the house and to thank her for all she does. I'll show you with my actions how to treat a woman right, and give you a role model for when you grow up and are searching for someone of your own. I'll make sure you know the right way to disagree, and the joys of making up afterward. I promise you'll know nothing but love from your parents. I might not have been there when you were born, but I'll damn sure be here from here on out.

Another night, Milena tiptoed out of the master bedroom to JT's room and peeked in. TJ was sitting in the chair she'd spent many a restless night in with JT. He was holding their son against his chest and slowly rocking back and forth as he talked to him.

JT was fast asleep, his thumb in his mouth, but that didn't stop TJ from telling him all about how wonderful his life was and how he'd do his best to make sure it was always wonderful, no matter what obstacles might be thrown in his path.

Milena had backed away, overcome with emotion. *This* was what she'd dreamed about when she'd thought about having a family. A father who loved and cared as much about their children as she did. A man who was hands-on, who wouldn't expect her to do everything in regards to the kids. Her own parents had been such a wonderful example, she hadn't ever wanted to compromise.

But TJ had given her no choice. He'd left when she'd needed him the most. And that had hurt. But he was here now. Doing his best to make up for the time he'd missed.

After a week, Milena knew she had to put a stop to TJ's late-night visits with his son. As much as they made her heart melt, it wasn't good for either man or boy. They both needed to get back into a routine. TJ of sleeping through the night, and JT not being coddled and rocked to sleep when he woke up.

They'd eaten dinner, and had settled on the couch to watch the news and relax before heading to bed when Milena brought it up.

"I appreciate you getting up and taking care of JT in the middle of the night, but you can't do that every night."

"Why?"

"Because. You're spoiling him."

"So?"

Milena sighed and turned to face TJ. "Do you want to raise a boy who can't sleep unless he's rocked? It's cute right now, but when he's four, five, eight…it won't be so cute anymore. He won't be able to go to sleepovers because he needs his daddy. He'll end up being addicted to video games and afraid of girls. He'll be living with us when he's in his thirties. He'll probably be a serial killer who kidnaps women and forces them to rock him to sleep before killing them because they didn't warm his bottle of milk to the right temperature."

TJ blinked, then threw his head back and laughed.

Milena couldn't stop staring at him.

After he'd controlled himself, he saw the way she was looking at him and asked, "What?"

"I've never seen you laugh like that before."

"Yes you have," he countered.

Milena shook her head. "No, I haven't. When we were together before, you never laughed. Maybe chuckled, but you never let yourself go like that."

At her explanation, TJ sobered. He took a deep breath and looked away from her. "I don't think JT will grow up to be a serial killer, and I'm pretty sure he'll be a hit with the ladies, but your point is well taken. I just...I missed so much time with him, and feel as if I don't get my cuddles in now, I'll miss out on them altogether. Like you said, before we know it, he'll be a teenager and won't want his old man loving on him."

"Maybe just love on him before he goes to bed then."

"Okay, I can do that." TJ looked at Milena. "I still don't sleep well."

"What?"

"I can count on one hand the number of nights in the last three years I've slept all the way through."

Goosebumps broke out on Milena's arms. She'd

never seen TJ this serious. It was a night for firsts. "Why?"

She didn't think he was going to answer. Several minutes went by as TJ collected his thoughts. Then he did something else she'd never seen him do before. He bent his knees and put his feet on the cushion at his ass. He wrapped his arms around his up-drawn knees in a defensive position. She'd never seen him so vulnerable. So unsure.

"It's a long story. One that started before we met," he said softly, resting his chin on one of his knees.

Milena wanted so badly to go to him. To wrap her arms around him, much as she did with JT when he was upset. But she sat as still as a statue, not wanting to interrupt. Not wanting to do anything that would stop him from explaining, finally, what had put him in the VA hospital. What had happened on his fateful last mission.

"I joined the Army right out of high school. I wasn't ready for college and the Army seemed like the natural choice. My parents were awesome about it."

"You don't talk much about your family."

TJ shrugged. "They're alive and well. Mom and Dad live in Montana. They love the open spaces. I can't deny it's beautiful up there. I love them, but I'm not close to them like you are with your folks. They're supportive of me, and every now and then we'll talk on the phone, but I guess they're a lot like me…not very touchy-feely."

Milena nodded. She could see that. TJ wasn't the most demonstrative man when it came to outward displays of affection, but that made the little things he did all the more precious. Hand holding, his palm on the small of her back, the way he always greeted her by pulling her into him with a hand on the back of her neck…yeah, she definitely loved the little things. She was sad for TJ, however, that he didn't have a closer relationship with his parents, but she understood. He'd been away from Montana for a long time. "Any siblings?"

"Nope. Guess we have that in common."

Milena nodded. "So you joined the Army right out of high school…" she prompted.

"Yeah. I was surprised to find that I really enjoyed it. I liked the camaraderie with the men in my unit. I excelled on the shooting range and after sitting through a recruitment session for Delta Force, decided to try out.

"It was one of the toughest things I'd ever done, and the only reason I made it through was because of the men who were going through it with me. We helped each other, held each other up when we had to, and talked smack until we graduated. I worked with those men for several years on my Delta Force team. We became closer than brothers. I was the sniper for our group. I was responsible for having their backs from afar."

He took a breath and held it for a few seconds before letting it out and continuing. "One day, my unit was tasked with manning a checkpoint. Not something we usually did, but the powers that be were running low on manpower because of a convoy that had headed out earlier in the day. My captain volunteered the team. I was on a roof a mile away, watching the vehicles and people that came in and out of the checkpoint.

"It was hot. Really hot, and I was baking on that rooftop in the sun. It wasn't anything I hadn't experienced before, but for some reason, that day it was super irritating. Sweat kept dripping into my eyes, which for a sniper, isn't exactly ideal. I heard something behind me and when I turned to look, I saw a little boy. Probably around five. He was holding a canteen, and when he saw me looking at him, he offered it to me.

"I knew better, but I gestured him closer and took the water. I'd seen the boy around before, in the village near the base. He was cute. Had dark hair and big brown eyes. He loved to play football—soccer to you and me—and was always waving at the soldiers. I gratefully took a large gulp of the water. I'd swallowed before I realized something was wrong. The little boy was shaking so hard, I could easily see it when he got closer to me. He began to speak. I could only understand a small bit of Arabic, but his words weren't necessary when he pulled up his T-shirt."

Milena's heart was breaking for TJ. She had a feeling she knew what was coming, and she wanted to put her hands over her ears and yell at him to stop, but she did neither, just waited for him to get through what he needed to say so she could comfort him.

"He was wearing a belt filled with explosives. I just stared at him for a minute, not truly understanding what was happening. He said he was sorry—then blew himself up.

"I was thrown backwards right off the roof. That's how I got the back injury I was in the VA hospital with. I didn't lose consciousness though. I saw that kid's body parts flying through the air, mixed in with the debris from the building I'd been on top of moments before.

"Then I heard the explosions from the direction of the checkpoint. The fucking terrorists knew I was on the roof. They knew I'd kill anyone who looked suspicious before they could get close enough to take out my team. So they sent a kid, an innocent little kid, to do their dirty work for them."

TJ turned to look at Milena then, his eyes so full of self-loathing it made her own eyes fill with tears.

"I killed them, Milena. Every single man on my team was wiped off the face of the earth because of my inattention."

She couldn't stand it any longer. Moving slowly so

she wouldn't spook him, Milena crawled across the couch until she was right next to him. She shoved one arm behind his back and the other she pressed between his up-drawn knees and belly. He didn't move from his defensive position, but she hugged him anyway. Laying her head on his shoulder, she squeezed him as hard as she could.

"Tell me about them," she said softly.

TJ cleared his throat, and after a long pause, spoke. "Lurch was the goofiest guy. He was tall, around six-six, and he had these long arms that we all swore touched the ground when he walked, hence his name. But he'd give the shirt off his back if someone needed it. Rey was an asshole most of the time, thought he was the fucking king of the world, but he was amazing in the field. He always had these 'feelings.' If something was off, he knew it way ahead of time. Saved our asses more than once for sure. I've always wondered if he knew something was going to happen that day.

"Mouse was the smallest of the group, but he was super deadly with his knife. He could throw that thing and hit a bug at twenty meters. Bud had a bad habit of smoking weed whenever he went on leave, and he loved his wife and kids so much. All he could talk about was how fast his girls were growing and how much he missed them."

Milena squeezed TJ harder when his voice hitched,

but he didn't stop.

"Knight loved to play chess, and always won, no matter who he played. Fritz was our language expert. He knew at least ten different languages, and was trying to learn Noongar, some aboriginal language only about two hundred people still speak in Australia. Crazy motherfucker. And then there was Rooney. He didn't say a lot, but when he did, it was always philosophical."

TJ dropped his legs suddenly, scaring Milena, but he didn't pull away. He wrapped his arms around her and buried his face in her hair. "I miss them, Doc. And I'll never forgive myself for getting them killed."

"How did they die?" Milena was trying to wrap her mind around how TJ thought he'd killed his team.

"From what I was told when I was in the hospital in Germany, it was a coordinated attack. The explosion in the village was their signal. Several men attacked at once. Including a fucker with a truck full of explosives."

She thought about that for a second, then asked. "So, what could you have done to prevent it?"

"What?"

"You said it yourself, it was an ambush...so what could you have done to prevent it?"

"I might not have prevented it, but I would've shot as many of those fuckers as I could."

"All of them?"

TJ growled, but he didn't lift his head. Milena

pushed. "Because it seems to me if they had a truck filled with explosives, there wouldn't have been much you could've done about that. Yeah, you might've shot the driver, but wouldn't the truck still have crashed into the checkpoint? And what about the other men? You couldn't kill everyone who was attacking at the same time, right?"

"I could've killed most of them."

Milena squeezed him. "Most of them, maybe. But not all."

"Enough to give the guys some time to get to cover."

"TJ, I wasn't there. I've never had to shoot someone. Never had a group of people I've been as close to as you obviously were to your friends. But what if the situation was reversed? What if the ambush didn't happen, and you were killed on that roof? Would you want your friends to feel guilty that they hadn't been there to protect you? Would they be upset that you were by yourself instead of one of them being by your side?"

"It's not the same thing."

"Of course it is," she scolded lightly. "I'm not a psychiatrist, but I spent a lot of time with veterans at that hospital. I know survivor's guilt when I hear it. The bottom line is, maybe you made a mistake, but you didn't force that boy to distract you. You didn't *make* him blow the building up; he would've done it if you'd allowed yourself to be distracted or not. And you certainly didn't have anything to do with those men ambushing the checkpoint. They would've done it no matter who was there. It sucks, and I hate that it had to happen to you and your friends. But you didn't kill them. Those asshole terrorists did. Not. You."

She had no idea if she was getting through to him or not, but she couldn't shut up. Not about this.

"This doesn't compare to what you went through, not in the least, but after I had JT and he wouldn't stop crying, I got really depressed. I kept thinking, *why me?* What had I done to deserve this? To deserve a baby who wouldn't stop screaming. My mom forced me to talk to a counselor who specializes in dealing with parents with colicky babies. The first thing she said was, 'This is not your fault. He doesn't have colic because of anything you did or didn't do. It just is.' Her words stuck with me. They made things easier to deal with, knowing the drink I'd had before I knew I was pregnant didn't cause him to have colic. That all the stress I was under and the crying I did after you left hadn't injured him somehow. There are a hundred different things that you might've done differently that day, but the outcome might still have been the same. And if the terrorists hadn't succeeded then, they would've just tried again. Maybe killed more men. More children."

Milena took a deep breath and hurried on, bolstered

by the fact he hadn't interrupted her.

"I'm sorry that happened to you. I'm sorry you got hurt, and I'm sorry that you lost your friends, and their families lost their brothers, husbands, and sons. But look at where you are today. You're a respected highway patrolman. You're a father. You have a loyal and amazing group of friends who sound exactly like your Delta Force team…they'd do anything for you. There's good and bad in everyone's life, TJ. Sometimes you just have to concentrate on the good and let the bad go."

He didn't respond, but he didn't pull out of her arms and storm away, as he would've three years ago.

Instead he shifted, pulling her with him until they were both lying on the couch. Milena was tucked against his side with the cushions behind her. She felt cocooned and protected in his embrace. And she was well aware that he'd probably done it unconsciously, put himself between the room and her.

She told him something she'd been thinking, but hadn't verbalized until now. "Thank you for telling me what happened, TJ. But you should know, it hasn't changed my feelings toward you in any way, shape, or form. I might have been mad at you for leaving. I might have been confused about why you left so abruptly. But from the moment I realized it was *you* who had pounded on that window when Cruz was interrogating me about the school, I trusted you."

She felt him jerk under her, but didn't stop. "I didn't even hesitate to ask if you would stay with JT the other night when I had to go into the clinic. Even though I didn't think you'd ever been around toddlers before, I knew nothing would happen to him while he was in your care. There's no one I trust with his life more than you."

"God, Doc, you need to stop." TJ's voice was raspy with emotion.

"No. I won't." She braced herself on an elbow so she could see his face better. "You might not know the little things, like exactly how to change a diaper or how much cream to use on his tush, but you know the most important thing of all. How to love and protect him. And that is precious to me. If push ever came to shove, I have no doubt you'd do everything in your power to make sure he was safe, even if that meant you got in trouble or your life was in danger."

That's when the tears fell from his eyes. As if she'd turned on a faucet, they leaked out the corners of his eyes and soaked the cushion under his head. But he didn't look away and he didn't hide his emotions from her.

Milena dropped back down and hugged him, trying to show him with her actions how much he meant to her, and how much his opening up meant as well.

It might've been five minutes later, or it might've

been an hour, but when his words came, they made any doubts she'd been harboring that she was doing the right thing by involving him in her life once more and moving in with him disappear as if they'd never existed in the first place.

"I love you. I'm sorry that I hurt you back then, but know that I'm a different man now. Better. I can't promise to ever get over whatever part I might've played in my team's death, but I swear to you here and now, that I'll be there for you and our son when you need me. If you doubt anything else I say, don't doubt that."

"I won't."

She felt one hand snake up her spine and rest on the back of her neck. She smiled, knowing what was coming even as he tugged her closer to him. She lifted her head and was rewarded with a kiss on her forehead.

"It's no wonder you can't sleep through the night on this lumpy couch," she joked. "Think you might be able to sleep better in your own bed?"

He didn't play dumb. "If you're in it with me, yes."

Milena looked into his eyes. "I don't think I'm ready for more than sleeping yet."

"As long as I have you in my arms, I'll be content."

She narrowed her eyes at him in mock chastisement. "I didn't say I'd *never* be ready, just not yet."

He grinned, and she was so relieved to see it, she almost gave in and asked to be ravished.

"You let me know when you're ready, Doc. I'll let you use and abuse my body however you want."

She grinned at him. "Promise?"

"Abso-fucking-lutely."

Milena shook her head. "I kinda doubt that. I remember how bossy you were in bed. You never let me play."

He laughed. A low, rumbly sound that she felt between her legs. "You loved my bossy."

She did. But refused to admit it.

"It's almost scary how much I love that boy," TJ said. "You're gonna have to give me quite the incentive not to sneak out and go cuddle with him in the middle of the night," he teased.

Milena raised an eyebrow. "Sleeping with me isn't incentive enough?"

"Depends. If you mean sleeping next to you with one-point-three feet between us, no. If you mean holding you all night with you wearing only my old Army T-shirt, yes."

Milena couldn't help the low moan that escaped. "I missed you," she whispered, her turn to feel overly emotional.

"I missed you too, Doc. Every fucking day."

They lay on the couch in silence for a few more minutes before TJ rolled off and helped her stand. Without a word, they went to their son's door and checked in on him before continuing to the master bedroom.

Milena changed in the bathroom and got ready then crawled under the sheets as TJ took his turn in the bathroom. She almost swallowed her tongue when he reappeared wearing only a pair of red boxers. He turned off the lights and climbed onto the mattress as nonchalantly as if they hadn't spent a night apart in the last three years.

He didn't hesitate, but pulled her into his arms. Milena curled into him as naturally as she'd done when they'd been dating. His earthy smell wafted up and she sighed in contentment. Right before she fell asleep, she heard him say against her hair, "I've got your back, Doc. Your back, front, and everything else in between."

She fell asleep with his heartbeat thudding heavily against her cheek.

Chapter Fourteen

TJ COULDN'T REMEMBER the last time he'd slept so deeply. He woke up at four-thirty, just as he did every morning, and for a moment he was confused. Then he remembered the night before. He was currently wrapped around Milena, his front to her back. One of his arms circled her chest and she was holding on to him as if he were a teddy bear. He inhaled and was rewarded by the lemony scent of her hair.

The smell immediately made his blood flow south and his dick hardened against her ass. It was such a visceral reaction, he almost growled. Memories flowed through his head of all the times they'd made love in the mornings. He'd taken her just like this more than once, easing into her body from behind. Sometimes their loving would be sweet and easy, and other times he'd take her hard, with her moans encouraging him to pound into her.

TJ inhaled a long, slow breath, trying to get control over his libido. When he'd graduated from the academy and first become a highway patrolman, he'd tried to put Milena out of his mind. He'd gone on a few dates, and even went home with a woman he met at a bar one night. But as soon as he'd walked into her apartment, he knew he'd made a mistake. He couldn't touch her. Not when he still loved Milena. He'd made some lame excuse for needing to leave and had gotten out of there as soon as he could.

Even going home with the woman had made him feel as if he'd cheated on Milena, which was crazy since he hadn't even known where she was at the time, but the feeling was there all the same. He'd been on a few more dates since, but had kept everything casual.

Having Milena back in his arms, and his son sleeping down the hall, made him feel complete once again. He couldn't believe he'd shared as much about his last mission as he had the night before, but he also knew it was necessary. If they were going to move on as a couple, which he wanted more than he wanted to breathe, he had to open up to her. Try to explain why he'd been so angry three years ago.

And typical of Milena, she'd taken it in stride. She'd made some excellent points and deep down, TJ knew she was right. He'd made a mistake, but *he* wasn't the one who had killed his team. The terrorists were ruthless, and if their plan hadn't worked that day, they would've tried again. And again. It wasn't as if they played fair.

As he lay there with Milena in his arms, TJ had an epiphany.

He had a son. He and Milena had created a human being together. He wouldn't have JT if he hadn't been in that VA hospital in Austin. He wouldn't have met Milena, wouldn't have fallen in love with her. If he hadn't been hurt, he wouldn't have been sent to Austin to recover. She had always said that everything happened for a reason, and he finally, truly understood what she meant.

His arm tightened around Milena and he closed his eyes. For the first time since the men who'd been like brothers to him had been murdered, he'd thought of something good that had happened because of their deaths.

The idea almost felt sacrilegious, but then TJ imagined Mouse smiling at him. He could practically see Bud, high as usual, grinning in that mellow way he had, telling him to just chill. Each of his buddies flashed in front of his eyes. Alive and whole.

"Morning," Milena said softly, interrupting his thoughts.

Yeah, he could practically feel his friends watching over him. He grinned. *Fuck off, assholes, don't look at my woman.*

"Morning, Doc. Sleep well?"

"Yeah. What time is it?"

"Early. You can sleep for at least another hour and a half."

"Mmm, kay." She turned to face him then, curling her arms up in front of her and tucking her head so it was notched under his chin. She was lightly snoring within seconds.

TJ's heart felt like it stopped beating in his chest for a second, then when it started up again, it was beating at twice its normal rate.

Even after everything he'd done to her and everything he'd told her the night before, she still cuddled up to him as if she didn't have a doubt in her head that she was safe. Her capacity to forgive after all she'd been through was astounding.

TJ lay in bed holding Milena for another fifteen minutes, memorizing every nuance of how she felt. His cock still throbbed, but he ignored it as best he could. This moment wasn't about lust. It was about coming to grips with his past and finally putting it behind him once and for all.

He would've stayed there all morning if it hadn't been for the soft babbling that came through the baby monitor next to the bed. Not wanting Milena to wake up, he immediately eased back from her, making sure to place a pillow in her arms as he left. It was a poor substitute if her groan of protest was anything to go by, but when he ran a hand over her hair, she immediately settled.

TJ had loved before. He loved his parents. He'd loved his Delta teammates even if he'd never come out and said it. He supposed he even loved his new friends. But nothing had ever come close to the kind of love he felt for Milena and their son. It was all-encompassing, as if the world had so many more possibilities than he'd ever been aware of before.

TJ knew he was being corny, but didn't care. He leaned over and kissed the side of Milena's head and made his way into the bathroom, grabbing the baby monitor on the way. He quickly took care of business and pulled on a pair of sweats before heading out of the room and down the hall.

When he opened the door, JT was standing in his crib. When he saw his dad, he smiled and bobbed up and down, holding up his arms. TJ lifted him and brought him over to the changing table. "How about we try this again, huh buddy?"

"Food, Daddy. 'Ungry."

"I know, buddy. Let's get you changed then we'll go see what we can find for you. Okay?"

"'Kay," JT echoed.

Even though he was still grossed out by the whole changing-a-diaper thing, TJ smiled throughout the entire process...and he managed to get it right on the very first try.

By the time Milena wandered into the kitchen an hour and a half later, TJ had fed JT, cleaned him up, read him three books, and was now supervising him playing with some toys on the floor in front of the couch.

"There's coffee on the counter," he told her when she stood staring at him and JT. "I already put sugar in the pot, so you don't need to add more."

"You drink your coffee black," she said, tilting her head in confusion.

"Yeah, I know. I poured myself a large cup, then added the sugar. The rest is all yours."

Without a word, she moved to the kitchen as if in a trance. He kept his eyes on her as she filled a mug. She then wandered back into the living room and settled on the couch next to him as if she'd done it every day of her life.

TJ put his arm around her shoulders and felt a contentment he hadn't known before move through him as she settled against him, giving him her weight. She pulled her feet up and her knees came to rest half on his thigh. "You awake?" he asked with a chuckle.

She shook her head and took a sip of the coffee. Then she sighed and said, "It's perfect. Thank you."

"You're welcome."

"You have any trouble with his diaper this morning?" she asked.

"Nope."

"Did he eat?"

"Yeah. He had some Cheerios and I made some scrambled eggs too."

She looked up at him then. "He ate eggs?"

TJ shrugged. "Yeah. With lots of ketchup."

She chuckled. "No TV?"

"He watches a lot. I figured maybe I'd read to him instead this morning. When he got tired of that, he played with his cars for a while, now he's obviously moved to his blocks."

Milena looked from him to JT, and back to him. He braced himself for her ire. He knew mornings were usually her time with their son, but he'd wanted to let her sleep in for once. He might love her and she might trust him, and hopefully like him more than a little, but they were still finding their way to being a family.

But she didn't say anything. Simply sipped her coffee and rested against him.

"I know mornings are usually your thing with him, but you looked so peaceful sleeping, I wanted you to have an extra few minutes," TJ said quietly.

"I like this."

TJ blinked. That wasn't what he was expecting to hear.

"I love that you were able to have some time with him. And you're right, he does watch too much TV, but it's an easy way to keep him occupied. Admitting that might make me a bad parent, but…" Her words trailed off.

"It doesn't make you a bad parent," TJ reassured her, giving her a squeeze.

She looked up at him then. "Are you all right?" she asked quietly.

That gooey feeling inside him grew even larger. "I'm good."

"Because you were pretty upset last night."

"I'm good," he repeated. "Promise. Are *you* okay with everything we talked about?"

"Why wouldn't I be?"

"We talked about that last mission of mine, but we didn't talk about what it was that I did in the Army."

Her brow furrowed, and TJ wanted to kiss away her confusion, but he needed to bring this last thing up. Then he wouldn't ever again talk about what he used to do for a living if she didn't bring it up first.

"What you did? TJ, you were a soldier, I know that."

"I was a *sniper*," he said firmly. "I can't tell you how many people I've killed, but I can tell you it was more than a regular soldier has."

Milena sat up and placed her mug on the table in

front of her, then she turned to TJ. She framed his face with her hands and leaned toward him. "I don't care, TJ. It doesn't surprise me that you were good at what you did. And it's not like you were out there shooing innocent people. I'm fairly certain everyone you killed probably deserved it."

"They might've had kids. A wife. Family."

"Then maybe they should've been at home taking care of that family instead of running around trying to kill American soldiers," Milena fired back.

TJ stared at her for a heartbeat then grabbed her. Ignoring her grunt of surprise, he hauled her over him until she was straddling his lap. He didn't care that she would feel his erection, he just needed to hold her.

Once she'd gotten over her surprise, she melted into him, putting her arms around him and laying her cheek on his shoulder. He felt the warm puffs of air against his neck as she spoke.

"I'm proud of you, Thomas James. Proud of your service to our country. Proud of the man you've become. And proud that you're the father of our son. You might confuse me sometimes, and frustrate me, but never doubt my support of both your military career and law enforcement one."

"You're too good for me," he told her.

"Nah," she countered. "We're perfect for each other."

He couldn't have stopped himself if he tried. One hand moved to her neck to hold her still and his head dropped. TJ poured every ounce of love he felt for her into the kiss. Showing her without words how much she meant to him. That he'd protect her from the Joneses and anyone else who might ever dare try to harm her. She was his.

He half expected her to protest, to pull away, but she didn't. Milena gave as good as she got. Moving her hands to his head and running her fingers through his short hair as they kissed. Her hips gyrated against his erection, and he could feel the heat of her body seep through his sweats to kiss his already rock-hard cock.

Just when he was preparing to roll them over on the couch, TJ heard a laugh. A high-pitched, happy sound. Then he felt a little hand smacking his cheek. Laughing, TJ dropped his hand from Milena's neck to reach out and grab his little boy. Then he fell over onto his back, pulling the two most important people with him. JT thought it was a fun game and squealed with laughter. Milena's eyes sparkled with a mixture of humor and lust. It was a look TJ wanted to see every day for the rest of his life.

JT squirmed until he was face to face with his daddy, and then mimicked what he'd just seen. "Daddy, kiss. Daddy, kiss," he babbled as he leaned forward and kissed TJ's scruffy cheek. Then he kissed TJ's chin, then his forehead. He was drooling and laughing as he did it, his little hands patting his daddy's face and chest as he smothered him with kisses.

Milena laughed and sat up, scooping her son as she went. "How about we let Daddy get up and get dressed, huh, little man?"

"Daddy, dress!" JT repeated.

TJ stood and curled an arm around Milena, bringing her and their son into his embrace. He kissed Milena hard on the lips, then kissed JT on the forehead. "I love you guys. I'll be back in a bit."

Then he let go and sauntered toward the master bedroom to get ready for the day.

He never saw Milena bite her lip and her eyes fill with tears as a result of his casual but heartfelt words.

Chapter Fifteen

MILENA SAT WITH Sadie in the breakroom at the downtown clinic. They were exhausted from seeing patients nonstop that morning, and needed ten minutes or so to regroup before they saw the last couple of patients. Sadie usually stayed at home with her parents and JT on her days off from the coffee shop, but this morning had asked if she could come along and volunteer.

Hayden was on security duty, hanging out in the lobby and keeping her eye on them.

"So…it's been two weeks since you moved in with TJ. I take it things are going well?" Sadie asked.

Milena tried not to blush, but knew she failed when her friend smiled. "Yeah, they are."

"Details, woman. Is he as good in bed now as he was three years ago?"

Milena bit her lip, then shrugged. "I don't know, but I'd have to say probably."

"Probably? What do you mean? You don't know?"

"We haven't slept together. I mean, we have, but not *slept* together."

"I'd call you a liar, but I know you wouldn't lie about that. Why in the world not?"

"For the first couple of nights, he slept on the couch. Then he shared what happened on his last mission, and we slept together in his bed. I told him I wasn't ready for more. Since then, we've gone to sleep in each other's arms every night. He wakes up before me, gets JT up, spends time with him, and showers when I get up and take over toddler watch."

"So, that's it? You just sleep?"

"Well, no. We've made out a few times, and the last couple nights I've tried to show him I'm ready to move on, but he hasn't gotten the hint."

Sadie shifted in her seat until she was sitting on the edge and her elbows were resting on her knees. "No more hints, Milena," she scolded. "Either tell him straight out that you're ready for more, or grab hold of his dick so he can't misunderstand what you want."

"What if that's not what *he* wants? I mean, he's been so happy with JT and our routine, I'm afraid he's content with keeping the status quo."

"He's not," Sadie said definitively.

"How do you know?"

"I've seen the way he looks at you when you aren't paying attention. When you guys drop JT off, he can't take his eyes off your ass. When you pick him up in the afternoon, he's happy to see his son, but his attention is always on you. Has he said anything about wanting more?"

Milena looked away from her friend, embarrassed for some reason. "He's told me he loves me a couple of times."

"What?" Sadie's screech was so loud, Milena was afraid everyone would come running to see what was the matter.

"Shhhh," she scolded.

"He's said he loves you, and you think he's happy with a little kissing and just sleeping next to you every night?"

When she put it like that, it sounded stupid. "No. But…I haven't said it back. I think he's waiting until I'm sure."

"Do you love him?" Sadie asked bluntly.

"Yes." The answer was immediate. She didn't even need to think about it.

Sadie didn't respond with words, merely lifted an eyebrow.

Milena laughed. "All right, all right, I've been an idiot. I need to tell him."

"Do we need to have the birth control talk? I mean, I know you work at a women's clinic and all, but…"

Milena shoved her friend's shoulder. "No, dork. I'm

covered. Thanks for being concerned though."

Sadie smiled, then said softly, "I'm giving notice at the coffee shop. I'm headed back up to Dallas next week."

Milena frowned. "So soon?"

Sadie laughed. "Girl, I've been here for months."

"I know, but I just…I've enjoying having you here."

"And I've enjoyed being here. I'm not moving to the moon, Milena. It's only like four and a half hours to Dallas."

"Did I ever thank you for coming down to visit and staying to help with JT?" Milena asked.

"No, but you'd do it for me."

"Of course I would, but I think you've got enough helpers up there with your uncles and their friends."

Sadie rolled her eyes. "Ain't that the truth. How about a girls' night out before I leave? You think Hayden or any of the girlfriends of TJ's friends would want to come along?"

"We won't know until we ask," Milena said with a sparkle in her eye. It had been a long time since she'd gone out. Getting to know Mackenzie, Corrie, and all the other women would be fun. Especially since Sadie was leaving soon. Milena knew she needed to work harder on finding friends. It was something she hadn't even thought about until Sadie came to town. She'd missed the girl talk.

"Cool. This weekend?"

"Absolutely. I'm so excited," Milena gushed.

They both laughed. Sadie stood, and when Milena did the same, she hooked her arm in her friend's and they left the break room laughing.

An hour later, they'd finished up with the last of the morning patients and headed out to the waiting room. TJ was there with Hayden, and they both looked up as Sadie and Milena entered.

Milena went straight to TJ and stood on tiptoes to kiss him. He seemed surprised at first, but quickly recovered, his hand going to the back of her neck to hold her against him as he deepened the quick hello kiss she'd intended to a longer, more intense one.

"Hey," she said when he'd let her go.

"Hey, Doc," he echoed. "Did you have a good morning?"

"Yeah." Milena turned to Hayden, not moving out of TJ's embrace. "Sadie's headed home to Dallas next week. We thought we would have a girls' night before she leaves. Want to come?"

"Yeah, that sounds fun. What night? I work Friday," she told them.

"Then not Friday," Milena said, laughing. "How about Saturday?"

"That works. Would you mind if I invited Mackenzie and some of the other girls?"

"No, I was hoping you would."

Hayden looked at TJ. "And so you know, I'm not going to be 'on duty' when I'm there, so you'll need to arrange something."

Milena couldn't keep the huge smile off her face. She hadn't even thought about the fact Hayden was an officer, despite how much she'd been around when TJ couldn't be, watching over her. She was thrilled that Hayden wanted to be "one of the girls" rather than on duty. She glanced up at TJ. He was also grinning.

"No problem, Hayden. I'll talk to the others."

"Anyone have any ideas on where we should go?" Sadie asked.

"There's a new club not too far from here," Hayden told them. "It's called Five."

"I've heard of that!" Milena exclaimed. "It's gotten really good reviews." She looked up at TJ. "For safety as well as for the atmosphere."

"That's good, Doc."

"What time? Nine?" Hayden asked.

"Perfect!" Milena said enthusiastically. "Thank you so much for coming with us."

"You work hard," Hayden said. "You're always going out of your way for the women here, don't think I haven't noticed. And from what TJ has said, you haven't had a lot of time in the last three years for yourself."

Milena felt TJ's arm tighten around her waist. It

made her feel good that he'd been talking about her with his friends. She didn't know them all that well, but she hoped this weekend would change that. "I haven't. I'm looking forward to it."

They all headed out of the clinic. Hayden's car was parked on the street, and they said their goodbyes then continued down the street to TJ's Mustang. Milena loved the feel of his hand in hers as they walked.

When they were almost there, Milena saw a familiar figure sitting on a bench a little ways down from TJ's car. She tried to tug her hand away. "Hang on, I'll be right back."

TJ didn't let go of her. "What's wrong?"

"Nothing's wrong. I just want to go say hi to Blythe."

TJ's eyes narrowed as he looked to where Milena had gestured. "Is that the woman who brought in the pregnant girl the other week?"

"Yeah."

"And she's homeless?"

"Yeah. She doesn't say much about where she stays or what her deal is. But I'm fairly certain she hasn't always been on the streets. She's too…soft."

As if he knew exactly what she meant, TJ nodded. He dropped her hand then reached for his wallet. He pulled out the forty bucks he had in there and handed it to her.

Milena almost blurted that she loved him right then and there. She'd been out with men in the past who'd looked down their noses at the homeless. Who didn't care about stray animals, or giving money to disaster relief funds, or in any other way giving to those less fortunate than them. TJ hadn't thought twice; he'd given her money as if his bank account was bottomless.

"Thanks," she murmured.

"You're welcome. I'll be impressed if she actually takes it though. Go on. I'll keep watch from here."

Milena nodded then headed for Blythe.

The other woman had short black hair cropped close to her head. It was uneven, as if she'd given herself the haircut, which Milena supposed she probably had. She was wearing a dirty, beat-up T-shirt and had a sweatshirt wrapped around her waist, even though it was hot outside. Her jeans were just as dirty, but didn't have any holes in them. A pair of gray sneakers rounded out her outfit.

"Hey, Blythe," Milena said softly as she approached. She'd never seen the other woman with a shopping basket full of her stuff, or even a backpack. She had to have some belongings somewhere, but Milena didn't know where she kept them.

"Hi, Milena," Blythe answered.

Her words lacked the pep that Milena was used to from her. Her hazel eyes were dull and her shoulders were slumped, as if she had a great weight upon them. Milena sat on the edge of the bench next to her. "How are you?"

"I'm good. You?"

The words were automatic, and Milena knew she was just being polite. "I'm okay. I haven't seen you around much lately."

Blythe shrugged.

Not able to stop herself, Milena put a hand on the other woman's knee. "If you ever need anything, you know all you have to do is reach out and I'm there, right?"

Blythe nodded. "I've been hearing that a lot recently."

Milena didn't know who she had been hearing it from, but it was more than obvious she was reluctant to accept any kind of help from anyone. "When I was pregnant with my son, I thought I could do it all myself. But then the doctor told me that if I didn't go on complete bed rest, I'd lose him. I *had* to ask for assistance. It sucked, and I felt like a failure when I had to move back home to have my parents wait on me hand and foot, but it not only helped me, it made *them* feel good. They wanted to help and hated watching me suffer."

Blythe glanced away from her fingers in her lap and looked Milena in the eye. "It's not the same."

"Bull," she chided. "It's exactly the same. I wouldn't have JT today if I hadn't accepted that help. This isn't you," Milena said, gesturing to the street in front of her. "I don't know you, but it's obvious to me and anyone else who cares to look. I don't know what happened to bring you here, but dammit, Blythe, let me help you. Let whoever else has told you they're there for you to help too."

Blythe looked away and took a deep breath. "I used to think that not having any sugar for my coffee was the end of the world," she said quietly. "But now I would give anything for that to be the worst thing that has happened to me."

Milena hadn't removed her hand, and she squeezed Blythe's knee once more. "Me and my friends are going to that new nightclub Five on Saturday night. Come with us. We're not going to hook up with guys or anything like that. Just us girls hanging out. We'll eat and have a few drinks. I consider you a friend, and would love to introduce you to everyone."

Blythe looked at her as if she'd lost her mind. "Are you insane? I'm homeless. I could be a crazy person. Besides, look at me. They'd never let me in a place like that."

"I'll bring you something. Nothing fancy, a pair of jeans and a blouse. Please?"

Blythe hesitated, and it looked like she was going to

agree. Her gaze suddenly focused on something down the street and her mouth tightened.

Milena looked around, but didn't see anything out of the ordinary.

"Thanks, but no, I don't think so."

"At least come see me tomorrow then," Milena begged. "I'll see what I can do about finding you a place to stay for a while."

"I'm meeting someone today. He said he's got a place for me."

Milena didn't like the look of desperation on Blythe's face. "Don't go with him," she said immediately, not liking the odd tone in her new friend's voice. "Let *me* help you. I'm not going to hurt you."

"I can't."

"Blythe," Milena said desperately. "Look at me."

It took a minute, but the other woman finally turned her head and met Milena's gaze.

"I'm your friend. You've been nothing but kind to the girls around here. You're the first to offer to hold their hands when they're scared and desperate."

"Why are you so nice to me? You shouldn't be," Blythe said, her words hitching. "You're making this so much harder."

"What? *What* am I making harder?"

Blythe shook her head. "I don't have a choice. It seems like I never have a choice anymore."

Milena didn't like the absolute devastation in the other woman's voice. She shifted and pressed the money TJ had given her into Blythe's hand. "That's all I have right now, but come see me tomorrow and I'll have more. I can get you a hotel room away from here and help you start over. Please, Blythe."

The other woman didn't look up, but Milena saw the tears escape her eyes and cascade down her cheeks, the tracks leaving white marks on her dirty face. "I don't have a choice," she repeated. "I never wanted anyone to get hurt." Her head came up, and Milena froze at the ferocious look on the homeless woman's face.

"I'll make it right though. I swear. I know it's too late for forgiveness, but I swear to God I'll do what I can to make sure no one gets hurt."

Before Milena could respond, Blythe stood and walked away.

"Blythe!" she called, but she didn't slow nor turn around.

Milena felt TJ come up behind her and put a hand on her hip. "Are you all right?"

"Yes, but Blythe isn't," she said, distressed.

"Did she take the money?"

"Yeah, but something's wrong. She was so depressed, and she said she didn't have a choice about something." Milena looked up at TJ. "I'm worried about her."

"I can have Hayden or Cruz see what they can find out about her if that would make you feel better."

Milena struggled with indecision. She wanted to run after Blythe and force her to come with her, to tell her what was wrong, but she'd already disappeared. She knew the alleys and streets way better than Milena did. If she didn't want to be found, she wouldn't be.

Sighing, she shook her head. "I don't even know her last name. I don't know what kind of information they'd be able to find out anyway."

"You'd be surprised, Doc."

"Come on, let's go get JT. Sadie is going to need our support when she tells my parents she's leaving. I think they've unofficially adopted her. They're used to a house full of people, then I left with JT and now she's leaving too. They aren't going to take it well."

"Then we'll stay over there today. You can hang with your mom, and me and JT will watch football with your dad."

His answer was matter-of-fact and so TJ. Milena knew Sadie was waiting for them, but she couldn't have held back her words if her life depended on it. "I love you."

TJ's eyes widened and his hand tightened against her side.

She went on. "I know I haven't said it yet, but I don't think I ever stopped. You broke my heart, TJ, but

I never stopped loving you. Not for one second. Please, please don't hurt me like that again. I couldn't survive losing you a second time."

"I won't, Doc. I swear to God, I won't." He pulled her into his arms, and they stood locked together for a long moment before they heard a whistle from behind them.

Smiling, Milena pulled back. "Looks like Sadie is getting impatient."

TJ brushed the backs of his fingers over her cheek, then nodded. "Come on. We'll pick up some grub on the way to your folks'. Got a preference?"

"I don't. But Sadie is gonna want the Blanco Café. She loves that place, and since she's headed back to up Dallas, I know she's going to want to get her fill."

"I could go for a breakfast taco for lunch."

Milena grinned at him, not surprised he'd heard of the eclectic Tex-Mex café.

They headed back toward his car and an impatient Sadie. When they got close, she asked, "Is Blythe all right?"

Milena shook her head. "No, I don't think so, but I'll tell you about it later."

Sadie looked like she was going to protest for a second, but eventually just nodded.

"You up for some Blanco Café this afternoon?" Milena asked.

"Do bears shit in the woods?" Sadie returned even as she was climbing into the back of TJ's Mustang.

Milena and TJ shared a smile before she sat. He closed the door behind her and went around to the driver's side.

None of the occupants of the car saw the man in the alley across the street watching them, and they didn't see him head off down the sidewalk where Blythe had disappeared.

$$\backsim$$

"SO?" THE MAN asked belligerently when he found Blythe in an alley a couple blocks from where she'd been talking with Milena.

"She said that she'd be at that new club, Five, on Saturday night."

"And the redhead too?"

Blythe shrugged. "I guess so. She said she was going out with her friends."

Jonathan smiled. It was an evil smile, one that Blythe knew she'd never forget.

She hated betraying Milena like this. She'd always been nice to her. The money she'd pressed into her hand burned a hole in her pocket. All Blythe wanted was enough money to get off the streets for more than a night. She used to want her old life back, but that was impossible. The Blythe she used to be didn't exist anymore.

She felt the cell phone she'd accidentally stolen vibrate in her pocket, but ignored it. She couldn't talk to the only person who made her life worth living right now. She needed to concentrate on Jonathan.

He lifted a hand and brushed it over her head before Blythe took a step back, out of his grasp.

"I told you what you wanted to know. Where is he?" Blythe demanded.

Jonathan chuckled. "That's not how it works, and you know it. I'll tell you where you can find the brat if the information you provided proves to be correct."

Blythe's hands curled into fists.

When Jonathan had first cornered her, and said he had information of interest to her, she'd blown him off. But when he'd found her again a day later, and shown her the picture of a child belonging to another homeless woman Blythe had gotten to know, she'd forced herself to listen.

Hope Drayden was thirty-two and, while they hadn't had any long chats about their circumstances, Blythe surmised that Hope seemed to be on the streets after a series of unfortunate events, rather than from something she'd specifically done. She wasn't an alcoholic, didn't do drugs, and she'd been doing everything she could to try to keep her and her son safe.

But the streets weren't the place for a kid—not that

they were a place for anyone, really.

Seven-year-old Billy had disappeared from the shelter one night. Hope had been frantic, and Blythe had reassured her that she'd do her best to help find her son. He'd been gone three days and everyone assumed the worst.

Then Jonathan had shown her the picture. It was Billy. He was blindfolded and sitting in a small closet, his arms tied behind his back, the tracks of his tears easily visible on his little cheeks. The picture could've been taken in any of the numerous empty buildings downtown, or anywhere in the city for that matter.

Jonathan told Blythe he'd set the little boy free if she snuck into the women's clinic and left the back door unlocked for him. She'd refused. He'd glared at her, then said he'd be back.

She'd used the cell phone she had to call the cops and report poor Billy's kidnapping. It had taken a bit to convince them she was serious. Hope had refused to come to the police station with her, as she was afraid once they found Billy they'd take him away from her and place him with child protective services. So Blythe had spent all afternoon at the station downtown, and had even agreed to wear a wire to record Jonathan's threats.

But she couldn't find Jonathan. She had no way to contact him, and previously, he'd found *her*. After a full day of waiting for the man to show up, the cops had blown her off. Accused her of making the entire thing up. They'd warned her that if she kept up with her "ruse," they'd arrest her for making false reports and wasting taxpayer money.

When Jonathan did find her next, he told her he'd seen the plainclothes cops. He warned her that if she ever tried to screw him over again, not only would *she* pay, but he'd kill Hope, Billy, and several of the other homeless people she hung around with.

With no support from the police, and with Jonathan's threats hanging over her head, Blythe knew she'd do whatever he wanted.

And what he wanted was Milena and Sadie.

She didn't *want* to do it. Was horrified that she was even *considering* telling him anything about the two women, but Billy's life was depending on her. Hope had made herself sick worrying about her son, and besides, Milena and Sadie were adults. They had a better chance of getting out of whatever this sicko had planned for them. At least that's what Blythe tried to tell herself.

So she betrayed them, telling Jonathan exactly where the women would be Saturday night. In a loud, busy nightclub surrounded by hundreds of other people. She felt horrible, but didn't know what else to do. If the police didn't believe her, who would?

At the back of her mind, she knew who *might* be

able to help her…but it would hurt so badly if he didn't believe her either.

Just as she thought about him, the phone in her pocket vibrated again, as if he could read her mind and knew she was doing something reprehensible and wanted to stop her.

"Tell me now where he'll be Saturday night," Blythe demanded instead of answering the phone.

Jonathan stared down at her, then shrugged. "No."

Blythe shivered but held her ground.

"You meet me at Five on Saturday night. When I'm sure they're really there, I'll tell you where to find the brat."

Blythe didn't have a choice but to agree. "He'd better not be hurt," she warned.

Jonathan just laughed. "You have no say in what happens to him. If he's good and does what he's told, he'll be just fine. Just like you. If I get there Saturday night and Sadie and her friend aren't at the club because you lied to me, you won't see him again—and you'll wish you hadn't ever laid eyes on me."

"I already wish that," Blythe hissed.

Jonathan smiled and leaned toward her. Blythe took a quick step backwards. "See you Saturday. Oh, and…you might want to shower. You stink."

With those parting words, Jonathan turned and strode out of the alley.

Blythe wanted to run after him and kill him. If she had a knife right then, she might've. His words weren't a lie, she *did* smell awful, but for someone as evil and slimy as him to point it out, that was just rubbing salt in the wound that was her life.

Without checking to make sure she wasn't about to sit in something foul, Blythe backed up against a wall and slid to the ground. She curled her arms around her updrawn legs and buried her head in her knees.

She was tired. So damn tired. She never would've thought her life would turn out like this a year ago.

The stolen phone in her pocket began to vibrate once more, but she ignored it. She'd talk to him when she had Billy's location.

Chapter Sixteen

"**I**'LL GET HIM," TJ said softly when they pulled up to his apartment later that night.

They'd done just as he'd suggested. Picked up lunch, gone back to her parents' house and hung out. Her mom was sad that Sadie was leaving, but after she promised to keep in touch, seemed to rebound.

Dinner was a loud and happy occasion, and Milena rejoiced at the way all of her favorite people got along so well. JT fell asleep while they were watching a movie and they finally left around eighty-thirty.

Milena watched TJ unbuckle their sleeping son from his car seat and lift him into his arms. He easily carried JT while still managing to grab the diaper bag, shut the door, and wrap his arm around her when he got to her side.

They walked up to his apartment complex and Milena thought of what they'd talked about that night. Her father had brought up the subject of the Joneses and asked TJ for an update.

No one had seen either Jonathan or Jeremiah since Milena and Sadie had seen Jonathan outside the clinic, which was frustrating. TJ told her dad that he wasn't sure they were still a danger, but he wasn't willing to let down his guard just yet.

His words had made her feel all tingly…but then her dad had asked how long he would be able to take a break from his job to look after her.

TJ had said to let him worry about that, but Milena couldn't help but think about it now. The last thing she wanted was TJ getting in trouble or, God forbid, being fired because he was keeping watch over her instead of doing his job.

They were silent as they headed up the elevator and entered the apartment. TJ immediately headed for JT's room. She followed him and watched as he lovingly placed the toddler in his crib. He stood there for a long moment before leaning over and kissing his little forehead. He turned on the baby monitor next to the crib and joined her in the doorway.

"I don't want you to lose your job," Milena blurted quietly.

TJ simply looked amused at her outburst. "How long have you had that thought in your head, Doc? You were going to burst if you didn't say it, weren't you?"

"Be serious, TJ. I haven't seen Jonathan since that one time, and there's no reason for them to come after me. Cruz said the same thing. Spending every day following me around and getting your friends to watch me is ridiculous."

"Your safety isn't ridiculous," he said, closing their son's door and using his hand to push her down the hall toward their room.

"What has your boss said about this? When do you need to go back to work?"

TJ's brow furrowed, but he didn't answer her.

"TJ?" Milena asked as he shut the door to their room.

"Go ahead and get changed."

"You're not going to answer me, are you? And that makes me think you've already been asked to go back to your regular shifts, and you *will* get in trouble if you don't."

TJ kissed her forehead then turned her and gave her a gentle shove toward the bathroom. "Get ready for bed, Doc. I'll tell you everything when we're settled for the night."

Milena sighed but did as he requested. *This* she remembered. His stubbornness and absolute refusal to do or say anything he didn't want to. She brushed her teeth and changed into her night T-shirt—well, *his* old T-shirt—and went back into the room. TJ passed her and entered the bathroom.

Sighing, Milena made sure the baby monitor was on

and climbed under the sheets on her side of the bed. Within moments, TJ was back, looking as amazing as ever in his boxers. He left the light on his side on and got under the covers with her. He hauled her into his arms.

Without beating around the bush, he said, "I was asked to go back to my normal shifts next week. But I told them that I wouldn't. Not until Jonathan and Jeremiah have been caught."

"TJ, you can't do that," Milena said, her brows drawn down in concern.

"You didn't let me finish, Doc."

She sighed and gestured for him to continue.

"My supervisor isn't unreasonable. I can't blame him for wanting me back. The other deputies at my station have been taking up the slack since I left. I owe them big, but not one has complained. It's just the way they are."

He took a breath to continue but she asked before he could, "So you don't have to go back to work?"

"Impatient," he teased, pulling on a lock of her hair. "I called Cruz on speaker and had him tell my supervisor everything he knows about the Joneses. Why the FBI is concerned about your safety. All the information they have on where those two assholes might be, which isn't much. When he was done, my supervisor agreed there's a chance you might still be in danger, and he agreed to let me stay on guard duty for another couple weeks. We'll reassess at that time and make the decision as to your safety then."

Milena melted into him, more relieved than she knew how to put into words.

"You like that," he said.

"Yeah. I'm glad you won't get in trouble. I honestly don't feel as though I'm in danger. I mean, it's been weeks since the school was raided and shut down. I know you saw that one guy hanging around my parents' house, but you said yourself that you can't be positive it was Jonathan or Jeremiah. It could've just been a regular ol' burglar. But I can't deny that I like having you around. It's been nice getting to know you again. I also have to admit that I feel more comfortable with you and your friends watching over me just in case."

"I called Captain Chase Jackson and let him know Sadie will be going home soon."

Milena wrinkled her brow in confusion. "Who?"

"He's an Army guy I know who called and asked me to keep my eye on the school. I had no idea you were living in the same city I was, and when he said your name, I was floored. He and I have been in touch regarding the situation, and he wanted me to keep him updated about Sadie's situation."

"Why?"

TJ grinned. "Why do you think?"

Milena was having a hard time wrapping her head around this new information. "He likes her? But he's never met her, right?"

"As far as I know, no."

"Why would he care if she's here or back up in Dallas, then?"

"He cares that she's here because of what happened. He wants to make sure she's safe. But now that he knows she'll be going back home, I have a feeling he's going to find a reason to go up there and introduce himself to her uncle and the other men who work at McKay-Taggart."

"Is he nice?"

TJ nodded. "Yeah, Doc. He's nice. He's definitely one of the good guys, and she'd be hard pressed to find a better man than him."

Milena grinned. "Should I warn her that she has a secret admirer?"

"Nope. I think Chase is on his own on this one."

"Maybe just a little warning?" Milena asked, holding her hand up and indicating a small amount with her thumb and pointer finger.

TJ reached down and began to tickle her as he said, "No, not even a little,"

Milena shrieked in surprise as his fingers dug into her side. She tried to squirm away from him, but he had a tight hold on her. "TJ, oh my God, stop...you know I hate that!" She was giggling as she begged him to stop, but she couldn't get away from his talented fingers, and he knew just where she was the most ticklish.

TJ rolled until Milena was straddling him. She pushed up and looked down at him. Her fingers were splayed on his chest and she could feel his heart beating under her palm. His hands were on her waist as he held her firmly and safely on top of him.

Remembering Sadie's words from earlier, Milena inched her hips backward until she felt his erection pressing against her core. Without breaking eye contact, she pressed herself into him and slowly circled her hips. Her panties were wet with arousal, and she felt him grow harder under her.

"Milena," he warned, tightening his grip on her waist.

But she didn't stop. "Sadie told me I should be clear about what I want. That I should stop giving you vague hints." Milena ground down on his cock as she did. One hand reached between them and she awkwardly caressed as much of it as she could reach. "I want you, TJ. I've dreamed of having you inside my body again. Of getting my hands and mouth on your dick. I love you…and I want you."

She held her breath as she stared down into his eyes. He said that he loved her, but he'd been holding back from moving their physical relationship forward. Milena hoped he was just waiting on a clear signal from her, like Sadie suggested, and it wasn't because he wasn't sure he wanted to be in a full-fledged relationship with her again.

It seemed as if time stood still while she waited to see what he would do.

TJ'S FINGERS TIGHTENED on Milena's waist as he tried not to throw her onto her back and fuck her brains out. He'd been trying to go slow. Trying to let her get used to him again. To show her that he could be gentle, loving, and that he wanted her for more than just sex.

But her hand on his cock and the feel of her absolutely soaked panties rubbing against him threw him over the edge. For a split second, the only thing he could do was stare up at her, wondering if he'd heard her right.

He'd never get tired of her saying that she loved him. *Never.*

But at the moment, he wasn't thinking about that. No, all he could think of was burying himself inside her as far as he could get and not letting her up for air until she'd taken every drop of his come.

"Fuck," he said, but it was more an exhalation of air than an actual word. Rolling them once more, TJ stared down at Milena. He lifted one of her legs, placing it on his hip as he leaned over her.

Bracing himself, he reached down with the other hand and, without hesitation, shoved aside the gusset of her panties and eased a finger inside of her. Milena moaned and grabbed his biceps while arching into his touch.

He slowly finger-fucked her, loving how she pressed up and how her legs widened, welcoming him.

"Look at me," he ordered, adding another finger and making sure his thumb brushed over her clit with every press inside her body.

Her head came down and her eyes opened into slits as she stared up at him.

"I love you, Doc. I've *always* loved you. Even when I was an angry asshole, I loved you. I'm going to marry you and, if the doctor says it's safe, give you another baby. I'll be by your side every step of the way this time though. I want to spend the rest of my life making you happy, and doing everything in my power to make sure you have everything you need and want."

"TJ," she sighed.

"I'm clean," he told her, hating this part, but needing to say it before he took her the way he wanted to. "I got tested after I fucked up and tried to get you out of my head by going home with someone one night. I didn't do anything with her, but I still felt dirty afterwards."

"I haven't been with anyone since you."

Her words made him feel even more possessive. "Thank fuck," he breathed. "And this probably isn't the time or place, but you should know that I haven't been with anyone either. How could I when you still owned my heart?"

"Really?" she asked.

"Really," TJ confirmed immediately. "This pussy has always been mine, hasn't it?" he growled.

"Yes! God, yes," Milena moaned.

The noises his fingers were making were loud in the quiet room. She was soaked, and TJ wanted inside her. Now.

"Are you on birth control? Do I need to get a condom?"

She hesitated for a second, and TJ was worried he'd broken the mood, but she finally swallowed and said, "I'm on the pill. Have been since JT stopped breastfeeding. The doctor thought it would help my hormones and moods get back to normal."

The scent of her desire was thick in the air, and with every breath he took, TJ swore he could actually taste her. "Take that shirt off," he ordered, even as he eased her leg down and tugged on her panties.

Working in tandem, they got her stripped, and at the sight of her body beneath him, TJ couldn't hold back any longer. He shoved his boxers down without bothering to take them all the way off and lined his cock up to her opening.

Milena spread her legs, showing him everything, giving him all of her.

He hadn't ever seen anything more beautiful in his life. Her tits were fuller than they'd been three years ago. Her belly had a pooch that hadn't been there before. He could see stretch marks on her body. Her thighs were soft and he could feel how smooth the skin was against his thighs as he crowded closer to her.

Slowly, so he could memorize the moment, TJ pushed inside her body. He slid in easily, her excitement bathing his cock as he entered her.

She winced, and he stopped when he was halfway inside. It physically hurt to stop, but there was no way he would do anything to cause her pain.

"You all right?"

"It's been a while," she whispered.

"There's no rush," TJ told her, lying his ass off. He felt as if he was going to come any second. The memory of being inside her was nothing like the reality. He could feel her muscles flexing against him, trying to keep him out at the same time they were pulling at him to finish what he'd started.

He reached between their bodies and gently stroked her clit as he stared down at the woman under him. She was familiar, yet not. TJ had thought her beautiful when they were together before, but she was even more so now. She'd carried his son in her body for almost nine months. She'd nursed him with her body. It was a miracle, and he felt unworthy simply being in her presence.

What most women didn't understand was that a man loved his woman's body. Loved her tits, big or small. Loved her curves, loved her belly and thighs. Loved her ass and especially loved her pussy.

And TJ was no exception.

Milena moaned as his thumb stimulated her clit. He felt her inner muscles relax around him, and he took advantage, sliding farther inside her body. She immediately clenched down and he stopped.

"You are so beautiful," he told her. "Even more so than three years ago. I honestly didn't think you'd forgive me, and wouldn't have blamed you. But you giving me this means so much more as a result." He pressed harder against her clit. "Let me in, Doc. All the way."

At his words, one of her hands came down to where they were joined, and he groaned as she found out for herself how much more of him she needed to take. She looked into his eyes. "Do it, TJ. Take me."

"I don't want to hurt you," he said between clenched teeth.

Then she took matters into her own hands. She

grabbed hold of his ass and pushed up against him as hard as she could.

His cock slid deep inside with her actions, and they both moaned at the same time. TJ fell forward on his hands and held himself as still as possible. He could feel his heartbeat in his dick, and her warm, wet pussy felt a million times better than his hand ever could.

"Move, TJ. Fuck me."

Her words were all he needed to hear. He pulled almost all the way out of her, then slammed back inside. Then he did it again, and again. He couldn't stop if he had a gun to his head. He should be taking her softly and sweetly their first time, but he couldn't. Milena's moans and her fingernails in his ass urged him on. He felt like he was a virgin again. He had no control and knew he was seconds away from his orgasm.

He tried to stop, to make sure she came before him, but he was too far gone and she felt way too good around him.

"I'm close," he told her. "Fuck, I know you haven't come, but I can't stop."

"Keep going," she ordered. "Take me. Take what's yours."

That was it. Her words hurdled him over the edge. TJ pounded into her twice more, then held himself as far inside her as he could get and came. His balls actually hurt as they drew up and released his come. He felt her squeezing him, milking every drop out of his cock. If possible, her tight channel got even hotter with their combined juices.

His arms shaking, TJ closed his eyes and simply enjoyed the feeling of being inside Milena once more. When his dick twitched one last time, he sat back, pulling her ass over his bent knees and onto his lap.

Her legs were spread so far apart, TJ knew it had to be uncomfortable for her, but she didn't complain. She simply smiled up at him and brought her arms up to rest over her head, leaving herself open and vulnerable to whatever he wanted to do to her.

And boy did he want to do lots of things to her. But first, she needed to come. He'd been selfish, which wasn't like him. But typical of Milena, she didn't complain, just gave him what he needed.

Knowing he'd eventually slip out of her tight pussy, TJ shifted until he was as close to her as he could get. His cock was still lodged inside her body, but he could feel their combined fluids slowly dripping onto his boxers. He wished he'd taken the time to take them off, but it was too late. He wasn't going to stop now.

His hands went to her breasts and he palmed them, learning their new size and shape. He pinched both nipples and smiled when she jerked on his lap. But she didn't move her arms or otherwise protest his touch.

He played with her tits for a long moment, loving

how her nipples peaked, how a pink flush moved up her neck and into her cheeks. She squirmed on his lap and he moved a hand to her belly, pressing down. "Stay still," he ordered.

"TJ, please."

"Please what?"

"Make me come. I'm so horny."

Loving how open she was about her needs, TJ took pity on her. Lord knew he'd gone off like a rocket because he was so excited to be inside her again. If she was feeling half of what he was, she had to be desperate. Using one hand to continue to play with her nipples, he moved the other between her legs.

Dipping his finger to where they were still joined, he scooped up some of his release and smeared it over her clit. He could just see the small nub peeking out from its protective hood. He caressed it with a light touch as he asked, "You want to come, Doc?"

"Yes. Oh God, yes."

"Then that's what you'll do." And with that, TJ stopped fucking around. Remembering how she needed a rough touch to climax, he used two fingers and a circular motion to stimulate her.

Milena's hips immediately bucked upward as far as they could in his tight hold, which wasn't far, and he grinned. Using the hand that had been at her breasts to hold her down, TJ continued his direct assault on her clit. She writhed and squirmed in his grasp, but he didn't relent.

He could feel her inner muscles clenching his dick as she neared her climax. Amazingly, TJ felt himself growing hard again. He almost laughed at how easily she aroused him, but didn't want her to take his laughter the wrong way. He pressed down harder and she exploded.

She strained against him and every muscle below her waist tightened. Her thighs squeezed his hips and she shook as she came. It was absolutely beautiful, and a sight TJ hadn't realized how much he'd missed.

Instead of letting her come down from her orgasm, he paused for a couple of seconds, then pressed down on her clit, forcing her into another orgasm right on the heels of the first.

"TJ!" she screeched as she came once more.

Now fully hard again inside her, TJ grabbed her and rolled, making sure not to lose his connection with her. He held her above him and, as she looked down at him with half-closed eyes, he ordered, "Fuck me, Doc."

She obeyed without hesitation. Even though she was still orgasming, she ground herself down on him and moved her hips in circles. It wasn't exactly what he meant, but he'd take it. Milena was too far wrapped up in her own pleasure to do more than writhe on his dick.

Surprisingly, even without pumping in and out of

her, TJ found himself on the edge of another climax. Seeing Milena's pleasure, and feeling it around his cock, was enough.

"I love you," he ground out before letting another load of come loose deep inside her body. This orgasm was less intense than the first, but no less satisfying. He'd regularly masturbated, but nothing felt as amazing as being inside his woman when she got off. Nothing.

Suddenly, Milena fell boneless on top of him, and he didn't hesitate to wrap his arms around her and hold her safe against his chest. They were both sweaty and the elastic band of his boxers was digging into him uncomfortably, but he couldn't have moved if his life depended on it.

How long they lay like that, he couldn't have said, but eventually his softening cock slipped out of her warm body and he groaned.

Milena giggled, and he felt the movement against his skin. She raised her head and looked down at him with a satisfied expression. "So, I guess my not beating around the bush worked, huh?"

TJ ran a hand over her hair and nodded. "Oh yeah. And for the record, I highly approve."

She smiled, then sighed and snuggled back into him. "I love you."

He would never get tired of hearing those three words. Never. "I love you too, Doc. You have no idea how much."

"Oh, I think I do," she said, and he could feel her smile against his neck.

"No, you don't. I was only half living the last three years. I'm good at what I do, and love being a highway patrol officer. I've got good friends and family who love me. But I had no idea what I was missing until you came back into my life. Everything seems brighter. Smells seem more powerful. And I'm finally happy again. *You've* done that. You and JT."

He felt a tear on his shoulder, but wasn't alarmed. Especially not when she protested, "You can't say those kinds of things to me, TJ."

"Why not?"

"Because. I can't handle them."

"Bullshit. You can handle anything. You've already proven it. You are one of the strongest women I've ever met, and that includes some of the women in the Army who kicked serious ass."

"Seriously, you need to stop."

TJ chuckled. "Okay, Doc." He turned his head and kissed her forehead. They were silent for several minutes before he asked, "You need to clean up?"

She mumbled something he didn't hear.

"What was that, Doc?"

"If you move, I'll have to kill you," she repeated clearly this time.

The smile on TJ's face grew. His boxers were damp with the evidence of their lovemaking and her body weight was heavy on him, but he didn't care. "Okay, sweetheart. Sleep."

"Is the alarm set?" she mumbled.

"I'll be up, no worries."

"'Kay," she said and nuzzled closer.

Everything about Milena was special to him. She trusted him to get up on time in the mornings. She trusted him with their son. She trusted him to keep her safe.

As she fell asleep on top of him, TJ tightened his hold around her, hoping every night for the rest of their lives would end this exact way. With her lying dead to the world in his arms, trusting him to keep their family safe from whoever and whatever might want to do them harm.

Chapter Seventeen

"I'M GOING TO be hanging out with the guys tonight while you're at the club," TJ told Milena. "An agent who works with Cruz will be with you. Stay with the group. Don't go anywhere by yourself, and don't leave the club for any reason."

"I know," Milena told TJ. He'd gone over everything with her three times now. She wasn't about to be one of those "too stupid to live" chicks in the movies who had stalkers after them but still wandered off by themselves, or who didn't think for one second they were being lured somewhere.

"I just don't want anything to happen to you," he said, pulling her into him with a hand on the back of her neck. They'd just left JT at her parents' house. They'd had dinner and JT had been sound asleep in his crib, her parents happy to look after their grandson for the night. Sadie was in the car waiting for them. They were standing between the front porch and his Mustang.

"Nothing is going to happen. Hayden's going to be

with us. And that FBI guy as well," she told TJ.

She felt him sigh, his warm, minty breath wafting over her face like a caress before he stood up straight. He grabbed her hand and they walked to the car. He held her door as she got settled into the passenger seat, then walked around the car and climbed in on his side.

As they drove downtown to Five, TJ asked, "Who all is going tonight?"

"Mackenzie, Mickie, Hayden, Erin, Sophie, two of her friends, me, and Sadie."

"Sophie's going?" TJ asked.

"Yeah. Why? Is that bad?"

"No, not at all," TJ said.

"From what I understand, she heard about the outing from Mackenzie and wanted to know if she could invite her friends from work."

"Hmmmm. I wonder if Chief will be there too."

"No!" Milena said. "No boys allowed!"

TJ chuckled. "Okay, okay, I was just wondering. Corrie isn't going?"

"No. Corrie said that clubs weren't her thing. I can't blame her. I suspect her hearing is super sensitive since she's blind. Who are *you* hanging out with?"

"Dax, Cruz, Conor, and Quint. Squirrel was going to come too, but agreed to take a shift at the station for one of the others who had something come up."

"Squirrel?"

"Yeah, he's one of the firefighters we hang with sometimes."

"That's a weird name," Sadie piped up from the backseat.

"No stranger than those my buddies had in the Army."

Milena was momentarily worried thinking about his lost teammates would send him into a funk, but he didn't seem to react adversely. He truly was healing. She was glad. "Wait, what was *your* nickname?"

"Rock."

"Really? That's so…normal."

TJ looked over at Milena. "What were you expecting?"

"I don't know. The Terminator. Or something more badass."

He chuckled. "Sorry to disappoint you."

Milena hit him lightly in the shoulder. "Whatever."

The rest of the ride went by quickly, with conversation light and easy between the three occupants. TJ pulled up next to the curb and Milena took out her phone and texted Hayden. Within moments, she was standing next to the car, ready to escort Sadie and Milena inside.

They climbed out of the car, and Sadie stood back a little ways as TJ said goodbye to Milena.

"Call if you need me."

"It's going to be fine."

"Don't accept a drink that you don't see the bartender make."

Milena rolled her eyes. "Now you're being ridiculous. I wouldn't do that anyway. We're going to have some drinks, dance a bit, and enjoy hanging out with each other."

"I just worry," TJ said softly.

"I know. And believe me, it's appreciated, but we're going to be fine. I don't know exactly what time we'll be done, but I'll call when we're ready. I'm guessing around midnight, maybe? I'm not much of a night owl anymore. Besides…" She smiled at him and ran her fingers up the middle of his chest suggestively. "I've got plans with my boyfriend tonight."

"You do, huh?" he asked, clasping her fingers in one of his big hands.

"Yup. You went down on me the other night, but wouldn't let me return the favor."

TJ's grip tightened for a split second before he relaxed his hold and leaned in, making sure his words were only for her. "You want to suck my cock, Doc?"

Milena swallowed at his crude words. "Oh yeah. Then I want you to fuck me so hard I'll feel you between my legs for the next few days."

He groaned. "Christ, you're gonna be the death of me."

She grinned up at him and patted his cheek. "You love it."

"I do," he said immediately. "And I love you."

"I love you too."

"Have fun and be safe," he ordered.

"I will. You too."

"Watch out for each other," he told Hayden and Sadie, who were standing nearby with huge smiles on their faces.

"We will," they said in tandem.

"Bye, TJ. Drive safe." It was silly, but she almost hated to let him go. After all her talk about looking forward to girls' night and how she would be perfectly fine without him for a few hours, she suddenly felt as if letting him drive off without her was the wrong thing to do.

"I will. Talk to you later," TJ said, and kissed her briefly on the lips before stepping away and walking around his Mustang to the driver's side.

Sadie hooked an arm around one of hers and Hayden did the same to the other.

"Come on, girlfriend. It's time to get our drink on," Sadie said enthusiastically.

Shaking off the weird feeling of doom, Milena forced a smile on her face and nodded. "Let's go. I can't wait to talk to the others and get to know them better."

"Oh, believe me, they want to know all about you

too. They've been dying to meet you," Hayden said as they all walked toward the entrance to the nightclub.

"…AND *THEN* HE said, 'I'm sorry you had a bad day at work, and far be it from me to add to your craptastic day. I'm only going to give you a warning.' I was so relieved, I think I thanked him a million times before he said he had to get going. Good Lord, there I was babbling on and on, and all he wanted to do was get rid of me so he and Daxton could go eat."

Milena smiled at Mackenzie. The woman was hilarious. Of course, letting her off with a warning was something TJ would do, especially since she hadn't been going too much over the limit. And if she'd babbled at him, as she'd done through most of the night, it wasn't surprising he'd let her go.

Mickie wasn't quite as outgoing as Mackenzie, but she was still super friendly, having no problem telling story after story about TJ. It was Hayden, however, who told the most interesting tale of the night. Apparently, TJ had been asked to go up to the Fort Hood area and help out with a "situation." Hayden hadn't come right out and said it, but she implied he'd used his skills as a sniper to help out a Delta Force team up there. One of their women had been kidnapped by a crazy former Army guy as some form of revenge. Hayden's respect for

TJ was easy to hear in her voice.

Milena also liked Erin. She was a bit standoffish at first, but when their second round of drinks had arrived, and tasted really watered down, she'd stalked to the bar and told the bartender off. She'd ended up making their drinks herself. When she came back to the table, she explained that the bartender had said if she thought they sucked so much, maybe she should just make them herself. Of course, since she worked part time at The Sloppy Cow, a bar on the other side of the city, she'd taken him up on his offer.

Sophie and her friends had hit it off with Sadie, and the four talked for most of the night. Milena had learned they all worked in a lab not too far from the club. When she overheard Sophie talking about how she'd moved in with her firefighter boyfriend who lived next door to her, and a former homeless couple was currently living in her old house, Milena made a mental note to ask her more about that later.

"Who else needs to pee?" Sadie called out over the music. They'd been taking turns, so they didn't lose their table and somebody was always there to keep watch over their drinks. Other than someone sending a round of free drinks to their table, the night had been uneventful.

Milena and Erin raised their hands.

Giggling, as much for the fact they were grown

women raising their hands in a bar as they were for falling into the stereotype of going to the restroom in a group, the three women got up and began to shove their way toward the back of the club where the bathrooms were located.

It took a while to get there because of how packed the place was, but they held hands and stuck together and eventually made it to the back hallway. There was a line—of course there was—so the three women shot the shit as they waited. Finally, they were able to squeeze into the small room.

They were washing their hands and laughing when they heard it.

Milena looked at Erin. "Is that what I think it is?"

The other women in the restroom apparently didn't hear anything, because they continued to laugh and talk as usual.

Milena felt Sadie's hand on her arm. "I heard it."

"Come on, let's go see what's going on."

They hadn't taken two steps outside of the small bathroom when all hell broke loose inside the club.

JONATHAN HAD BEEN waiting for the perfect opportunity to make his move, and when his redhead and Jeremiah's bitch made their way to the bathroom, he knew it was time.

He'd sent a round of drinks to the women's table to mess with them. He wanted to see the agent, who stuck out like a sore thumb, look around and wonder who sent the drinks. He'd been sitting at the bar waiting for an opportunity to get to his redhead and the other bitch when the cop got up and stomped toward the bar to interrogate the bartender about who sent the drinks to the table.

Jonathan had gotten up to avoid being near the bartender when he was questioned when he saw the two women he'd come for get up and head for the bathroom. It was dumb luck, but he wasn't going to let the moment slip by.

He positioned himself between the bathrooms and the rest of the club and pulled out the revolver he'd smuggled in. He had six shots. He had to make them count. Had to create as much chaos as possible.

Turning and aiming at the first person he saw, he pulled the trigger.

He watched the woman fall to the ground in front of him, blood immediately spreading on the concrete floor beneath her.

It took her friends a second to understand what had happened, and when they did, they immediately started screaming and backing away from him.

Needing to get the crowd moving in two different directions, toward the front doors as well as the back, he quickly aimed at a man standing near the women who were backing up.

As soon as he fell, more people screamed. The music was still blaring, making it hard for anyone who couldn't see what had happened to know what was going on.

Then Jonathan turned and shot at someone standing behind him. He didn't even look to see who he'd killed. It didn't matter. All that mattered was his redhead and the bitch. He didn't really give a shit about the woman his father wanted, but if he left to start his own family and didn't deliver the bitch his father wanted, Jonathan knew without a doubt his father wouldn't rest until he'd hunted him down. So he'd take her too, but once he gave her to his father, Jonathan was out of there.

The screams around him increased, and Jonathan moved toward the bathrooms. The only part of his plan that was unpredictable was if anyone else had managed to smuggle in a firearm, or if the FBI was able to get through the panicked crowd before he could get away with his prize. Weapons weren't allowed inside the club, but this *was* Texas. Jonathan hoped like hell no one killed him before he'd achieved his goal.

Smiling at seeing the now panicked crowd doing exactly what they were supposed to—blindly running for the two main exits—Jonathan shot someone else, just for fun.

He saw his redhead before he saw the other bitch. Tucking the gun into his waistband, he headed straight for them. He caught up with them as the crowd was moving slowly toward the doors, not everyone able to squeeze through them at once. He purposely tripped the third woman who was with his targets.

When his redhead turned and held out a hand to help her friend up, he caught it in his and said urgently, "We've got to get out of here! That guy is still shooting. You can catch up with her outside!"

He had his collar pulled up on his neck and was wearing a ball cap pulled low over his eyes. He hoped it was enough to keep his identity a secret from the two women until he got them where he wanted them. By then, it wouldn't matter if they realized who he was.

"Erin!" his redhead yelled, looking back at her friend, but Jonathan pulled her along, not giving her a chance to stop.

"Go!" she yelled back. "I'll catch up with you out-side!"

"I'll get us out of here," Jonathan told his redhead. He was somewhat surprised when she didn't yank out of his hold, smiling inside when he saw she was holding on to the bitch with her free hand. Everything was working out exactly the way he'd planned.

The three of them made their way with the throng

of people pushing and shoving to escape what they thought was a continued massacre behind them. He stayed in front of the women, making sure neither got a good look at his face.

They made it out of the club through a set of doors and as soon as they were in the dark alley at the back of the club, he pulled them quickly to the left, away from the people moving to the right toward the front of the club and the main street.

"Wait, we need to go the other way," his redhead said, pulling at his hand, but Jonathan didn't stop. He tightened his grip and got almost to the end of the alley before she finally yanked her hand out of his and came to a halt.

Without pausing, Jonathan turned and pulled the revolver out of his waistband. He held it up and aimed it at the center of the bitch's forehead.

"Don't make a sound or she's dead," he said calmly without raising his voice.

"Oh my God, it's you," his redhead said.

Jonathan smiled. "It's me, baby. Now, here's what's going to happen…"

BLYTHE HID IN the shadows and watched the chaos explode around the nightclub. She held on to Billy's hand tightly, refusing to let go of him for even a second.

She'd met Jonathan earlier and, after he'd verified that Milena and her friends were inside, he told her where he'd stashed the little boy.

She'd immediately gone to the abandoned building and found Billy right where Jonathan said he would be. His hands were tied behind him, he was blindfolded, and his feet were bound together. Unless he had figured out how to get himself untied, he would've been stuck there, and probably died.

He'd been overjoyed and relieved to see her, and even though Blythe wanted to take him straight to Hope, she couldn't until she saw what Jonathan had planned.

As she watched the panicked mob exit the club, she had a pretty good idea what he'd done. He'd caused one hell of a distraction so he could get her friend away without being noticed. Blythe reached for the cell phone in her pocket. She managed to keep it charged by going to the public library every couple days.

A few months ago, when she was at a fire in an old building next to a hospital, one of the firefighters had given her his sweatshirt because he'd noticed she was cold. She'd shamelessly stolen it—the nights were chilly, after all—but she hadn't realized his phone was in the pocket until later. By then, the fireman was long gone and it was too late to return the sweatshirt or phone. She'd felt bad for not being able to give the expensive electronic back.

Blythe hadn't expected the owner to text his own phone. He gave her the code to unlock the cell and encouraged her to talk to him. So she had.

They'd only texted at first, but eventually he'd convinced her to pick up the phone when he called.

They'd formed a friendship of sorts. He wanted to help her. When she refused, he'd offered to give her money. She'd refused that too. Finally, he'd stopped treating her as someone who was pathetic and needy, and instead talked to her like he would a friend. It had been a long time since she'd had that.

Now, Blythe called *him*. She was ashamed of what she'd done, but he could help. He'd offered it often enough before, and she needed him.

She clicked on his name and waited for him to pick up.

"Hey, Blythe, long time no hear. Everything okay?"

She searched the crowd for Jonathan and Milena, but couldn't see them anywhere. "No," she told the only friend she had. "I need your help."

TJ LAUGHED AT the joke Daxton had just told. It was the first time since the school had been raided, and he'd found Milena, that he'd let down his guard and hung out with his friends simply for fun.

Daxton, Cruz, Quint, Calder, and one of the fire-fighters, Chief, were all sitting around a bar called The Sloppy Cow, hanging out until the women were done for the night. Conor was supposed to be there too, but he got called into work. The only single man there was Calder. He was a medical examiner who always had fascinating stories to tell. Earlier he'd said he couldn't make it, but his plans had changed.

They were waiting on an order of cheese fries to arrive when Chief's cell phone rang. "Hey, Squirrel, what's up?" He listened for a moment, and TJ stiffened when Chief's smile died and was replaced with an anxious frown. "TJ is here with me. Any word on the others?"

"Fuck!" TJ swore, then got up and headed for the door before he even heard what was going on. It was about Milena. He knew it down to the marrow of his bones.

Cruz caught him by the arm. "Wait. Don't go off half-cocked. We need to know what we're dealing with."

TJ controlled himself. Barely. He had to get to Milena. She needed him. He didn't know how he knew that, but he did.

He was so stupid for letting her go out. Yes, she was a grown woman. And yes, Hayden was there with her, as well as an FBI agent, but he should've put his foot down and insisted that he and the other men be there at the bar with them. He could've given her space, but still been there to protect her. Whatever happened was his fault.

Chief clicked off the phone, and he and the others at the table headed for the door of the bar. They reconvened outside and Chief didn't beat around the bush.

"That was Squirrel. Something's going on at Five. He wasn't sure what." He paused then turned to TJ. "Milena and Sadie have been taken."

TJ didn't ask how he knew. He'd known from the look on the other man's face that Milena was either hurt or worse.

"And the others?" Dax asked.

"Their whereabouts are unknown, but Squirrel is pretty sure they're good," Chief said.

"You're with me," Cruz told TJ.

"I'm coming too," Quint said.

"I'll be with Dax," Calder added.

"I'm going to head to the station and talk to Squirrel. I'll call Conor along the way and let him know what happened. I'll be in touch if I find out anything else," Chief told the group.

"Appreciate it. Let's roll," Dax said, already headed for his car.

While they were on their way to the nightclub, TJ took out his phone and dialed Milena's number. It went straight to voicemail, which wasn't a good sign, but not exactly surprising. He thought for a second, then dialed another number.

"Hey, Rock. It's a bit late to be calling, don't you think?"

"Sadie and Milena are gone," TJ informed Chase.

"What?"

"They were at a club downtown and something happened. They're gone. Are the Deltas around? I might need their help," TJ said.

"They're not. Last I knew, they were on a mission. But I'm on my way," Chase said.

TJ heard the other man moving in the background. Heard a door shut.

He sighed. He really could've used the Delta Force team Chase's sister was involved with, but he'd do what he needed to, with or without them.

"It'll take me about two hours to get down there. I'll call when I'm closer and you can tell me where to meet you. In the meantime, keep me in the loop."

"Yeah," TJ said absently, his mind already on what the next step in finding Milena and Sadie would be.

"Did you hear me?" Chase barked. "I mean it. You call and tell me what you know as soon as you know it."

"Done."

"I mean it, Rock," Chase warned, using his old Delta nickname.

"I heard you loud and clear," TJ reassured the other man. "When I know something, you'll know something."

"Thank you. Later."

TJ clicked off the phone without saying goodbye and tried to control the anger bubbling up inside him. It had been a long time since he'd been this scared and pissed off at the same time.

The mood in the car was tense, each of the men lost in their thoughts about their own women. He hoped the others were all right, but all his focus was on Milena.

Instinctively, he knew without a doubt in his mind that Jeremiah had made his move. The asshole had come out of whatever hole he'd crawled into and stolen Milena. For what end, he had no clue, but TJ was going to make sure it was the last mistake the man ever made.

Chapter Eighteen

———— ◆ ————

D AX HAD TO park three blocks away from the nightclub because the streets had been blocked by law enforcement. It had taken twenty more minutes for them to find Mackenzie, Mickie, Hayden, Erin, Sophie, and her two friends, because of the chaos and pandemonium in the area.

The FBI officer who had been in the club keeping his eye on the women was standing off to the side, obviously frustrated and worried. He said that by the time he'd realized something was happening, there was no way he could get to the area of the bathrooms where Erin, Milena, and Sadie had gone, because of the stampede of people blocking his way. He'd been trying to find out who had ordered the cocktails for the group, and had fucked up by not noticing the three had gone to the bathroom.

It was Erin who actually had the information they needed.

"We were in the bathroom when we heard the

shots," she told Dax, Cruz, Quint, Calder, and TJ. We ran for the back exit, along with everyone else, and I fell. Sadie tried to help me up, but I told her to go on and I'd meet her outside. A guy had grabbed her hand and told her to keep moving, and by the time I was up, I'd lost sight of them."

"What did he look like?" Cruz asked. Mickie was curled into his side, and the two hadn't taken their hands off each other since they'd been reunited.

"I'm not sure. He was fairly tall and was wearing a black baseball cap."

"What color hair?" TJ asked impatiently.

"It was dark back there, but I think it was light. Blond maybe?"

TJ turned to Dax and Cruz. "It was Jonathan."

"We don't know that—" Cruz began, but TJ interrupted him.

"Who else could it have been? It's why we've been guarding Milena."

Before anyone could say anything else, TJ's phone rang. Looking at the screen, he saw Milena's mother's name. A sick feeling swept through him as he answered. "What's wrong?" he asked without preamble.

"TJ?"

"Yeah, Missy, it's me." He tried to tamp down his pissed-off tone, but was having a hard time doing so.

The older woman's breath hitched on a sob as she

said, "JT's been taken! There was a knock on the door, and it was a man in a police uniform. He said that something had happened to Milena, and we needed to get her son and come with him. So Bob went and got JT and came downstairs. Then the cop pulled a gun on us! He made me tie up Bob then he did the same to me. *He took JT!* We've called the police but I don't know what else to do! We're so worried!"

TJ didn't think he could get any more upset. But hearing that his son had been taken did it.

"Did the fake officer have black hair and a mostly black beard?" he asked.

"Yes! Was it…*him*?" Missy asked hesitantly.

"Yeah. That was Jeremiah."

Milena's mom sobbed.

"I'm going to get him back, Missy. Mark my words."

Something in his tone must've gotten through to her, because she stopped crying. "I know. That's why I called. Find him, TJ. Bring my grandson home."

"I will. I'll call later."

"Okay…"

TJ ground his teeth together when he hung up. He hadn't told Milena's mom that her daughter was also missing. Both she and Bob had enough on their plate at the moment. He'd see if he could get an SAPD officer or someone to go over and sit with them.

He turned to the others and informed them of what he'd just learned. Outwardly, he sounded in control, but under the surface, he was more pissed than he'd ever been in his entire life.

It was bad enough Jeremiah had taken Milena, but to touch his son?

No. *Fuck* no.

"So Jonathan grabbed the women and Jeremiah took the boy? Why?" Dax asked.

"I don't give a shit why. All I care about is getting them back," TJ said.

"Where would they take them?" Hayden asked. She sounded calm, but it was obvious she was angry. TJ figured she was probably upset Milena and Sadie had been taken practically from under her nose. He didn't blame Hayden. Not in the least. Milena hadn't gone off by herself, she hadn't done anything stupid, but she'd been taken just the same. Jonathan had snatched the girls from under *everyone's* noses.

"That's the million-dollar question," Quint said, answering Hayden. "Where would they take them? They've managed to elude not only the police, but the Feds for weeks."

"A motel?" Calder asked. "There are a ton of flea-bag, cheap pieces of shit. Believe me, I've been called for DOAs at a ton of them."

"Mexico? Maybe he'd try to take them over the border?" Dax chimed in.

"I doubt it," Cruz said. "They'd be way too obvious and I've already called in a BOLO for Milena and Sadie. And a two-year-old would be way too conspicuous at the border."

The group was silent for a moment, then TJ asked, "What about the school?"

Cruz looked sharply at TJ. "Why would they go back to someplace they'd been busted at?"

"Why not? If Jones thinks Milena ratted him out and got his operation shut down, why not go back to where he was king? Where he felt the most powerful?"

"Yeah," Dax agreed, sounding enthusiastic. "He knows every inch of that place. Somehow, he and Jonathan escaped the raid. They obviously have hiding spots there."

"How do we get close without being seen?" Cruz asked. "The last thing we want is to go in with sirens blazing and have them disappear into some hidey-hole again, or just flat-out kill the women or JT."

"*We* need to check it out," TJ told everyone. "Just us. Not the whole fucking FBI and every cop in a ten-mile radius. We'll see if there are signs of anyone being there recently."

"And if there are?" Dax asked.

TJ smiled, but there was no trace of humor on his face. "Then they're dead for touching what's mine."

MILENA TRIED NOT to panic. Jonathan had shoved them into a van parked in an alley near the club, and before she or Sadie had been able to do anything more than freak out, he'd had their hands tied behind their backs. Then he'd knocked them out by holding a cloth over their faces. The only thing she remembered before she'd passed out was the look of horror on Sadie's face as she'd watched while Jonathan had rendered Milena unconscious.

Now Milena was sitting in a chair alone in a large room she didn't recognize. Her hands were cuffed behind her. She could get up and walk around, hunched over, dragging the chair with her, but she wouldn't get far that way.

But she couldn't just sit there like a helpless victim. She stood and wobbled over to one of the windows in the large room and peered outside. One look at the empty land and building on the other side of the window made her stomach clench in horror. She recognized where she was immediately.

The Bexar County School and Orphanage for Girls.

Jonathan had brought them back to the school. At least she assumed he'd brought both her and Sadie there.

Worried about her friend, Milena frantically struggled against the cuffs for a long moment, doing nothing but hurting herself. Frustrated, she sagged against the back of the chair.

The door to the room opened, scaring Milena half to death, and she looked up expecting to see Jonathan, but instead it was Jeremiah who came through the door.

Her breath hitched in her throat at seeing him—but it was the fact he was holding her *son* in his arms that really scared the shit out of her.

Her mind spun as she tried to figure out what was going on and how the hell Jeremiah had gotten his hands on her baby.

The older man stepped inside the room and closed the door behind him softly. JT was asleep—at least Milena prayed he was—his head resting on Jeremiah's shoulder, one arm dangling limply.

"Hello, Milena," Jeremiah said in a perfectly normal voice.

For a second, Milena wondered if this was all a big joke. First, she'd been in the middle of an FBI raid on a school that was merely a front for a child-porn and sex ring. And now she'd been kidnapped from a nightclub shooting and her son had also apparently been taken from her parents' house.

Her parents!

"Where are my mom and dad?" she asked frantically.

"Shhhh," Jeremiah said, walking toward her.

"They're fine."

"Take off these handcuffs and give me my son," she demanded hotly, wanting nothing more than to feel her son's weight in her arms.

"No."

She hadn't really expected him to do what she wanted, but his immediate and emphatic answer still frustrated her. "What do you want?" Milena asked.

"What do I want?" Jeremiah repeated. "What I want is to have my girls back. I want to still be living and working here at my school. You have no idea how long it took to train my girls. We all had a wonderful life here."

Milena gaped at him. He was delusional. "A wonderful life? You were molesting and raping children."

Jeremiah shook his head. "You don't understand. My girls loved me. Would do anything for me. They had a good life. They were fed, clothed, and cared for. Do you know the statistics about the abuse babies who are born to unwed teenage mothers go through? Trust me, it's astounding. Here, they were loved. They didn't go to bed hungry. Didn't have to deal with mothers who were too busy to care about their daughters."

"You were abusing them in ways far worse than anything they might've experienced with their mothers," Milena insisted.

A vein in Jeremiah's forehead began to throb, but he

didn't raise his voice. "No, you're not listening to me. My girls were *loved* here. They were precious. They experienced nothing but love and respect from me and the visiting Misters. They were treated as if they were princesses. They were proud when they were chosen to be with a Mister."

Milena'd had enough. "You raped them!" she screeched. "You're a disgusting, perverted, miserable excuse for a human being! They weren't *proud*, they were scared to fucking death. You and your asshole so-called 'Misters' hurt them. Stripped them of the joy of being kids. You had no right to touch them. None at all!"

"That's where you're wrong," Jeremiah said, his face red from anger, his voice rising. "I had *every* right. They were *mine*. Mine to raise. Mine to punish. Mine to enjoy and mine to get rid of when they no longer suited my purposes. But *you* ruined that for me. I did you a favor, and you stabbed me in the back!"

Milena was just now realizing that she shouldn't have yelled at the older man. He was clearly unstable and mentally damaged. *And* he was holding her son. She should've praised him for what he'd created with the school. Built up his ego. But it was too late for that.

"I didn't turn you in, Jeremiah," she said in what she hoped was a conciliatory tone.

"It's *Master* Jeremiah," he returned, icily. "You will

address me properly at all times."

Milena gulped. Fuck. She mentally kicked herself for goading him. She knew better. She immediately acquiesced and made sure she used as respectful a tone as she could muster. "Master Jeremiah, I didn't turn you in. I swear. I had no idea what the school was about. I was only here to help the teenagers give birth."

"You knew, bitch," he said, scowling, seemingly forgetting about the toddler he held in his arms. JT's head fell off his shoulder and dangled off to the side at a weird angle. Milena actually jerked in the handcuffs, wanting to go to her son, protect him, but of course she couldn't.

"You knew—and you told! You got all my beautiful girls taken away. I didn't even get to keep *one*. You have to pay for that. Someone has to *pay!*"

Jeremiah straightened then, hitching JT up more securely on his shoulder. He ran a hand over her baby boy's light brown hair in what would've been a caress if Jeremiah wasn't fucking insane.

"I need to start over. Get new girls. Train them all over again. But this time I'm going to keep them all for myself. I'm not going to let outsiders in. They'll be all mine. Mine to teach, to train, to love. Well…mine and my son's."

"Where *is* Jonathan?" Milena asked, not liking the gleam in Jeremiah's eyes.

"Who?"

"Jonathan. Your son."

"Oh, him." Jeremiah shrugged. "Don't know. He's not important."

"But you said you were going to start a new school with your son."

A smile spread over Jeremiah's face then. One so evil Milena shivered in the overly warm room.

"I am. *This* is my son." He turned JT in his arms then, resting his little bottom on his forearm. The toddler's head once again wobbled to the side, but Jeremiah didn't bother propping it up on his shoulder this time. "You took my girls from me, so I'm taking the most important thing *you* have. His name from here on out is Joel. I will teach him how girls should be treated. Teach him how to discipline them and the best way to make them obey. From around age nine or so, he'll be able to begin participating and have some girls of his own."

"No," Milena whispered in horror.

"Yes," Jeremiah countered. "Master Joel has a lot to learn, and I'll teach him everything I know. We'll work side by side and be a team. Me and him will be Masters of a new school for girls."

The awful future her son faced if she didn't get him away from this psychopath had her panicking. Milena jerked frantically against her bonds. "Let me go! You can't do this! He's just a little boy. Leave him alone!"

Jeremiah laughed then, an evil, maniacal laugh that sent chills down Milena's spine. "I can do whatever I want, bitch." He leaned over and put JT on the ground. Her little boy was limp, completely out of it from whatever Jeremiah had used to drug him. And it was very obvious the toddler had been drugged.

Jeremiah moved his hand and wrapped it around the toddler's neck.

Milena could only stare at him in sheer horror.

"Here's what's going to happen," Jeremiah said in a perfectly normal tone. "I'm going to uncuff you from that chair and we're going to take a walk. I'm going to show you what I created here, room by room. Prove to you that the girls liked what I gave them. What the Misters gave them. You will walk in front of me without protest. If you do anything I don't like, I'll hurt him. His life is in your hands. If you try to run, I'll choke him. If you try to hurt me, I'll choke him. If I drop him, he'll die. Understand?"

Milena tried not to hyperventilate. "I understand," she said weakly. Her mind was going a thousand miles an hour, trying to figure out what she was supposed to do and how she was going to get her and JT out of this.

She held completely still as Jeremiah walked behind her. She felt him unlock the handcuffs and didn't move. She was going to wait for him to tell her when to move and where.

"Stand, bitch. It's time you got an education."

Milena slowly stood, ignoring the tingles in her hands from loss of circulation. She turned around and bit her lip to try to stop a whimper from escaping. Jeremiah was holding JT under his arm like a sack of potatoes.

If he dropped the boy, he'd surely break his neck.

Milena was suddenly glad her son was unconscious. There was no way he'd sleep through being manhandled as Jeremiah was doing, and he'd likely be screaming bloody murder. He'd known nothing but comfort and gentle touches throughout his life. He wouldn't be dealing with their current predicament well if he was conscious. And she had no idea how Jeremiah would deal with a hysterical child. Didn't want to find out either. Thank God for small favors. Milena hoped her son stayed knocked out.

"After you," Jeremiah said, holding out his free hand in what would've been a gallant gesture if he wasn't scaring the shit out of her.

Milena took a step toward the door, her heart in her throat.

She was way out of her league. She had no idea what to do and how to escape without either getting JT killed or having Jeremiah disappear with him forever. Both were unacceptable.

For the first time since she'd regained consciousness, Milena thought about TJ. She didn't know how long it had been since she and Sadie had been taken from the nightclub, but the second TJ knew something was wrong, he'd come for her. She didn't know how he'd find her or how he'd get them out of their predicament, she just knew he would.

He'd trained his entire life for this kind of situation. But Milena had no idea how he'd be able to take out Jeremiah while he held JT. If something happened to his son, he wouldn't be the same person afterward. She wouldn't either, but TJ would blame himself and she'd lose him all over again. She knew that down to her soul.

He needed help, and she'd do whatever it took to make sure JT survived whatever Jeremiah had planned. All she had to do was wait for an opening. She had to stay alert and ready for Jeremiah to make a mistake. She'd do what she needed to do in order to make TJ's job easier. She wasn't a former Special Forces soldier or a badass highway patrolman, but she was a mother. And if an opportunity arose when she could help, she would.

Following Jeremiah meekly and silently, she mentally pleaded, *please be out there, TJ. For the sake of our son, please be out there somewhere.*

Chapter Nineteen

———◆———

A N HOUR AND a half had gone by since TJ had been at The Sloppy Cow with his friends. Daxton had gone to the school long enough to scope it out to see if their hunch had been correct—it had—and then he'd returned to help put together a plan.

After planning their approach to Bexar and how things would go down, TJ had to stop at his apartment before he could finally head to the school. Too much time had passed. Time during which Jeremiah could be doing God knew what to the two people TJ loved most in the world. But he was too trained to go into a situation as dangerous as this without a solid plan.

He'd done as promised and called Chase as soon as they had a plan in place. The other man was nearly to San Antonio and had merely said he'd meet them at the school before hanging up.

Putting Chase out of his mind, knowing the others would brief the Army captain, TJ eased his Mustang into the small alcove he'd used when he'd done surveillance on the school months ago. The entrance off of the winding road was barely visible. He parked, making sure his car was completely out of sight of anyone driving by, and climbed out, all his thoughts centered on the task ahead. Cruz knew where he was going and what his plans were, and TJ knew he'd tell the others.

He opened the trunk and pulled out the sniper rifle he'd taken time to collect from his apartment. He'd bought the weapon after he'd gotten out of the academy. He hadn't been sure why he'd felt the need to have it, and he'd only shot it once since he'd purchased it, but he had no doubt his skills were just as good today as they were when he'd been on the Delta Force team. They had to be.

TJ made sure the rifle was loaded even as he headed for the trees. He walked for a hundred feet then got down on his hands and knees for the last ten. He ducked under the scrub bushes that grew along the edge of the rise and settled on his stomach. He brought his rifle around and balanced on his elbows. He removed the cover to the scope and took a deep breath, completely in the zone.

It was pitch dark and almost eerily quiet. The only lights came from the school below him. But the night-vision scope on his rifle lit up the area as if it were two in the afternoon instead of two in the morning.

Daxton, Cruz, and Quint were driving down the

dirt road that led to the school as he got settled.

Moving the scope to the building itself, TJ took a few moments to check it out. He saw two vehicles parked along the side of the main building. The rage threatened to overcome him, but TJ ruthlessly held it back. He had to keep himself calm in order to do what he had to do.

There was no sign of Jeremiah or Jonathan other than their cars, but TJ was patient. They'd most likely use their vehicles to get out of there eventually. They might have walked out when the school was raided, but TJ had a feeling today would be different. Maybe he was channeling Rey, or his Delta buddies were guiding him from the grave, but TJ knew that if he didn't take Jeremiah Jones out today, he and Milena would have to continue to watch their backs.

TJ trusted the others—Daxton, Cruz, even Chase— to get Milena and JT out of the building safely. He trusted them as much as he did his former Delta Force team. They'd proven time and time again they were reliable and would do whatever it took to make sure their friends' women were safe.

TJ's job was to eliminate the threat once and for all.

A line of sweat beaded on his forehead and slowly slipped down his temple, but he didn't even notice. The bush he was lying under tickled the back of his neck and the rocks under him dug into the skin of his elbows and belly, but TJ didn't feel any of it.

He was in the killing zone. Jeremiah was going to die today. It wasn't a matter of if, but when.

MILENA FELT SICK. Jeremiah had walked her through the entire school, showing her what he'd created and telling her how much better the new school he was going to rebuild would be. It was deathly quiet and eerie. The dormitories where the girls were kept were heartbreaking. The cribs that had once held babies were empty, but the starkness of the room was startling. There weren't any bright colors to stimulate tiny minds, no mobiles over the cribs. Nothing to indicate the babies were given any kind of love whatsoever.

The room for the littles was even more depressing. There were eight beds lined up in two rows of four. No dolls, no toys. Nothing but white sheets and gray walls. The shackles on the beds told their own story. Milena didn't need Jeremiah's explanation of how the girls had to be taught not to get up in the middle of the night and try to wander away.

As the girls aged, their sleeping accommodations didn't get any better. Austere and depressing. Even once the girls graduated to the smalls, there was no evidence of any kind of entertainment. Milena had no idea what the girls did day after day to occupy themselves, and was scared to ask.

But it was the "classrooms" that made her want to run screaming out of the building. Each room had a king-size bed and was extremely luxurious compared to the living quarters of the girls. There was dust on all the surfaces, but it didn't disguise the expensive comforters and sheets on the beds. Milena didn't even want to think about what the girls went through at the hands of perverted men in those rooms.

She didn't say anything. After antagonizing him earlier, she didn't want to risk upsetting Jeremiah further. She simply let him talk on and on about how he was going to make his new school bigger and better. She forced herself to look in the direction of the disgusting man when he was talking to her, but kept her eyes on JT.

Her son was now being held back up against Jeremiah's shoulder and still seemed to be out of it. Milena was scared to death that something was wrong with him. That he wasn't just knocked out. She'd been relieved he was asleep earlier, but he'd been so still for a long time. Too long. She kept her eye on him, and sighed in relief when she saw his back moving up and down with his breaths.

"Are you listening to me?" Jeremiah asked.

Milena jerked and brought her eyes up to his. She had no idea what he'd just said. "Of course."

Jeremiah tightened a hand around her son's throat. "Liar," he said.

"I'm sorry!" Milena begged. "I was just thinking about how well run this school must have been."

"It was," Jeremiah said, moving his hand.

Milena sighed in relief, but knew Jeremiah was only one tantrum away from killing her son right in front of her eyes. The only thing that had kept him alive this long was the fact that Jeremiah wanted to use the toddler to help start a new perverted school.

"This was the second school I've started, and the most renowned. Did you know I was awarded the key to the city of San Antonio? I was revered and respected. I was helping my girls. Then *you* had to go and ruin it."

"I know you think I turned you in," Milena repeated her earlier claim quietly, "but I didn't. I swear."

Jeremiah shrugged. "It doesn't matter. But hiring you was obviously a mistake. You were here, what, a few months before I got shut down? It's taught me not to bring in outsiders, no matter what. I'll just have to help my girls give birth myself."

Milena tried not to react. The last thing a pregnant teen or girl needed was her abuser helping her bring a new life into the world. And God forbid the baby was male. She had a feeling he wouldn't live even an hour. There would be no more adoptions. No more of Jeremiah even attempting to fold himself into whatever town or city he settled near.

Jeremiah looked at his watch. "Come on. We don't want to be late."

"For what?"

He ignored her question, but motioned for her to proceed him out of the room. She trudged through the door, hoping like hell TJ had had enough time to figure out where she and JT were and to arrive with the cavalry. It had been about an hour since she'd woken up; Milena had been sneaking glances at her watch, trying to keep track of time.

They went down several hallways, through a cafeteria kitchen, and into a large ballroom. Their footsteps echoed eerily in the empty room, and Milena shivered. She hadn't heard anything from outside the school the entire time they'd been there. No sirens, no one yelling for the Joneses to give up. Nothing but silence.

Her heart sank with the thought that she was on her own after all. That TJ hadn't found her yet.

At the far end of the room, they approached another door, and Milena stopped in the doorway. Standing on the other side were Jonathan and Sadie.

"Sadie!" Milena exclaimed. She stumbled when Jeremiah pushed her roughly from behind and barely caught herself from falling by grabbing a chair.

"Are you all right?" Milena asked when she'd recovered.

"Yeah. You?" Sadie asked.

Milena nodded.

Sadie's head jerked up, and Milena gasped when she saw Jonathan holding on to her hair. He'd tugged it, forcing Sadie's head back. He held a knife up to her throat, and Milena swallowed hard.

She was terrified for her friend, but saw that Sadie looked more pissed off than scared. Milena wasn't sure that was the smartest reaction, but she had no idea what Sadie had been going through while Jeremiah had been giving her the grand tour.

"Father," Jonathan greeted solemnly.

"Jonathan," Jeremiah returned.

The four of them stared at each other for a long moment before Jonathan spoke again. "I'm not coming with you."

"I know you're not," came Jeremiah's calm response.

Milena didn't know what was going on between the two men, but there was an extremely weird vibe in the room.

"I'm taking Sadie," Jonathan said belligerently, as if he was afraid his father wouldn't agree.

Milena watched as Jeremiah eyed Sadie. His gaze went from her feet up to her head and back down, before he finally said, "Her hair is the exact shade of red you like, and she's got nice wide hips."

Jonathan smiled then, and Milena shivered. The

other man might be younger than his father, but he was no less evil and perverted.

She suddenly felt as if she might be sick. This is what Jeremiah had done. He'd raised Jonathan to be just like *him*. And he wanted to do the same thing with JT.

No. She'd rather both of them were dead than allow him to be taken from her and made into a monster like Jeremiah had done with Jonathan.

"She'll give me beautiful red-haired babies," Jonathan agreed.

Sadie struggled in his hold then. "I'm not going to give you anything, asshole!" she snarled.

Jonathan dropped the knife he'd been holding and moved his hand from her hair to her throat. He kept her head forced back as he cut off her air.

Sadie immediately began to fight. But even though she was tall, Jonathan was taller, stronger, and easily able to keep her off balance.

Milena took a single step toward her friend before she was stopped by a hand on her shoulder. She turned and looked at Jeremiah, and saw that he'd put his hand around JT's neck again.

"Stop, please!" she pleaded. "I'm not moving. Let him go. *Please!*"

She stared into Jeremiah's dark blue eyes, hoping she'd see some sort of compassion there, but when she saw nothing but evil, she started to panic.

He waited a beat, letting her know he was in charge, then slowly moved his hand to JT's back.

JT's eyes opened into slits, and Milena could see the confusion in them. She willed her son to go back to sleep, to pass out, something, but instead he awakened further.

"Mommy," he said in the most pitiable voice.

"There, there," Jeremiah said, turning so JT couldn't see Milena anymore. "You're okay now, son. Just relax."

Milena's hands curled into fists, but she'd learned her lesson.

TJ is here somewhere. Don't do anything rash. She didn't know how she knew, but she did. There was a sense of…expectation in the air. She hadn't heard anything outside, but she could *feel* that TJ and his friends were there. They simply had to be. There was no other alternative.

"It's time for us to part ways," Jeremiah told Jonathan. "I wish you the best of luck."

"You too, Father," Jonathan responded.

Milena felt as if she was in the middle of the twilight zone. The two men were being extremely polite and remote to each other. It didn't make any sense. But she didn't have time to wonder about what was happening because Jeremiah grabbed hold of her upper arm and was propelling her out of the room.

She managed a quick look behind her to see Sadie being dragged out of the room by Jonathan. He'd taken hold of her hair once again and was forcing her to walk hunched over as he headed for a door on the opposite side of the room.

Right before she left the room, Milena's gaze swept over the lone window…

She blinked—whatever she'd seen, it was there one second and gone the next.

But it was enough.

Confirmation that what she was feeling was true. Help was here.

She hadn't recognized the face at the window because it was too dark outside, but Milena knew without a doubt rescue was at hand. The man had a look of absolute fury and concentration on his face. He'd been looking at the doorway Sadie and Jonathan had disappeared through.

Taking a deep breath, Milena tried to concentrate. The next few minutes were crucial. She couldn't screw up. She wished JT was still unconscious, but maybe it was better that he was awake. Her boy was normally easygoing and happy, but when he was scared or uncertain, he turned into a little demon. That might work in their favor. Milena had a feeling Jeremiah didn't deal well with tantrums.

Jeremiah dragged her through another room and down a long hallway. Then suddenly they were outside. Milena blinked and tried to get her eyes to adjust to the darkness. They'd exited out the front of the school and the dim glow above the door didn't do enough to light up the area around them. Milena couldn't see anyone else. No cars other than the van she and Sadie had been transported to the school in and what was obviously Jeremiah's sedan.

She couldn't hear any other voices, as if the three of them were the only living things around for miles. Not even the birds were chirping. There was no wind. It was as if Mother Nature was holding her breath.

Milena reassured herself that she'd seen someone in the window. TJ and the others were there. They simply had to be.

Jeremiah turned then and faced the school. He looked up and shifted until JT could also see the building. "Look at this, Joel. This is what we will make again. You and I. Together."

JT, of course, wasn't paying any attention to the man holding him, he only had eyes for his mother.

"Mommy!" he yelled, holding his arms out for her.

Milena stood stock still, trying to figure out her next move. The hair on her arms was standing straight up. The air felt electric. She might not be able to see anyone around them, but she knew they were there. Knew *TJ* was there. Somewhere.

"No, you have no mommy," Jeremiah told the toddler. "I'm your daddy, and you'll do as I say."

"No!" JT screamed. "I want mommy!"

"Get over here," Jeremiah ordered Milena, pointing to the dirt at his feet.

Milena moved as if in slow motion. She instinctively knew whatever reason Jeremiah had for wanting her on her knees in front of him wasn't a good one, but she didn't resist. Not looking away from the evil man's eyes, she moved as slowly as she could, without making him more unstable than he already was.

He'd turned until his back was to the school, and she was now facing him and the majestic front door.

Jeremiah was having a hard time controlling a squirming and screaming JT. Her son didn't stop trying to get away from the man holding him and there was a real chance he'd fall, but Milena tried not to panic. Jeremiah didn't want to kill JT. He was only trying to control him. She couldn't overreact. Not now. Not when this was about to be over.

She didn't know how she knew that, she just did.

She took a deep breath and slowly sank to her knees in front of Jeremiah. She waited without a word to see what he was going to do next.

"Your mommy doesn't exist anymore," he told her son. "We don't need women. Women aren't good for anything. *Girls* are what are precious. Women are expendable. You and me are a family now. I'll teach you everything I know. Long after I'm gone, you'll carry on my legacy, Master Joel. Schools for girls will be opened everywhere. You'll make sure of it."

Milena tuned out Jeremiah's words, but didn't take her eyes from him. JT was frantic now, which would've broken her if she wasn't concentrating so hard on Jeremiah.

The pedophile leaned over and pulled a gun out of an ankle holster. He stood and held it up to her head, but the gun wavered. He was having a hard time controlling the thrashing toddler in his arms and aiming at the same time.

"I've waited a long time for this moment," he told Milena. He stared down at her for a second, then ordered, "Beg for your life. Beg for your son's life."

"No," Milena said firmly, breaking her meek-and-mild demeanor for the first time since she'd been handcuffed to the chair. "You aren't going to spare me, no matter what I say."

Jeremiah sneered then. A look so evil, Milena felt dirty just for seeing it.

"He's mine, bitch. You're going to die knowing your sweet little boy is a rapist pedophile…just like his dad."

Milena opened her mouth to respond—

But didn't get the chance before Jeremiah's head exploded.

It was literally there one second, his evil grin seared into her brain, and gone the next.

Blood sprayed everywhere, but Milena didn't scream or even blink. Her hands were reaching out for her son as he fell.

She managed to grab JT from the dead man's arms before he'd even hit the ground.

TJ LET OUT the breath he'd been holding but didn't take his finger from the trigger. There was a chance he'd miscalculated the wind, the distance, something. But the sight that greeted him after he blinked made him sigh in relief.

Then he calmly put down the rifle, turned to his right, and vomited up everything he'd eaten that day.

It was the first time in his career that he'd gotten sick after killing someone, but then again, he'd never had to shoot a man who was inches away from the two people he loved more than life itself.

JT WAS SCREAMING. The kind of sound that made Milena's head hurt and want to put her hands over her ears, but she didn't. Milena felt strangely calm as she attempted to soothe her son.

She heard noises to her right and stood on wobbly legs. She backed away from what was left of Jeremiah, holding JT close to her chest as the little boy screamed in terror and confusion.

Even in the dark, she recognized TJ's friends, Daxton and Cruz, as they rounded the side of the building, their pistols at the ready.

"Shit! Are you all right?" Cruz barked as he neared her. His words were loud, to be heard over JT's wailing, and Milena simply nodded.

"You're covered in blood. Are you sure you're okay?" Daxton asked in a slightly calmer tone than his friend.

"It's not mine," she reassured him. She'd felt Jeremiah's blood and brain matter splatter on her as he was shot, but at the moment it wasn't registering.

She wanted TJ.

Wanted him more than she'd wanted anything else in her entire life, but he'd be here as soon as he could. She knew that without a doubt. The second Jeremiah had led them outside, Milena had known they were going to be okay. TJ was out there with his rifle. She knew it.

Knew without a doubt that he'd use the skills he'd honed throughout his time in the Army to save their lives.

It was obvious the two men in front of her knew it as well, since Daxton merely nodded, taking her word for it that the blood wasn't hers.

"Milena!"

She spun at the sound of her name, and was relieved to see Sadie coming around the opposite corner with Quint and the man she'd seen at the window earlier. He had her hand clasped in his—and didn't look like he was going to let go anytime soon.

Surprisingly, Sadie didn't seem inclined to let go of him either.

"Jonathan's disappeared," Quint said as soon as he got close to his friends. His voice was also elevated because of JT's crying, so Milena could still hear him. She'd learned long ago how to carry on perfectly normal conversations with a screaming baby in her arms.

"What happened?" Cruz asked.

"Crazy asshole thought he had me cowed. That's what happened," Sadie said. "He took me into a room with a huge bed and told me he was going to put his baby in my belly right that second. That he couldn't wait another minute to start his future family. The motherfucker had one of my arms attached to the headboard—with restraints that were permanently mounted to the bed, I might add—when he turned around to reach for something in a drawer next to the bed. I…"

Sadie looked unsure for a moment, looking down at the ground. She took a deep breath then continued. "I kicked him in the head and he fell backwards. I ripped off the Velcro cuff and ran. Straight into *him*." She gestured to the man still holding her hand.

Sadie tilted her head and looked at her friend. The words she was saying were typical Sadie. Strong and confident, but there was something about the way she wouldn't meet her eyes that made Sadie uneasy. She opened her mouth to ask her friend if she was really all right, when Quint spoke.

"After she literally ran into us, I went after Jonathan while Chase got Sadie out of there," he told the group. "I had to have arrived no more than thirty seconds after Sadie escaped, but he was gone."

"Gone? How is that possible?" Dax asked, clearly frustrated.

"I have no clue. But he wasn't in that room. There was a small pool of blood from some sort of wound— maybe from his head where Sadie kicked him, or from where his teeth used to be—but he was gone," Quint explained.

In the distance, sirens could finally be heard.

"You're going to the hospital," the man holding Sadie's hand told her.

"No, I'm not. I'm fine," she insisted.

"You're going to the hospital," he repeated.

Sadie merely rolled her eyes then tugged at her hand. "Whatever. Let me go."

They stared at each other for a heartbeat, and Milena knew at any other time, she would've smiled at the thought that her stubborn, badass friend had apparently met her match. But the smile wouldn't form. She was hanging on by a thread. She needed TJ.

She closed her eyes and tried to hold herself together. JT was still screaming, although he'd stuffed his face into her shoulder so his cries were somewhat muffled. She could almost pretend he was a couple months old again and she was dealing with his colic, but it was impossible to forget what had just happened. Not when she could smell the coppery scent of the blood in her hair and on her body. Not when she could still see Jeremiah's evil grin. Not when she still heard all the things he'd planned to teach her son echoing through her mind.

And not when all she had to do was look behind the wall of men standing protectively between her and the dead man on the ground to see how close she and her son had come to a very different outcome.

The sirens were getting louder, but it was the crunch of tires on the gravel surrounding the school that had Milena opening her eyes and turning.

Headlights were headed toward them at a breakneck speed. Milena didn't even flinch when gravel went flying as the black Mustang came to an abrupt stop. Everyone around her faded into the background. She heard the men talking, even heard Sadie's voice, but she only had eyes for TJ.

The second the car came to a stop, he was out and moving toward her. Milena stayed right where she was. He'd come to her. He'd always come to her.

The second he got close enough, one of his hands went to the back of her neck and she immediately felt comforted by his familiar touch. The other palmed their son's head, his hand engulfing it. TJ pulled his family into his embrace, not caring that Milena had Jeremiah's blood spattered all over her.

Milena sagged against him. She wrapped her free arm around him and held on to his shirt at his back with an iron fist.

Neither spoke. Milena knew she didn't really have any words anyway. She was simply so grateful to be alive. For her son in her arms. That TJ had done what he'd done.

After a long moment, Milena felt TJ take a deep breath and drop his hand from her neck and pull away slightly. "Are you all right, Doc?"

She looked up into his brown eyes and nodded.

"He didn't hurt you?"

"A few bruises. Nothing that won't heal," she said quietly.

At her words, his eyes darkened, but his hold stayed gentle. Caressing JT's head, he asked, "And our son?"

"I don't think he's hurt. Just scared. He was also unconscious for a bit too."

TJ's jaw tightened, but he didn't pull away from them. "We'll get both of you checked out at the hospital," TJ said softly. Then he asked, uncertainly, "Can I hold him?"

Without any qualms, Milena shifted and allowed TJ to take their son from her arms. The thought of anyone else taking him from her at that moment made her want to hold on tighter, but handing her son over to his father was as natural as breathing.

"Hey, bud," TJ murmured into JT's ear. "You're okay. Daddy's got you."

It took a while, but amazingly, with TJ's words in his ear, the toddler eventually stopped screaming and collapsed into his dad's embrace. His little arms went around his dad's neck and he looked like he was trying to burrow into him.

Milena's eyes filled with tears for the first time that night.

"Cruz is going to talk to the Feds," Dax said quietly from next to them. Milena turned her head to look at the other man. "They're going to want to know what happened."

Milena stiffened, but TJ didn't even flinch. "Then

tell them."

Dax frowned, but the man attached to Sadie's side came up to them. Having obviously overheard the short conversation, he said, "I've already called my colonel. The base general has this, and you, covered," he said. "He's not happy that Jeremiah was former Army and doesn't want any negative publicity. Because TJ's a highly decorated former Delta Force soldier, and Jeremiah was obviously not an upstanding citizen, he's willing to do what he can to help make sure there aren't any repercussions about what happened here tonight."

Milena was completely confused, and she looked up at TJ for reassurance.

"Doc, this is Chase Jackson. He's a captain in the Army. He's stationed at Fort Hood, and we've crossed paths before."

"Oh...hi," Milena said, frowning.

TJ held out a hand to Chase. The two men shook and TJ said, "I wasn't worried, and I don't care if there's blowback. I would do the exact same thing again."

Chase and TJ eyed each other for a moment, then the Army captain nodded. "I'll see you back at the hospital. We can talk more."

"Milena, you're good, right?" Sadie asked before Chase could drag her away.

"Yeah. You?"

"I'm fine. Just pissed that Jonathan got away."

"Speaking of which, I need to go organize a search for that asshole," Cruz said before turning and striding toward the first police cars that were pulling into the area. "He has to be here somewhere. We'll find him this time, even if we have to take this place apart brick by fucking brick."

Milena watched as Chase hauled Sadie toward one of the ambulances pulling into the increasingly crowded area.

She felt numb. Like what had just happened was something she was watching on TV.

TJ lifted her chin and stared down at her. His thumb brushed back and forth over her cheek. She didn't know if he was trying to remove some of the blood that had splashed onto her face or if he was absently caressing her. She supposed it didn't matter because either way, she loved his touch.

"Are we okay?"

Milena's brow wrinkled. It was an odd question. If he had asked if *she* was okay, she would've nodded immediately, but she wasn't sure what he was asking. "Are *we* okay?" she echoed.

"I lost you for three years because of something stupid I did. I'm telling you right now I can't lose you again."

Milena took a page from his book and reached up and wrapped her hand around the back of his neck.

"You aren't going to lose me."

"I shot him, Doc. I was over a mile away and I shot him while he was holding our son," he said quietly. He paused as if waiting for her to yell at him.

"Thank God you did," Milena said.

TJ looked unconvinced. "He was holding our *son* and you were right in front of him."

"Why do you think I kneeled right where he told me to?" Milena asked. "I could've refused. Could've stayed standing and demanded he just shoot me. But I didn't. You know why?" She didn't give TJ a chance to answer. "Because I knew you were out there somewhere. Knew I needed to get out of your way and give you a clear shot. I knew you wouldn't hit our son. No way. So I kneeled and waited. And you didn't disappoint me."

TJ's eyes closed and his head dipped.

Milena stood on her tiptoes and leaned into him. "From the second I woke up and saw Jeremiah, I knew you were coming for me. Yes, you killed him, but from where I'm standing, you saved hundreds of other girls from his abuse. He told me all about his future plans. About how he wanted to use our son. How he wanted to turn him into a pedophile like him. I'm not sorry you killed him, TJ. I didn't feel safe until Jeremiah walked us outside. Because I knew you were there. Watching over us. Waiting for the perfect shot. All I had to do was stay alive and out of your way long enough for you to do what I knew you were doing to do. I love you, Thomas James. All of you. Every single part."

"I don't deserve you," he choked out.

Milena saw the tears on his face. He wasn't trying to hide them from her, but it was more than obvious he wasn't comfortable with his emotions. "We deserve each other," she told him easily and without a single doubt.

At that, he took a deep breath and straightened. He kissed the side of JT's head and nodded. "Yeah, we do."

"Daddy, cry?" JT asked, patting one of his dad's cheeks.

"Yeah, buddy. Daddy's crying. But they're happy tears."

"Bad man."

"Yeah, he won't hurt you again," TJ reassured his son.

"Daddy save."

It was Milena's turn to blink back tears now. She leaned up and kissed JT's cheek. "Yes, Daddy saved us. He'll always save us." And with that, she wrapped her arms around her entire world.

The three of them stood there for a long while, watching as the police searched for Jonathan...without luck.

Finally, TJ pulled away and urged Milena toward an ambulance. "Come on. Let's get you both checked out. I called your mom when I was on my way to you and told her JT was safe."

Milena jerked. Shit. She hadn't even thought of calling her parents. "Thank you."

"You're welcome. I know it's still the middle of the night, but what do you think about all of us heading to their house after we're done at the hospital? She feels guilty about JT being taken, even though there was nothing she or your dad could've done, and I know she needs to see for herself that her grandson is okay. I didn't tell her that you had also been kidnapped, and I think she needs to hear that piece of news in person. I told her I'd call if she needed to meet us at the hospital, but reassured her that JT seemed to be okay."

Milena's love for TJ was already rock solid, but at his concern for her parents, it grew even more. "I'd like that," she told him.

TJ nodded and turned them, not letting go of her waist, and headed for one of the ambulances. The other vehicle, with Sadie and presumably Chase, had already left.

JT refused to let go of his dad after they'd climbed inside, so TJ simply sat on one of the gurneys. Milena's eyes met his as the paramedic began to take vitals from JT.

She mouthed, "I love you," to TJ, and smiled when he returned her silent words. Milena knew she should be freaking out about everything that had happened, the fact that Jonathan was missing, and that she'd narrowly escaped death, but she couldn't. She was alive, her son was alive, and they were with TJ. They were as safe as they could be right there with him, and always would be.

Epilogue

TJ WAS NERVOUS. And he wasn't a man who got nervous. His hands were fucking shaking. He was a sniper, for God's sake. Was known for being unflappable. But tonight, he was way out of his league.

Erin had arranged with her boss at The Sloppy Cow to close the popular bar to the public for the evening. TJ and all his friends were having one hell of a huge party. All of his law enforcement friends were there. Dax and Mackenzie, Cruz and Mickie, Quint and Corrie, Hayden and her man, Boone, Erin and Conor, and even Calder had shown up. He'd been shying away from big events like this because he said he felt weird not having a significant other, but tonight, he'd come.

And the cops weren't the only ones who'd been invited. The men—and woman—from Station 7 Firehouse had come too. Sledge and Beth, Crash and Adeline—and her service dog, Coco—Chief and Sophie, Squirrel, Driftwood, Taco, Moose, and Penelope had also shown up.

The two friends who were with Sophie at Five, the night Milena and Sadie had been taken, had also joined them. Milena had even invited her parents. Since it was a private party, JT was allowed to tag along, although at the moment, he was fast asleep in a stroller sitting next to Milena's parents in a dim back corner of the bar.

Even TJ's own parents were there. Milena had encouraged him to call them after the incident with Jeremiah. They needed to know they were grandparents. They'd been shocked and overwhelmed, but also extremely emotional. They'd wanted to fly down to Texas immediately to not only meet Milena, but their grandson as well.

The only people missing, as far as TJ was concerned, were Sadie and Chase, but Milena understood why her friend couldn't be there.

After Jeremiah was killed, the FBI had spent an entire day searching for his missing son. They were determined to figure out how he kept disappearing from right under their noses. And they'd finally found the reason. The escape tunnel system under the school was as impressive as it was frightening. The number of weapons that had been found was equally scary. It seemed the government was right to be concerned about the school in the first place. Yes, it was a haven for child abusers, but Jeremiah and Jonathan had also gotten their hands on quite a few illegal and deadly weapons.

The Feds didn't appreciate RPGs being stockpiled by anyone, for any reason.

Chase had whisked her up to the Fort Hood area before anyone could protest. It had been a little over a month since anyone had seen Jonathan, but no one was going to underestimate him this time. TJ had talked to the Army captain recently, and he'd said that Sadie and her uncles had agreed to let him keep her safe until Jonathan had been caught. No matter how long it took.

TJ figured the Army captain had his hands full with Sadie. If Jonathan wasn't found quickly, she wouldn't be content to be "looked after" for long. From what TJ had heard, she was almost as badass as her uncles...at least in attitude if not physically.

However, Chase's challenge to not only win Sadie's heart but keep her safe as well was as far from TJ's mind as it could be at that moment.

The ring he'd been carrying around since the day after he'd saved Milena from Jeremiah Jones was burning a hole in his pocket. He wanted her to remember the day he'd asked her to marry him, for the rest of her life. Wanted it to be memorable and romantic...unfortunately, he wasn't the most romantic of men. But he wanted to try. For her.

Clearing his throat, TJ took Milena's hand in his and stood. It took a bit, but finally his friends noticed them and stopped talking.

"What are you doing?" Milena asked as he turned to face her.

Not taking his eyes off hers, TJ forgot the fancy speech he'd memorized and spoke from his heart. "I love you, Doc. I think I've loved you since the moment I met you. I was lying in that bed at the VA hospital, in pain, bitter and angry about what had happened to me and my team, and you came into my room with a huge smile on your face. Even when I grumped at you to leave me alone, you smiled."

"TJ..." she started, but he talked over her.

"I don't deserve you. You could have any man in the world, and they'd be the luckiest son of a bitch to call you theirs. But you chose *me*. Even when I hurt you, you let me back in. And that's a miracle, Doc. A fucking miracle."

"Don't swear," she whispered, tears shining in her eyes as she realized what was happening.

He smiled at her. "Sorry. You're a miracle, Milena. *My* miracle. I'll move heaven and earth to make sure you have everything your heart desires. I'll make sure you and our children hear every day how much you're loved." He dropped one of her hands and reached into the pocket of his jeans. He pulled out the ring he'd known was perfect for her the second he saw it, and held it between them.

"I already asked your dad, and he gave me permission." A bead of sweat rolled down his temple, but TJ ignored it. "Milena Reinhardt, will you marry me? Will you let me take care of you and our children for the rest of our lives? Will you give me the privilege to continue to hold you in my arms every night and walk down the street with your hand in mine?"

He had more he wanted to say, but Milena didn't give him a chance. Ignoring the ring he was holding out, she threw herself into his arms while saying, "Yes!"

TJ caught her easily and spun her around, holding her off the ground. He barely heard the cheers of their friends and family in the background. He placed her back on her feet and took her left hand in his. He eased the ring he'd chosen on her finger and couldn't help but feel extremely emotional as he saw it there. It solidified the fact that she was his. That she'd always be his.

He looked into her tear-filled eyes. "I told you this before, but I'm not sure you really heard me. I wasn't going to let you go again, Doc. No matter if it took years for you to forgive me, I wasn't going to give up. The only way I would've backed off was if you wore another man's wedding ring." He caressed the base of her finger next to his engagement ring. "You're mine now. My ring will rest here on your finger for the rest of our lives, telling everyone to back off."

"And will you wear *my* ring?" she challenged.

"Fuck yes. With pride and pleasure. Although you

never have to worry about me straying. I'm yours, just as you're mine."

He thought she'd look at the ring then. Ooh and ahh over it. It was big; really, too big for her dainty finger, but he didn't give a shit. He wanted everyone to know Milena was taken.

But she didn't even glance at it. She put her arms around his neck and stood up on her tiptoes, plastering her body to his. He felt himself harden against her. He couldn't help it. He loved everything about her. He felt as if he was always semi-hard around her.

Smirking, as if she knew exactly how horny he was and how much he wanted her, she put a hand on the back of his neck and tugged his head down.

Obliging, TJ bent and felt her lips against his cheek before she moved them to his ear. Her warm breath brushed over his sensitive lobe as she said, "I love you, Thomas James Rockwell. I can't wait to become Milena Rockwell. I'm going to change JT's last name too. As soon as possible. But…what would you say to giving him a brother or sister?"

TJ pulled back and gazed down at the woman he loved so much, he felt as if his heart would burst. "As long as the doctor says it's safe for you to have another baby, I'll give you whatever you want."

"I'm not sure we can wait for the doctor to give the all clear."

TJ knew his brows were furrowed in confusion, but he asked, "Why?"

"Because it's too late."

Clarity came to him then, and TJ felt an emotion he couldn't identify moving through him. His eyes widened and he swayed a bit on his feet. "But you're on the pill!"

Milena's smile was so huge it lit up the space between them. "Yeah, well…you apparently have the world's most potent sperm. I don't think they cared about something as pesky as the pill. They got into my womb and forced it to produce an egg they could impregnate."

Worry, excitement, and dread welled up inside TJ. He leaned over and picked up his fiancée, making her squeal in surprise as he strode toward the door.

"What are you doing? Put me down, TJ!"

Ignoring her, TJ called out to Missy and Bob. "You guys okay with keeping JT for the night?"

They smiled back, and Missy nodded and waved him toward the door.

"TJ!" Milena said again. "Stop!"

He ignored her and continued walking. Ignoring the catcalls and jibes from their friends, TJ pushed open the door to the bar and strode out into the cool night. He walked straight to his Mustang before finally putting her back on her feet.

He took her head in his hands and tilted her face up. "How far?"

He was having a hard time forming words, but luckily, she understood him.

"Only eight weeks."

"I'm going to take good care of you," TJ vowed. "You won't be alone this time."

She put a hand on his cheek, and TJ tilted his head, trapping her hand between his cheek and his shoulder. "I know I won't."

"You're really pregnant?"

"Yeah. I'm really pregnant."

"I fucking love you so much," TJ said.

"I love you too."

He kissed her then, a short, sweet kiss that he had trouble keeping short or sweet. He helped her into his car and shut the door behind her. When he was settled behind the wheel, he turned to her.

"Spread your legs and pull off your panties."

Milena didn't protest. Didn't complain. Simply did as he'd requested.

They'd done this before, and even though she'd been flustered and embarrassed at first, she'd come harder than ever before when he'd finally gotten her home. He'd made her play with herself throughout the ride home from wherever they'd been, and the second they were inside his apartment, she'd attacked him.

"Pull up your skirt."

She didn't say a word, just did as he ordered.

"Play with yourself." When she moved a hand between her legs, he stopped her. "No, with your left hand. I want to see my ring on your finger as you touch yourself."

Milena groaned then, but did as he asked. She wasn't left handed, and her movements were jerky and awkward, but she did it.

TJ swallowed hard and started the engine. He reached over and placed his hand over her flat tummy and closed his eyes for a moment. Pregnant. Milena carried their child in her body. He'd thought he was overwhelmed when he'd met JT for the first time, but this was so much more. More frightening. More exciting. Just more.

"I love you."

At Milena's whispered words, TJ opened his eyes and sat up in the seat. He needed to be inside her. Needed to have her taste on his tongue. Needed to feel her hot mouth around his cock. He needed all of her. Every way he could have her. The hard fucking he'd fantasized about giving her earlier faded from his mind. He wouldn't ever do anything that might hurt the child she carried.

"Don't stop," he warned as her hand slowed. He pulled out of the parking lot and headed for his apartment complex, her arousal mixing in the air with her soft lemon scent. A combination that never failed to make him hard as nails.

For the thousandth time, TJ thought about what a lucky bastard he was as he looked over at the woman he still couldn't believe was his in every sense of the word. He'd let Milena choose their wedding date, but he'd do everything in his power to get his wedding ring on her finger sooner rather than later.

On the other side of the city, Blythe Coopman huddled behind a Dumpster, hiding from the group of men she'd sensed were following her earlier. She was tired. Fucking exhausted. She hated living on the streets. Not knowing where her next meal would come from. Not knowing who was friend and who was foe.

Feeling melancholy and lonely, she pulled Squirrel's cell phone out of her pocket. She'd been to the library and charged it so it would last another couple of days. She wrote a short text to the only person she talked to on a regular basis these days.

Blythe: *Hey.*

It took a minute or two, but when he texted back, Blythe sighed in relief.

She'd been completely confused when she'd first

started texting him, since both phones were registered to "Squirrel," but eventually figured out how to change the name on the phone to her own.

> **Squirrel:** Hey, pretty lady. What's up?
>
> **Blythe:** That's what I was going to ask you. Working?
>
> **Squirrel:** No. TJ proposed to Milena tonight. He took off with her, but since he's paying, we're all partying at the bar. :)

Blythe knew he didn't mean the text to be anything other than what he'd written. A breakdown of where he was and what he was doing. But his words stabbed her in the heart anyway. She'd seen how worried TJ had been about Milena.

Had seen how much Chief had worried about Sophie when she'd been inside that burning building.

She'd been on the streets for a while now, but she was tired of it all.

She wanted to be at the bar with Squirrel and Sophie.

She wanted to see her friends, Tadd and Louise.

She wanted to *live* again.

Not knowing how to answer Squirrel, Blythe put the phone back in her pocket and rested her head on her knees.

She had some thinking to do. She could either feel sorry for herself and continue to push away the people who said they cared about her—or she could pull her head out of her ass, accept their help, and figure out how to start living again. Really living.

"THIS IS RIDICULOUS, Chase. I'll be fine up in Dallas. Uncle Sean and Uncle Ian will make sure I'm safe," Sadie told the man in front of her. She was frustrated she was missing TJ's proposal to Milena. She missed having a normal life. Living in Chase's small apartment and being watched every minute of every day had gotten old really fast.

They were standing just inside his apartment arguing about whether or not she should go back to her life in Dallas. Chase had his arms crossed and was glaring down at her. "I don't want you to go. I realize you're an adult and I'm not holding you hostage, but I truly believe you're safer here with me."

Sadie sighed. "I'm putting you out. I'm in the way. Let me go home."

His countenance gentled, but he still shook his head. "Jonathan was going to rape you. Had one of your hands tied to that fucking bedpost. You told the Feds yourself that he was obsessed with getting you pregnant and taking your babies for himself. Do you honestly think he's going to just give up and run away with his tail between his legs?"

She bit her lip and looked away from Chase's intense brown eyes. He wasn't. She knew it and Chase knew it. But that didn't mean she wanted or needed a babysitter.

Back in San Antonio, she'd only put up with TJ following her around because it had meant Milena would be safe. She never considered that *she* would be in danger.

"I can take care of myself," she protested.

"Let me do this," Chase said in a low tone that Sadie couldn't interpret.

"Why?"

"Why what?"

"Why are you insisting on this? It's not necessary, and you and I both know it."

"I don't think you're ready to know why," Chase said.

That got Sadie's hackles up. "I might be younger than you and not an officer in the Army, but I'm not a baby. And I'm not a victim either. I'm not going to cower, cry, and wait for that asshole to find me. What aren't you telling me?"

She'd expected Chase to be discomfited and look away from her. Expected him to apologize for treating her like a little kid and not wanting to tell her some of the horrible things Jonathan likely wanted to do with and to her. She could've handled that.

But when he spoke, his words shocked her to the core.

"You want to know why it's not a good idea to go back up to your badass uncles? Back up to Dallas, where they have an entire team of men who can keep you safe? Because yeah, I know they could."

He paused as if he was waiting for confirmation.

Sadie couldn't stop herself from nodding silently. She wanted to act stronger, but couldn't do anything but stare up at the alpha man standing before her. She'd been surrounded by them much of her adult life, but for some reason, around Chase, she melted.

He leaned down, and one hand went to the left side of her neck, holding her still. His head lowered until his lips brushed against her right ear. Then he rocked her world.

"Because you're *mine*. And I'm personally going to make sure that asshole is wiped off the face of this earth so he can't look at what's mine anymore. So he can't touch what's mine. So he can't even *think* about what's mine. Then, when he's dead, I'm going to marry you— and spend the rest of my life making sure no *other* asshole thinks he has a chance in hell of taking you from me."

Sadie gulped. Her nipples had tightened and she shifted in his grasp, trying to ignore the way her pussy immediately began to leak at his overbearing, controlling words.

This wasn't like her. She was Sadie Jennings. She wasn't submissive like her aunt Grace. Not at all. And when *Jonathan* claimed she was his, she hadn't liked it one bit.

So why had Chase's words turned her on so much?

She couldn't do anything but stare up at him as he pulled back. His hand still rested on the side of her neck, and she knew her pulse was hammering in her throat. Chase's eyes roamed down her body—taking in her peaked nipples and the way she shifted her feet, trying to assuage the lust in her loins—and he grinned.

"Now, are you going to let me keep you safe, or do you want to run away and hide behind your uncles?"

His words managed to douse the passion coursing through her body a bit…as she suspected he meant them to. Chase Jackson could read her better than any man ever had before. He seemed to know when she needed tenderness and when she needed him to pick a fight. It should've annoyed her, but over the last month or so, all it had done was intrigue and attract her to him more.

"I'll stay." Her response was more of a croak than actual words. She'd wanted them to come out belligerently, but she knew she'd failed.

His smile grew. Not a smirk, and not in a conceited way. She thought he actually looked relieved. "Good."

He stepped back. "Now…are you hungry?"

And just like that, the tension between them disappeared as if it hadn't ever been there. Chase was back to being the impersonal protector he'd done his best to be since he'd dragged her up to Fort Hood.

She was disappointed, but also relieved. Chase might only be two years older than her, but the more she was around him, the more he reminded her of her much older uncles.

Taking a deep breath, Sadie nodded, and tried not to squeal like a little girl when Chase took her hand in his and led the way out of this apartment toward his car. Maybe not so impersonal after all.

Look for the next book in the Badge of Honor: Texas Heroes Series, *Shelter for Blythe* in June 2018.

Discover other titles by Susan Stoker

Badge of Honor: Texas Heroes Series
Justice for Mackenzie
Justice for Mickie
Justice for Corrie
Justice for Laine (novella)
Shelter for Elizabeth
Justice for Boone
Shelter for Adeline
Shelter for Sophie
Justice for Erin
Justice for Milena
Shelter for Blythe (June 2018)
Justice for Hope (Sept 2018)
Shelter for Quinn (TBA)
Shelter for Koren (TBA)
Shelter for Penelope (TBA)

Delta Force Heroes Series
Rescuing Rayne
Assisting Aimee – Loosely related to DF
Rescuing Emily
Rescuing Harley
Marrying Emily
Rescuing Kassie

Rescuing Bryn
Rescuing Casey
Rescuing Sadie (April 2018)
Rescuing Wendy (May 2018)
Rescuing Mary (Oct 2018)

Ace Security Series
Claiming Grace
Claiming Alexis
Claiming Bailey
Claiming Felicity

Mountain Mercenaries Series
Defending Allye (Aug 2018)
Defending Chloe (Dec 2018)
With more to come!

SEAL of Protection Series
Protecting Caroline
Protecting Alabama
Protecting Fiona
Marrying Caroline (novella)
Protecting Summer
Protecting Cheyenne
Protecting Jessyka
Protecting Julie (novella)
Protecting Melody
Protecting the Future
Protecting Alabama's Kids (novella)

Protecting Kiera (novella)
Protecting Dakota

Stand Alone
The Guardian Mist
Nature's Rift
A Princess for Cale

Special Operations Fan Fiction
www.stokeraces.com/kindle-worlds.html

Beyond Reality Series
Outback Hearts
Flaming Hearts
Frozen Hearts

Writing as Annie George:
Stepbrother Virgin (erotic novella)

Connect with Susan Online

Susan's Facebook Profile and Page:
www.facebook.com/authorsstoker
www.facebook.com/authorsusanstoker

Follow Susan on Twitter:
www.twitter.com/Susan_Stoker

Find Susan's Books on Goodreads:
www.goodreads.com/SusanStoker

Email: Susan@StokerAces.com

Website: www.StokerAces.com

To sign up for Susan's Newsletter go to:
www.stokeraces.com/contact-1.html

Or text: STOKER to 24587 for text alerts on your
mobile device

About the Author

New York Times, USA Today, and *Wall Street Journal* Bestselling Author Susan Stoker has a heart as big as the state of Texas, where she lives, but this all-American girl has also spent the last fourteen years living in Missouri, California, Colorado, and Indiana. She's married to a retired Army man who now gets to follow *her* around the country.

She debuted her first series in 2014 and quickly followed that up with the SEAL of Protection Series, which solidified her love of writing and creating stories readers can get lost in.

If you enjoyed this book, or any book, please consider leaving a review. It's appreciated by authors more than you'll know.

CPSIA information can be obtained
at www.ICGtesting.com
Printed in the USA
LVHW041434020320
648715LV00014B/869

9 781943 562053